A Kind of Family

Between the Lines Publishing, LLC

Published by Between the Lines Publishing (USA)
as Willow River Press (imprint)

410 Caribou Trail, Lutsen, Minnesota 55612, USA

www.btwnthelines.com

Copyright © 2019 Bonnie Meekums

Cover artist: Jim Tetlow

Photograph by Phil Spence

A Kind of Family
Paperback ISBN: 978-1-950502-07-3

This is a work of fiction. All characters, organizations, and events portrayed are either a product of the author's imagination or are used fictitiously.

Without limiting the rights under copyright reserved above, no part of this publication may be reproduced, stored in or introduced into a retrieval system, or transmitted, in any form or by any means (electronic, mechanical, photocopied, recorded or otherwise), without the prior written consent of the publisher, except by a reviewer who wishes to quote brief passages in connection with a review written for insertion in a magazine, newspaper, broadcast, website, blog, or other outlet

For Phil

Together, we created our own kind of family

Prologue

Queenstown, New Zealand, 1914

Meekums

Ahurewa clung to her māmā. The little girl could smell the familiar, safe scent in her nostrils; a mixture of soap, honey and fresh sweat. She buried her face in her mother's breasts, blotting out the sound of the Pākehā as they approached her safe place. Ahurewa could feel her māmā's heart beating hard and fast, her own keeping pace. She could detect a strange smell on her mother's breath, and instinctively knew it meant fear.

Ahurewa heard them speaking the English language. The words sounded harsh to her ears. She and her mother only ever spoke to each other in their own tongue, in defiance of the ruling Pākehā. They did so secretly, whispering. It was their bond. Their link to their whānau. Their link to their whenua. Their land. Their sacred place. Their home.

Long fingernails dug into her back, either side of her ribs. They were pulling her. Simultaneously, her māmā's arms went limp. Why was she not pulling just as hard, to keep her close? Ahurewa clutched at the cloth of her māmā's dress. She heard a voice, screaming *Māmā! Māmā!* It was her own. She smelt the same scent of fear in her own body that had been in her māmā's. The Pākehā man stepped in and prised her fingers apart with a strength she could not hope to match. His words were saying it would be alright, but his spirit sang a different song. As she lost her grip, she heard her mother whisper in their secret tongue: *I will call your name on the wind. Listen for me. I will never leave you.*

As the Pākehā woman carried her out the door, she remembered her manners and did not protest, even though she wanted to kick and bite and punch and scream. Instead she looked back, seeing her own agony mirrored in the eyes of her māmā. The last sight she saw in that room was her māmā mouthing *I will call your name…*

Ahurewa could not remember much of the journey to the big boat, where she was handed over to another Pākehā. This woman slept on the bunk above her. Neither spoke. Ahurewa had lost her tongue along with her mother. When she needed to pee, she just did it in the bed, hoping it would simply drain away like the blood from her heart. It didn't. When she needed a tiko and could hold it in no longer, she stayed very still until the woman came in the door and shouted at her, cleaning her up roughly and putting her to bed on a bare mattress with a rough woollen blanket for cover. After that, she found her way silently to the privy, when the woman was not around. She never left her room.

When they had left Queenstown, the snow was on the ground but when they got to the place on the other side of the world, it was warm. All the people were Pākehā, it seemed, though there were some men whose skin was darker than her mother's, with different features. They were few and far between. A woman and a man approached her as she stepped falteringly onto the quay. The woman spoke quietly. She had bird-like features and smelled of an overpowering scent that was not grown in any forest. The man had kind brown eyes that looked right into Ahurewa's soul. But Ahurewa was not ready to be seen. She pulled an invisible cloak around her heart. *I will call your name on the wind. Listen for me.*

The couple told her they were her new Mummy and Daddy, and that from now on she was to be called Frances. *I will call your name on the wind.* They rode in a carriage with horses, to a house where the privy was outside, in a kind of shed. Before bed she was ordered to strip off and plunge into a bath made of metal, where she was scrubbed from head to toe by her new mummy before being clothed in a soft nightdress and given something to take to bed with her. It burned her hands, but she remained silent, hot tears stinging her eyes.

And so, her new life began. Ahurewa did not speak for a full cycle of the moon, which was no effort at all after the long journey across the seas. The day she arrived, she later learned, a war was started, which meant that lots of men were going off to fight. Her new daddy was not one of them. He had something wrong with one of his legs, which meant he was no use to them. Mummy seemed pleased.

Ahurewa listened all through the autumn, winter, spring and into the next summer, where she knew it must be winter for her māmā. She remembered her māmā's promise: *I will call your name on the wind. Listen for me. I will never leave you.* She knew her māmā never told a lie, but she could not hear her voice. Slowly, that beloved voice slipped from her memory just as her mother's dress had done. One day, she tried to whisper to her māmā on the wind and found that she had forgotten many of the words of her own tongue. When August 4th came and this upside-down world had been spinning for a whole year, she concluded that her māmā could not know she was now called Frances, and so even though Ahurewa knew her mother was calling her with the tenacity of a fantail bird, she could not be heard. The wind now sounded just like wind. The sound of her māmā's voice became replaced by her new mummy's bird-like singsong, and her new daddy's dark brown crooning. She found comfort in sucking her thumb, and occasionally clutching at her blankets though she knew not why.

A Kind of Family

PART ONE

Yorkshire, England, twenty-first century

A Kind of Family

A letter from Down Under

Rachel's hand shook. The letter, written on old-fashioned airmail paper, was as flimsy as the future she had once imagined. She remembered being twelve years old, looking up to her brother who by then was six feet one and a half inches tall as compared to her five feet six. Being the tallest in her class, it mattered to her that her big brother was bigger than her. He made her feel secure. He used to smile at her softly, telling her with his eyes that whatever she did she would always be his little sis. Loved. Or so she thought.

He had written in brown ink on shiny blue paper. When she saw the airmail envelope, her heart leaped. Perhaps he was coming home? Silly thought really. She knew he was settled in Perth. He had children. He had a new family. And he hadn't made it home when their parents had died on separate wards within hours of each other. Nearly a year ago. Rachel forgave him that, though. He was busy. Flying a plane all over the world, why would he want to fly back just to support his little sis? He told her he would say goodbye to their mother in his own way.

Why were you so stupid as to think he would still care about you?

Oh yes, she could always count on her inner, snide little 'best friend' at times like this. The voice that never quite left her alone. The voice that started the day her brother went to Australia. It got in there, now that no one was around to protect her from the bully inside herself.

Rachel decided to read the letter aloud, as if hearing the words spoken, she might more easily take them in. The top of her back hurt. There was a knot in her right shoulder. She tried to knead it with her left hand as she carefully laid the pages out in front of her on her oak table, smoothing each one out carefully, for fear of tearing them.

'Dear Rachel', she began. So formal. No 'Smuggins.' Not even 'Rache.'

'I write to say I will not return to the UK, now or at any time in the...' Rachel's voice cracked. Tears mixed with brown ink, tributaries that led to nowhere.

'...future. I find that, with our parents gone I wish to focus completely on my life here. It is a long time since we were brother and sister to each other, and you have never made the effort to come out here to see me. I can only conclude that I mean no more to you now than you to me – a mere memory of childhood. My family is here, and you must make yours there.'

Rachel stared into the garden, her eyes stinging as she screwed up the paper until it reduced to an insubstantial little ball. Annie sighed, and put her head on her paws as close to Rachel's feet as she dared.

'Rachel, I'm so sorry to hear that. God! What a shit!'

'Jane? You're fading in and out. Sorry to bother you when you're up there on Skye. I just needed to talk to someone, and Suzy's on shift at the refuge.' Rachel held the phone tightly in her right hand. She needed something solid. With her other hand she clutched the arm of her big, sturdy armchair, not daring to sit right back.

'Rachel. You know you can always call me, day or night.'

'Thanks, Jane. I really appreciate it.' Rachel knew her voice was breaking up. She sat up straighter in her chair. 'At least I have you and Suzy. You're like sisters to me.'

'No. We're better than sisters. We chose each other.'

'You're right. They say blood is thicker than water, but I'm not so sure.' But the line was dead.

Rachel texted Suzy: *Hey Suze. If not too zzzzz when you get in, call me?*

Meekums

As she lay in bed, her head dancing about in a half-wake, half-dream state the phone rang.

'Hey Rache! What's up love?'

'Oh, God! I'm so sorry to bother you. You must be shattered after a shift at the refuge and I know you're on duty tomorrow too at the care home. It's just—'

'Woah! Breathe! You're obviously upset. I'm not on until twelve tomorrow. Late shift. So, take yer time, lass.'

'It's my brother, Suze. He… he—' Rachel's jaw trembled.

Rachel would have preferred a large glass of wine, but she managed a smile as she looked up at the cup of tea Suzy handed her. Annie circled at her feet, seemingly unsure whether to rest or stay on guard. As she placed two hands round the solid mug Rachel felt its warmth and began to understand why some people find a cup of tea comforting in a crisis.

'I just want a family, Suzy. I feel so stupid saying that. I just want to be like other people and have a family. I mean you have your son. Jane has her cousins that she sees regularly. I have no one.'

Rachel looked up to see Suzy looking back at her with the same genuine empathy she had remembered from when they had trained together in counselling. A little bit of Rachel's stomach relaxed as she took a large mouthful and let more warm tea slide down. Annie settled her chin onto her paws.

'I mean, you and Jane *are* like sisters to me, and I don't know what I'd do without you. I hope you don't feel offended.'

Rachel looked up again from her mug to see Suzy smiling, a look of reassurance on her lovely lined face.

'I just wish I had my own family,' she continued, now looking straight at her friend, her eyes unashamedly wet. 'Here, in this house. I love being able to please myself, of course, but sometimes I get… well, I get lonely. And I feel so *hurt*, Suze. My brother was my world when we were younger. I thought he would never, ever leave me.' Rachel looked towards the window.

Her breathing slowed as she imagined her strong copper beech outside the window. That, and Suzy's calm presence enabled her to slow her thoughts and she became aware of an overwhelming tiredness. But there was one more thing Rachel needed to say to her friend.

'When he went away, I told myself we were still close. But in truth, I think that day was when everything changed. He never looked back, Suze. Literally. When he left us, he never looked back.'

Suzy nodded sagely, then smiled as she reached over and took the mug from her friend.

'Time for bed, mate. Let's talk again in t'morning. I'll give you a ring before I go on shift. Come on, I can see myself out. Let's get you upstairs.'

Ice cream

The next day was August 4th. Exactly a year since Rachel Drake's parents had died. Rachel stared out of her living room bay window to the tree beyond, clutching her belly. She still had not got used to being an orphan, despite her forty-two years. Born to older parents just as her mother's fertility was waning, she used to look on longingly as she saw other girls' parents go swimming, play tennis or go on long walks with them. Her parents sat indoors, as if fresh air was a dangerous commodity and exercise might just send them off to early graves.

Rachel had done her best to create her own 'family' through her friends. But somehow, it wasn't enough. Sundays were the worst. Everyone seemed to be out with their own families, or indoors doing Sunday lunch together. Rachel wandered round the park throwing balls for Annie like a lone old lady, then returned to read students' work, or review someone else's writing.

Today, a Friday, Rachel had to attend a mental health and art exhibition. Her colleague Felicity had said she would go and then at the last minute had asked Rachel to replace her because her daughter's ballet school needed chaperones for their latest show.

Why the fuck did you agree to attend this bloody art exhibition, Drake?

Her foul-mouthed inner critic, her 'best friend' put paid to her staring.

Rachel wandered aimlessly round the exhibition until one painting caught her eye. She was intrigued by the depiction of a hill that reminded her of her beloved Dun-I, the highest point on the isle of Iona in the Scottish Hebrides. The purple heather amidst vibrant grass made her want to don her walking boots and get up there. She wondered if the combination of green and purple suffragette colours was deliberate as she stood in front of the painting, her left elbow resting in the palm of her right hand, the fingers of her left hand lightly tapping her lips. What really grabbed her attention was the abandoned ice cream, melting in the foreground. While she was trying to figure out the symbolism, she noticed out of the corner of her eye a diminutive woman who had silently appeared at her side, her body tilted towards Rachel's.

'Oh, gosh, I wouldn't spend too long on that one! I only hung it to fill the exhibition space. It's actually a bit naughty of me to include it given that I painted it, but some of the workshop participants got really anxious when I asked them if I could show their work so I told them I would paint something and hang it along with theirs – to keep them company, if you know what I mean. I knocked it off in an afternoon working alongside them. It really isn't very good.'

Rachel turned and saw a pair of dark, velvety moon-eyes beaming back at her, the woman's face the colour of cappuccino framed by dark and shiny hair cut in a perfect bob. Rachel smiled, amused by the woman's guileless appraisal of her own work. Rachel had to admit it was simple, but it had a certain *je ne sais quoi*. She looked back at the painting, feeling inexplicably hot. Five minutes ago she was feeling pissed off, but now the evening was getting interesting, if unsettling. She gathered herself together and turned back to the artist.

'S–so, I know this was a workshop about women and mental health, but...' Rachel trailed off, uncertain what point she wanted to make.

'Fran's the name. Yours?'

'Sorry. Yes, I knew you were Frances. It says on the wall, there. Frances Baker. You prefer Fran, I take it? I'm Rachel. I got an invite through the university.' Rachel was aware she was rambling as she tucked a bit of wispy hair behind her ear. 'I'm a psychotherapist,' she added, unnecessarily.

'Oh, gosh!' Fran's body recoiled visibly – an almost imperceptible movement, but Rachel was trained to notice 'shadow movements'.

'Don't worry. I'm not trying to psych you out. Off duty!' Rachel quipped, knowing this wasn't strictly true. She wanted to understand this woman, and most of all she wanted to taste the ice cream in her painting. The realisation made her pulse race and the back of her neck go hot.

What are you thinking?

The stern voice of her inner headmistress.

Since being unceremoniously dumped at her PhD graduation by her first female lover, a lecturer in the department where she had studied, Rachel had avoided seeing anyone, male or female, as attractive. These days, she took solace in her work, her two closest friends Jane and Suzy, Annie the rescue dog, Radio Three, a good book and a decent glass of wine.

Rachel realised she had already given away far too much of herself to this delightful artist-woman. She now wanted to crawl under the floorboards, never to be seen again – and to banish all thoughts of the ice cream, whatever it might symbolise.

'Tell you what,' Fran ventured. 'If you really do want to know more about the work that went into this exhibition…'

Rachel noticed a blush seeping into Fran's cheeks, closely followed by an apparently strong interest in her sandals. Rachel found herself following Fran's gaze. Perfectly manicured toenails the same oxblood colour as her lips peeped out from under a pair of expensive-looking walking sandals.

'I'd love to!' Rachel blurted out, despite herself. 'Know more, that is. What are you doing this evening, after the exhibition closes?'

Whaaat? What are you doing, Drake? Are you insane?

Her best friend was now doing overtime. But Rachel uncharacteristically paid no heed.

'I don't live far away. I also make excellent coffee, but if you'd prefer a glass of vino, I have that too.'

You fool, Drake!

Her headmistress, back again.

'Great! Why not? I could explain the thinking behind the exhibition.' Fran beamed a delicious, innocent-looking, full-red-lipped smile.

'And, I hope, behind your painting,' Rachel found herself saying with surprising directness.

The two women paused, looking into each other's eyes as if only now they each saw what was happening. Rachel broke the silence.

'What time shall I pick you up here?'

'Oh, 10.30 to be safe. I'll probably have some clearing up to do.' Fran sounded nonchalant. Rachel nodded, wondering if she had been mistaken in what she had read in Fran's body language. But she was curious to know more about this woman – and her ice cream. She turned towards the stairs and hurried down them into the steamy street.

Rachel wasn't sure what to do in the intervening hours before going back to meet this Frances – Fran – Baker. How had this happened?

This sort of thing doesn't happen to you, Drake!

That best friend again.

Rachel wasn't even sure if she still fancied women – or anybody, for that matter. And yet, she had said she would pick up this undeniably hot woman at 10.30 pm. Rachel looked at her watch. It was now 5.45. Nearly five hours to kill. She decided to walk home across the park, to give herself time to think.

As she arrived at the large, Victorian terrace she called home she could hear Annie barking excitedly. She turned her key in the lock and as Rachel entered the kitchen Annie lumbered around her feet, impeding every step. Rachel gave her a reassuring pat as she shoved her hind quarters. The physical contact seemed to satisfy Annie as she formed the advance party through the hall into the living room, wagging her tail. Rachel flopped into her rocking chair overlooking the garden, kicking off her shoes. Annie took up her sentry position, sitting on Rachel's feet as Rachel considered the very nice Marlborough Sauvignon Blanc that was waiting for her in the fridge.

Best not get drunk and disgraceful, missy!

'Oh, OK. You're back, are you? Well sod it, I am going into the kitchen and I am pouring myself a glass. So there!' Rachel argued aloud.

The appearance of her inner headmistress always sent Rachel in the opposite direction, whereas she was much more likely to feel undermined by the best friend, much like the bullies at school. She shoved Annie off, who simply laid her head on her paws with a sigh, and headed back through the hall for the kitchen, opening her large but sparsely furnished fridge. Seconds later she was back in her rocking chair, taking a large gulp of her deliciously cold wine, Radio Three blaring out a soothing *Trois Gymnopédies* as she gazed at her lawn and the broad tree at its far end. As the wine took effect, she could feel every muscle in her body begin to relax; her breathing deepened and slowed. The working week was over with its endless emails with attachments as long as your arm requiring an instant response, the constant stream of students who had nothing better to do in the summer than try to convince her that their problem was the most urgent there had ever been, and the stupid posturing of certain colleagues. Admittedly there were essays to mark and a scientific paper to review for one of the journals for which she was on the Board but, for now, this moment was golden.

Rachel finished her glass, resisted the temptation to pour another and decided to run a bath.

'Stay!' she commanded Annie, who sat back on her haunches, wagged her tail and looked adoringly at Rachel as if she had just given her the most enormous treat.

A Kind of Family

The wind-up radio went on in the bathroom, this time on Radio Four. As she relaxed back into the bubbles, the Friday night comedy half hour began. It couldn't get much better than this.

After her bath Rachel pulled on some trousers and a shirt, then decided she had better eat something. She opened the fridge once more, doing her best to ignore the bottle that was screaming 'Drink me!' then decided she had better ring for a takeaway. She ordered her usual chicken karahi and two chapatis, then realised as she put the phone down that her breath would stink of curry. Not a good start to any evening. By the time the curry arrived at 8 o'clock her stomach was doing somersaults. Rachel peeled a banana and poured a cup of tea. She watched a rubbish movie on iPlayer, checked her watch, grabbed her jacket, and rushed out to catch a bus back into town.

When she arrived Fran was waiting, looking as fresh as when Rachel had left her.

'How come you don't look worn out, after such a long day?'

'Oh, gosh! Well, I went for a coffee downstairs, drank a load of water, and I confess I also took a break to do a yoga class on the first floor. This building is incredible! I guess that is one thing to come out of the decline of the industrial north,' she added, with a note of remorse.

Rachel smiled reassurance.

'So, where shall we go? Would you like me to show you where I live? Or shall we go out somewhere? I could buy you a wine or coffee? My treat.'

'I would love to come to yours.'

Rachel gazed at Fran, puzzled by the frankness of this woman. Was she coming on to her? Or just open and innocent as a child?

'If that's OK,' Fran added just as Rachel realised she had not answered. 'It's just that I'm all coffee'd out, if truth be told, and I've had enough of the hustle and bustle of the city for one day. Besides, Friday nights tend to be heaving. We won't be able to hear ourselves think.'

Fran was right, of course. Luckily, the buses were frequent. Rachel led the way, and within ten minutes she was turning her key once more. After negotiating Annie's enthusiastic welcome Fran followed Rachel into the living room, where the curtains were still open. Fran peered out into the darkness, the garden partially lit by a street lamp.

'Wow, it looks as if you have a lovely tree out there. What is it?'

'Copper beech,' Rachel replied, smiling.

'Oh my God! I love it! It's so beautiful! So… fulsome.'

Fran gazed longingly into the darkening garden, then without warning darted off towards the fireplace.

'Open fire? Do you ever light it?'

'Oh yes. I could light it now, if you'd like?'

Rachel didn't expect Fran's response, given the hot weather.

'I would absolutely love that!' Fran's face seemed to light up as her eyes met Rachel's.

The two women sat on the hearth rug, leaning their bodies against Rachel's two sturdy armchairs and staring into the fire. Annie had helpfully positioned herself between them, her tail resting on Rachel's knee. Rachel cradled her glass of cabernet sauvignon in two hands like a treasured possession. Fran's glass sat beside her, untouched after the first sip.

Rachel was reluctant to break the spell. When was the last time she had been able to sit in absolute silence with another human being? With Annie, yes, but she was… well, canine. When home, Rachel usually had her head in an academic paper with Annie lying at her feet, chin on one paw, apparently asleep but alert to the slightest shift in Rachel's position.

She breathed in, feeling a duty to entertain her guest.

'Would you like some music?' Rachel's voice crackled from lack of use.

'Um… yes, that would be lovely. What've you got?' came the dreamy reply.

'All sorts. What do you like? Classical? Jazz? Women singer songwriters?'

'Oh, gosh! Do you have anything by Kate and Anna McGarrigle, by any chance? I haven't heard any of their stuff in absolutely ages.'

Rachel beamed. 'As a matter of fact, I have. How about *Dancer with Bruised Knees?*'

Fran nodded, her face lighting up as she gathered her knees up under her chin and hugged them.

Fran asked to see the album cover and so, after Rachel had carefully placed her vinyl album on the turntable and adjusted the volume, she sat a little closer to show her. She knew she could just hand it to her, but she wasn't going to pass up this opportunity. As she sat down, shoving Annie unceremoniously out of her way, her hips brushed Fran's and a rush of energy rocked her body. Her eyes glazed over as she tried to open the album to get to the lyrics. As she fumbled, she felt Fran's hand on her hair.

'I love your hair. So fine, so fair, and curly! Mine's so straight.'

Rachel turned to look at Fran.

'I prefer your hair. It's so strong,' she replied, then gulped audibly as she reached out and touched Fran's silky straight bob.

'Thank you,' murmured Fran as they fell into a mutual caress of each other's hair, their eyes searching each other's faces. Rachel felt naked, her body shivering despite the heat.

Then, without planning it, their eyes closed as they leant towards each other and their lips touched. Oh, the softness! Rachel had forgotten what this felt like but decided in this moment it felt good. Very good.

Taking off their clothes seemed like the most natural thing in the world. Their lovemaking had a sense of inevitability about it that Rachel had not experienced since her youth, when sex just seemed to happen as regularly as brushing her teeth, and with as much pre-meditation.

When it was over, Rachel propped herself onto one elbow and looked with delight at Fran's body.

'You're beautiful,' she whispered. 'So beautiful and dark. Not just a tan, then?'

'No.' Fran sounded almost apologetic as she propped one hand behind her head to expose a dark nest under her left armpit. 'God knows where I get it from. Mum was as fair as anything, before she went grey.'

Rachel turned onto her back, grinning inanely to see Fran's face appear, shining above hers. She reached up and framed the delicate, exquisite face with her hands, then drew Fran's head down for a deep kiss.

'Ice cream,' she murmured.

A Kind of Family

Aggie

Fran called a taxi at about 2 am. Rachel wondered whether to invite her to stay, but decided it was too soon. Nevertheless, she found herself wondering what, or who, Fran was going home to.

Don't get ideas above your station, Drake. She is gorgeous, and you are lanky, spreading round the middle, with mousy flyaway hair. Don't call her, she'll call you – maybe.

Her best friend was doing overtime. Like a vicious teenage schoolgirl who delights in seeing another girl take a fall, she never missed an opportunity to undermine Rachel whenever she might be getting too sure of herself – or happy.

The next morning, Rachel woke to scratching on her bedroom door. Annie. She looked at the clock. Half past eight. Poor Annie must be desperate. She hauled her aching body out of bed, realising that last night she must have used muscles she had forgotten she had. She could no longer take fitness for granted. Thank God for Annie, who kept her on her toes.

Rachel pulled on yesterday's knickers, then a pair of jeans, and searched for her tossed-away bra. She finally found it adorning a plant pot, and a smile crept over her face as she remembered the unexpected passion of the night before. Despite the lack of sleep, she felt upbeat as she finally threw on her favourite oversized jumper, just in case the British summer had decided to change its mind and revert to type. Sure enough, when she looked out of her window, she saw heavy clouds.

Nevertheless, and despite her dislike of getting wet, Rachel decided her walking sandals would do. If it rained, it rained.

Rachel opened her bedroom door to go to the bathroom and found Annie blocking her path, excitedly moving back and forth in front of her. Rachel pushed the dog to one side, aware of her own urgent need to pee. After doing so she grabbed her keys, some doggie poo bags and Annie's lead which she attached to a very grateful bitch and headed out of the house along the canal.

Out in the air, Rachel was able to clear her head and think. Annie calmed down after a fair bit of sniffing, weeing and tail wagging and they settled into a companionable rhythm, only interrupted by Annie's need to follow some doggie trail undetected by humans, and of course to do the obligatory poo.

Yesterday evening had been amazing, but Rachel felt the need to put her foot firmly on the brake. She didn't want to assume anything about a relationship. For all she knew, for Fran that had been a one-off, just a pleasant fling. After tossing the events of last night around in her head several times and lingering (much to the consternation and disapproval of her headmistress) on some of its more unexpected delights Rachel concluded no harm had been done. She had had a wonderful time. She felt more alive now than she had in ages. She resolved to put the matter out of her mind and get on with her life. If Fran wanted to see her again, she would ring. Besides, Rachel had a PhD draft thesis to read – if she could keep awake long enough.

Later that morning Rachel sat at her desk, looking through the French doors leading from her study onto the patio and to the garden beyond, desperately trying to keep her eyes open. She felt a draught at her right side and turned to see the door leading into the kitchen slam shut. Rachel was about to turn back to her computer, making a mental note to buy some draught excluder when she thought she saw a shadowy movement at the corner of her eye. When she looked up there was nothing there, but it unnerved her.

Don't be an idiot, Drake. The door is locked. No one's got in. Get back to work. You know you're just trying to put it off. You really are a prize procrastinator.

Duly chastised by the headmistress Rachel turned back to her computer, willing herself to concentrate.

A cough. Annie cocked her ears in alert preparedness. Rachel was not 'hearing things'. She looked in the direction of the shadow she had seen earlier, her own pulse assaulting her ears. The cough had seemed to come from the kitchen. Had an intruder got in despite the locked door, or had she somehow forgotten to turn the key? She looked around for something with which she could defend herself if push came to shove. Nothing. She tried to remember the women's self-defence she had learned in her undergraduate days after a particularly nasty rape on campus. Her brain turned to mush.

Then an older woman appeared on the other side of the door from Rachel's study into the kitchen, and Rachel's fear turned to confusion mixed with a fair dose of irritation. It was as if she had come out of nowhere. Rachel could only see the top half of her through the half-glazed door. The old woman's face looked as if someone had scored deep marks on a dark canvas. Her eyes were like two dark pools that seemed to draw Rachel in despite her wariness. The visitor smiled and raised her eyebrows as if asking to be let in. Sighing, Rachel got up and opened the door as it occurred to her that this must be one of the people who had recently moved into number twenty.

'Fanks, love. I'm sorry. I must've give you such a fright. I don't mean to. Can I come in?'

Rachel looked beyond the woman to the outer door, which was closed.

She was already in.

'Oh, sorry, yes, sure. Do come through.'

Rachel led the way through her study into the living room and gestured towards an armchair. She herself sat in her favourite armchair, resisting the temptation to curl her feet up under her. The older woman seemed to hover on the edge of her chair.

Rachel prided herself on not being a snob, but she couldn't help wondering why this woman hadn't taken off her very old fashioned and slightly soiled all-over paisley pinafore, nor indeed taken her hair out of rollers, which poked out from under a headscarf. She looked and sounded as if she had stepped out of working-class life in 1960s London. Rachel also noticed the woman was wearing support stockings, except they were neither supported nor supporting. The thick, brown hosiery pooled around the woman's ankles, resting for the most part on her slippers.

Rachel realised she must be staring.

'My name's Rachel,' she offered.

Rachel raised herself from her armchair to greet the woman, but immediately felt a force like a hand in the centre of her chest, pushing her back down into her chair.

'Um… I'm so pleased to meet you,' she muttered as she collapsed, steadying herself on the arms of the chair. Then, remembering her manners:

'Can I offer you a cup of tea?'

The woman seemed to chuckle at the suggestion.

'My name's Agnes. They call me Aggie. How do you do?' She pronounced each word as if it were a rehearsed school speech spoken by an eleven-year-old.

'An' no fanks. I don't drink tea, ta.'

'Um – I could make coffee, if you prefer? Or a glass of water?'

'No, ta.'

Aggie shrugged her shoulders.

'An' I ain't from number twenty. Sorry to disappoint.'

Even more confused and irritated that this shabby old woman seemed to know what she had been thinking, Rachel's eyes moved to Aggie's right hand which held a cigarette, its ash trailing at the end. She was just about to say she did not allow smoking in her house when Aggie pulled herself up straight.

'Now, I know you might be wondering why I'm here.'

She pronounced the 'h' in here as if making a special effort to sound it. Rachel remained silent, staring at the ash which despite continuously burning never seemed to get any nearer to dropping. Neither did Aggie take a drag on her cigarette. Rachel also observed with bemusement there was no smell emanating from it.

Rachel felt increasingly unnerved, but her social conditioning dictated at least some degree of civility. She decided she should make small talk for ten minutes, find out why this rather strange woman had come to see her, then politely tell her she really needed to get on with her work.

'You see, ducks, I know all about you and Fran.'

Rachel bristled. How the hell did she know about last night? Was she the local delegation from homophobes anonymous, come poking her face into other people's business? She decided to confront her head-on.

'Sorry... how do you know Fran?'

'Oh, I know everyfink, my love. Don't worry though. I don't bite.'

Aggie emitted a self-satisfied chuckle as the non-cigarette hand moved to her untoned belly.

'Look, I have no idea who you are or why you feel it's OK to waltz into my house uninvited...'

'Correction. You invited me in.'

'After you had managed to get into my kitchen.'

'Ah. Yes. Well, I admit that might 'ave been a mistake.'

'A mistake? Is that what you call it?' Rachel checked herself, aware she was raising her voice. 'Are you in the habit of stepping into other people's kitchens?'

'Look, it's just as well you're sittin' down. I didn't mean to alarm you. It's just that... well, this isn't gonna be easy to understand, I know, but I… well, I've been assigned to you, you see.' Aggie pronounced the word 'assigned' as if it were in quotation marks. 'I 'ave to watch over you.'

'Really! Well I am perfectly capable of taking care of myself, thank you! And who, pray, has "assigned" you to me?'

Aggie turned squarely towards Rachel, a look on her face that spoke of both pity at her stupidity, and quasi-parental sternness.

'Rachel, you're a psychotherapist. Work it out. I know you already 'ear voices inside your 'ead. Well, consider this an extension of that, expect that I am per'aps a little kinder.'

Rachel was taken aback at this reference to her internal voices. True, they stayed firmly inside her head and so she had never entertained thoughts of madness. They were part of the internal chatter, she reassured herself, that we all suffer from. But if this new one was appearing – and speaking – as if actually there in the room, that took it to a whole new level. Was she, in fact, going mad? Was this a hallucination? The beginnings of a psychotic episode? Or was there some other explanation? Rachel realised even as she had this internal debate she was engaging in an internal conversation. Her best friend was the first to join in and declare her 'barking'. She made a deliberate effort to look at Aggie despite knowing her frown was impossible to erase. Aggie took this as her cue.

'I can see it's 'ard to take in, like I said. Look, when you get to know me, you'll realise I am – despite your prejudices – well, a bit wiser, shall we say, than either the 'eadmistress or the so-called friend you currently mix wiv.'

And with that, Aggie pushed her bosom up with her non-cigarette hand and turned away, her chin held in the air as she glided back through to Rachel's study and towards the kitchen. Rachel followed, feeling just a tad ashamed. Yes, she had to admit she had judged this woman. Wisdom was not a word she had associated with her on first seeing and hearing her. Rachel turned guiltily to look out at her garden

– a little sanctuary made possible through her middle-class professional lifestyle.

When she turned back, Aggie was gone. Rachel sank into her study chair, her eyes heavy once more as she tried to make sense of what had happened. Some years ago, she had attended a workshop about finding your inner 'wise person' or 'guide'. She thought of it as a load of hocus pocus but went along with it despite her scepticism. During one of the guided visualisations she had 'found' a long-haired hag but dismissed this as a stereotype. Since then, she had given zero thought or energy to the idea that she might encounter some part of herself that could guide her through life's vicissitudes. Until now. Was Aggie her 'wise woman'? Or was Rachel, as she first feared, going mad?

There was no way Rachel was going to be able to read the PhD thesis she had been struggling with. She looked down at Annie, who after her initial alertness had remained remarkably still throughout the encounter with Aggie. The light in her garden was beginning to dim.

'Walkies, old girl?'

Rachel didn't need to ask twice.

A Kind of Family

28

Careless whisper

Rachel went about most of the next day in her pyjamas, trying to make incisive comments on the PhD draft. In the midst of her distracted attempts to work she had a nagging feeling she was meant to be somewhere or doing something. Then it dawned on her. She had offered to cook a meal for Jane and Suzy. Rachel had known each of them for more years than she cared to add up; the two other women had become friends through her, despite being as different from each other as (an older) Sheridan Smith and (a younger) Dame Judy Dench.

Rachel dashed out to the supermarket, looking for inspiration. She had two and a half hours to get the house cleaned, herself in the bath then looking presentable, and food cooked. The first thing she reached for was a bottle of sauvignon blanc, and then some sparkling water for Suzy. Right. Couscous and roasted veg, maybe? The veg need not take long to prepare – chunky is best. With a bit of chicken? Or some goat's cheese? Rachel settled on trusty old chicken, with a goat's cheese starter. What to do with the goat's cheese? Panic set in, then she remembered she could look that up on her phone.

Mmmm. Thank you, Jamie Oliver.

Caramelised red onions, and a bit of iceberg lettuce. She decided to change this to watercress, on a whim. Now, for a dessert. Feeling uninspired, she grabbed some profiteroles and cream, but with a smile on her face changed this at the last minute to coffee-flavoured ice cream.

Once back home and having put the shopping away, Rachel started on a cursory clean of the house.

So long as it looks OK, one of her more helpful and supportive (and rare) inner voices suggested. The voice sounded like Aggie's; rough around the edges, but with a softness at its core. She looked around to see if anyone was there but could see no-one.

Slut, was the swift choral response from both headmistress and best friend.

Determined to listen for once to a voice other than theirs, she decided to concentrate on the floors and toilets, then called it a day with a soak in the bath. As she lowered herself into the hot bubbles, she could feel her aching limbs begin to let go.

With the dinner prepped and feeling relaxed, Rachel began to look forward to seeing her friends. She eased into a summer dress in flowery print with a delicate cardigan, then lovingly added some jewellery left to her by her favourite great-aunt Lizzy: amethyst earrings and matching necklace. When she opened the door, smoothing her clean hands down an imaginary pinafore she saw Jane. Bang on time as always.

'Rachel, you look marvellous!' Jane kissed first one cheek, then the other, stepping over Annie. Rachel took no notice of the compliment; Jane always thought everyone looked marvellous, other than herself.

'So do you, my love.' Rachel returned the kiss. Jane instantly made a noise that consisted of an exhalation accompanied by a dismissive grunt as she blustered past Rachel and into the kitchen.

Once there she asked cheerily, 'Anything I can do?'

Rachel knew Jane could guess the answer to this before it came; a firm 'No, all in hand!' delivered as pleasantly as possible, but a warning shot across the bow, nevertheless.

Jane, as always, looked awkward and at a loss when her offer of help was refused. She accepted the proffered glass of wine, and Rachel smiled knowingly. At least now her friend would feel a little more comfortable, having something to do with her hands. She watched as

Jane wandered round the very familiar living room as if exploring it for the first time, remarking on the books, CDs and vinyl as she did so.

'Oh, gosh! You've been playing Kate and Anna McGarrigle! Not listened to them for years!'

Rachel blushed and hurried over to replace the treasured album in its cover. She knew she looked flustered, which of course only made it a hundred times worse. She also knew Jane would not miss this, though she would be too polite to say anything. Yet.

The doorbell rang again, and Rachel was glad of the excuse to leave Jane to wander alone in her living room. This time, Annie just raised her head and went back to dreaming of rabbits.

'Oh, blimey, Rachel! I thought I was never gonna get parked. So many fucking cars in your street these days. How you doing, love?'

Suzy went from complaining to warmth with the rapidity of a toddler on a sugar high. She gave Rachel a big bear hug, smacked a kiss on her lips, then held her at arm's length, a look of frank appraisal on her face.

'Blusher? Or are you a bit hot and flushed, my love? Oh bless ya. You been slaving away in the kitchen? Christ! I could eat a horse!' And with that she let go, making her way into the house as if she owned it. As Rachel arrived in the living room her two friends were embracing.

'How's that gorgeous son of yours, Suzy?'

'Miles?' Suzy's face took on a look of pride mixed with consternation, as if she had just been given the honour of being the first woman on the moon. 'He's doing really well at uni. Top marks all round. But then, he feels he has to try twice as hard as everyone else.'

'I do hope the lecturers aren't racist,' Rachel interjected, a note of indignation in her voice.

'No, of course not, silly. But he has to go onto the wards, doesn't he? Joe and Joanne public aren't quite as enlightened. He rang me sounding very shaky the other day.' Her own voice trembled as she said this. 'Apparently, one of the patients said...' There was a pause, as Suzy visibly gathered herself together. 'He said, "I'm not being examined by no—" N word!'

'Well I hope he was put in his place!' This time it was Jane who leaped to defend the lad they had all seen grow into a fine, intelligent and dedicated young man.

'No. Apparently, the man was just offered another student. A white student, of course. Miles was devastated. I tell you, that lad's gonna need to grow a thicker skin if he's going to get through the training.'

The room fell silent. Rachel felt somehow responsible, being a white professional, for the errors of her colleagues. But then Suzy told them both the man in question was in the terminal stages of prostate cancer. The other two women muttered inconclusive statements about understanding but not condoning. But as she sat down, Rachel had a nasty taste in her mouth.

Despite this starter the meal went smoothly, the profiteroles and ice cream going down particularly well. Rachel and Jane got quietly pissed while Suzy remained as sober as ever, nevertheless cackling with loud, good-humoured laughter. During dessert, Rachel felt once again Aggie's presence. She wasn't sure if she was making it up but she sensed Aggie was waiting for something to happen. Jane planned to get a taxi home, but Suzy wouldn't hear of it, despite the fact that the two women lived on opposite sides of town.

They were still sitting at the large, oak table over coffee when Suzy raised her head and stared at Rachel, with what Rachel recognised as her friend's no-nonsense look.

'Right. You can cut the crap, Drake. Who is he? Or she?'

Jane also looked expectantly at Rachel, as if she had known this moment would come. At this point, Rachel spotted Aggie over Suzy's shoulder, her arms crossed as if to mirror Suzy's attitude. It was all Rachel could do not to look at her and scowl.

Both Suzy and Jane knew that Rachel had had neither boyfriend nor girlfriend for some years. Rachel hadn't told them the details of her last relationship, but they had somehow both deduced that it was abusive, and she sensed a special protectiveness towards her as well as a keen interest in seeing her 'settled' with the 'right' person. She felt cornered, her hot cheeks betraying her.

'Okay, okay. Shit! I can't hide anything from you two, can I?'

Her embarrassment was quickly replaced by a sense of relief at no longer having to pretend nothing had happened. She could feel a smile creeping across her face. And so, she told the two women a somewhat sanitised version of events. They seemed happy with her account despite firing questions like millennial fireworks:

'So what's she like? As a person, I mean?'

'Um… she's lovely.'

'What does she look like?'

'Petite, dark, gorgeous eyes you could drown in.'

'What does she do for a living?'

'She's a community artist.'

'Oooh! Was she involved in the Olympics by any chance?'

'Not that I know of.'

And so on. Rachel was aware that her answers were woefully inadequate. The truth was, she knew very little about the woman, and was as shocked at this turn of events as her friends were delighted. And yet Aggie, who stayed unobtrusively in the background throughout, nodded her head in sage approval.

The inquisition ended with a 'Sooooo happy for you' in unison, which only served to increase Rachel's rising sense of alarm.

'Look, you two… I have absolutely no idea where any of this is leading, so keep it under your hats!'

At which point Aggie smiled knowingly and disappeared.

As the days passed Rachel found herself both wanting Fran to ring and dreading it. Despite the joy of finally finding someone she was attracted to and who seemed to find her attractive, she found the not knowing impossibly stressful. Life was much calmer and more ordered before they had met. Before Fran burst into her life she could concentrate (more or less) on work, had clearly demarcated times for friends, and never spent time worrying about how she looked. Now, she found herself inspecting her waistline, grabbing hold of spare flesh and wondering if she should go on a diet. She plucked a couple of grey hairs from her head and fingered the hair dye at the supermarket. She bought some lipstick, remembering with a tingling between her thighs how enticing Fran's red lips had been. And she bounced out of her chair every time her phone rang.

But Fran did not ring. A whole week went by. Rachel considered ringing Fran, but the thought that she might be rebuffed made her feel nauseous. She decided it was best to simply leave it. It had been fun, but that was all. But every time her thoughts wandered to Fran, which was roughly as often as a small child asks, 'Are we there yet?' her body responded against her will with a humming electricity and a quickened heart.

God, Drake! You lust bucket! What has got into you?

Her best friend wasn't going to take this one lying down.

And then one day, the phone rang, and it was Fran, sounding nervous. Rachel's heart warmed to her. She was human after all, vulnerable like her.

'Hi. It's Fran.'

Rachel struggled with the myriad things she wanted to say but could not form the words. Inside, she was doing battle with herself. She was ecstatic that Fran had finally rung, but she didn't want to sound needy. She was aware of the silence she was creating as she searched for *le mot juste*. In the end, her response was:

'I know. Hi Fran.'

Huh! Is the best you can do, Drake? Where is your wise woman now, eh?

Another silence.

'It's good to hear from you.' Rachel continued, holding her belly in.

Was this too bold? But then she had done bold. Big time. What was there to lose?

'Oh. Good.' Fran sounded relieved.

Rachel's shoulders dropped. She hadn't realised she was tensing them. She let out a breath.

'How are you?'

'Oh. The exhibition went well. We got lots of people through the door. I should have got you to complete an evaluation form, actually. But not to worry. I've been trying to make sense of them. Over a hundred, but mostly positive. It should all help with the funding application. I hate that sort of thing.' Fran laughed a nervous, apologetic laugh.

'Oh, gosh, yes, I hate them too. I have to do funding bids all the time, for research.'

Oh my God, you pratt! Now you sound bloody condescending. Arsehole.

Rachel cringed at her own sad efforts to find common ground. They had talked so little. She had to admit they had had other things on their mind that night.

Remembering their time together, Rachel again found her body responding against her will. She worked to stay focussed on safe territory.

'Look, it would be lovely to see you again. Fancy a coffee some time? I'd like to get to know you.' Somehow, the suggestion of a date sounded far more forward than the rampant sex they'd already had. Rachel was glad Fran couldn't see her cheeks going the colour of an old-fashioned post box.

'I'd love that.' Fran's quick response allowed Rachel to relax a little.

'There's a new place opened in town,' Fran continued. 'It's one of those cafés selling food that's just out of date, all cooked by an amazing chef. You pay what you feel for the food, but the coffee's a fixed price. And it's amazing. Shall we go there?'

'Sounds good. My treat. How about Friday? I work at home Fridays. Are you free?' Rachel was holding her toes under, clutching at the carpet.

'I can be. I finish a group around twelve, but I have to write notes and see the staff. How about two?'

'Perfect. I think I know the place you're suggesting. I'll see you there around two.'

As she put the phone down, trembling like she used to do when she spent too long in the sea as a little girl, Rachel saw a hand out of the corner of her eye, holding a cigarette. Then the other hand came into view, with a thumbs up. So, Aggie was back! And she obviously approved.

The café was quirky, with an assortment of upright chairs and tables plus non-matching easy chairs and plants draped around the place, with art works on the walls. As she walked in Rachel saw Aggie standing right in front of one of the art works, her hair out of rollers but still partially covered by a head scarf. She had a coat on over her pinafore but had somehow omitted to change her slippers for shoes. Rachel glared at her. Aggie moved out of the way and then seemed to disappear. It was then she recognised the painting Aggie had been standing in front of, just as Fran walked in.

'So, this is where your exhibition ended up.' Rachel hoped she sounded suitably calm but appreciative, as her eyes avoided the painting that had started all of this.

'Yes. They needed some stuff on the walls, so it was a perfect opportunity. I've offered to change the exhibits every three months for them, and in the meantime the artwork is for sale. Except mine, of course. I wouldn't want to be making money out of my position as curator.'

Rachel felt a warm sensation in her chest. Here was a woman with principles she could relate to, who loved her job just as much as (despite her grumbles) Rachel loved hers. Fran seemed to genuinely care about the people she was serving; she talked with passion about the artists whose paintings adorned the walls of the café. At the end of their coffee, the two women parted company with a warm hug.

After their meeting in the café Rachel and Fran started dating more regularly – going to the cinema, theatre, and out for walks in the Yorkshire Dales. Annie loved the opportunity to show off her running, sniffing and herding skills to Fran, who obliged with regular strokes and soft words, and even threw Annie's ball with grace. Rachel found herself warming more and more to this woman who had walked into her life, and who now willingly hiked alongside her in the hills she loved. She also scored points for wearing proper walking boots, and like Rachel she made no concessions to what Fran described as 'gear whores'. Her boots were functional, as was her waterproof coat. Unlike Rachel, who wore walking trousers, Fran happily clambered over stiles in a dress and leggings. At the end of each walk they retired to one of the many country pubs in the area where Fran would inevitably begin chatting to an older couple or befriend some wayward four-year-old. Rachel found she was simultaneously attracted to, envious of, and embarrassed by Fran's outgoing nature. On these occasions Aggie appeared beside Rachel with a pint of stout. Rachel, after her initial fears of impending madness, was getting used to seeing Aggie around. Nevertheless, she was grateful she appeared to be the only person who could hear Aggie as on one occasion in a pub in Kettlewell in the Yorkshire Dales she loudly pronounced with a kind of proprietary pride:

'She's so bootiful, ain't she Rachel? You've gotta admit it.'

And in Grassington:

'Don't ya just love the way she ain't afraid to just go up to people and start chattin'?'

Rachel never would have dared to strike up a conversation with a complete stranger, yet for Fran this was as natural as breathing. As she watched and listened and was drawn into the conversations Fran started, Rachel realised her world was expanding.

On one occasion after a long walk they ended up at Rachel's house instead of a pub. Seeing an opportunity, Rachel suggested they have a bath together.

'Um. I'd better get off, actually. Got a lot to do. I have to prep a session for tomorrow.' Fran looked down at her socked feet, wiggling her toes.

'Ah. OK. No problem. It's just that I need a bath…' Rachel's voice trailed off as she gestured towards the bathroom. She knew she sounded pathetic, needy.

'Well, I guess… do you have a spare towel?' Fran's eyes refused to settle on Rachel but wandered towards the door.

'Fran, it's OK. Really. If you would rather just be friends, we can be friends.' Rachel knew she was lying. She wanted more. She had grown to like this woman. A lot. She had principles, she walked, Annie loved her.

And then there was the small matter of what was happening to her body and mind as she contemplated bathing with her.

Fran began peeling off her jumper, taking off her socks, and – then she was naked, standing in front of Rachel.

Rachel smiled softly and took Fran's hand, leading her into the bathroom. First, she selected some music on her phone, then began running the bath. The pipes made a noise that sounded like someone knocking out a rhythm on a steel drum. They both laughed as Fran reached across and pulled Rachel's fleece off her, then unbuttoned her walking trousers.

The bath was sensual, slow and all Rachel could have wished for. When Fran reached for the soap and lathered up her hands Rachel was more than ready to be caressed and kissed, returning Fran's passion with her own as they took turns to lie back in the bath and be massaged.

When Rachel came it was with a smile of abandon. The relief was not purely physical. She was glad to have broken the ice.

Rachel and Fran began seeing each other a couple of times a week. Rachel also called Fran most Friday nights after pouring herself a large glass of cabernet sauvignon. They seemed to enjoy each other's company and the sex was good, but Rachel felt Fran was holding something back. Rachel knew she wanted more from this relationship; she liked Fran a lot and feared she was falling in love, but she didn't know quite where she stood. Fran seemed happy enough to meet up mid-week and chat on the phone on a Friday night, but they never met at weekends and Rachel increasingly noticed voices in the background when she rang which both intrigued and unnerved her. On one occasion about two months after their first meeting, she thought she heard a whisper very close to the receiver. A woman's voice. Rachel wasn't sure what she had heard, but it sounded a bit like 'stroke me'.

Rachel broke out in a sweat as it hit her with a thud that she had not yet met Fran's friends, and come to that she had not introduced Fran to hers. This now struck her as odd given how important Jane and Suzy were in her own life. But then, such a move would be a statement about their relationship, and she wasn't sure if she was ready for that just yet. Still, the impact of hearing that other woman's voice had disrupted her complacency.

The next time Fran came around Rachel decided it was time to take action. As they lay in Rachel's bed Fran's body felt soft and warm against her skin, but Rachel's own body was held with the control of an Argentine Tango dancer. She gave Fran a gentle squeeze as, trying to sound casual she asked, 'Hey, Fran, would you like to meet my friends?'

Pause. Fran made no move, but Rachel could feel her body change from sleepy to alert, the skin tightening as its tiny subcutaneous muscles fired into action. Rachel tensed her core to continue:

'I could invite them all over for dinner one night. A weekend might be best, since they work the nine to five. What do you say?'

A Kind of Family

Fran stayed still for a while, then slowly propped herself up on her elbows so that she could look down into her lover's face.

'Love to,' she grinned.

And with that she got up, dressed, and within ten minutes was out of the door. Fran had still never slept over.

Home truths

Initially, Suzy said she could make it on the agreed date to meet Fran. But then she rang.

'Oh, God, Rachel. I am so, so sorry. I really want to meet Fran. It's just that t'refuge is short staffed at the minute, and they really rely on us volunteers to do some o' t'routine stuff so they can be available for women who are needing to be checked in and stuff. I feel a reet heel. But I guess I'd feel an even bigger heel if I let them down. I'll make it up to you, I promise. I'll get fish and chips in next time at mine. We can shove that great lumbering son of mine out o' t' living room. He needs to bloody well get his head in some books, any road.'

And so, it was back to the drawing board. Rachel managed to insist the meal was at her house, and finally found a Wednesday evening when no-one was busy.

'God, we are such a typical bunch of single women,' she quipped on the phone to Jane. 'It's no wonder we've all been unattached so long. How the hell am I meant to make room in my life for a serious relationship, Jane?'

Behind the quip, Rachel was feeling the strain. She wanted this relationship more than anything she had wanted in a long time, but she was behind with her emails, she had passed up being in a team that was writing a potentially lucrative research funding bid due to lack of time, and she knew she was cutting corners in terms of the feedback she was giving on students' written work. She felt as if she was juggling with fire sticks. She had noticed of late that the eczema above her left eye was beginning to get red and sore, and she suffered with chest pain whenever she ate in a hurry – which was most of the time.

When the day for the meal came Rachel spent the whole of it cleaning, shopping, preparing food and cooking, during which time she had several 'helpful' suggestions from Aggie.

'You wanna put some salt in with your spuds. What? You not *doin'* potatoes? A meal ain't a meal wivout spuds!'

'Are you gonna put a bit o' sugar in wiv yer peas? Now don't tell me you ain't doin' peas eiver.' Aggie shook her head slowly, her lips pursed.

Later, she turned up in the bathroom, when Rachel was cleaning.

'You don't need those bloody squirty things on mirrors. A nice bit o' newspaper and water is all you need to clean a mirror.' This, as she crossed her arms under her bosom, once more pursing her lips with her head tilted to one side.

And so it went on, with Rachel becoming increasingly irritated until she firmly shut the bathroom door on Aggie and said 'Keep out! I'm having some private time!'

As Rachel lowered herself into her bath with just one hour to spare, she felt exhausted, but wired. She felt a flutter in her chest and knew she would struggle to eat anything. The water felt soothingly hot, the bubbles caressing her tired body. She closed her eyes. As she felt herself sinking into near-sleep she heard a half whispered, 'Wake up!' in one ear. She forced her eyes open. There was no-one to be seen.

After her bath, and relieved to see that Aggie had taken a hike, Rachel spent precious minutes debating with herself over what to wear before settling on a plain black shift, to which she attached her great-aunt Lizzy's brooch. The brooch was very sixties, far too fussy and diamanté, but she liked it. It gave her some comfort, as if her auntie was watching over her, holding her hand to help her through the challenge of two worlds colliding.

It was ten minutes to eight when she finally made it downstairs, Annie racing ahead of her so that she nearly tripped. The doorbell rang just as she was tying her apron to do some last-minute food prep.

'Shit! No!' she shouted out loud, then realised she could be overheard.

She looked towards the door and saw the shadow on the other side shifting from one leg to another. The figure was petite. Fran. She opened the door. The concern on her face must have registered, because Fran apologised for being early.

'Um… sorry. Gosh, I've just realised what bad form it is to turn up early for a meal. Don't let me get in your way. I just didn't want to be making a grand entrance and all that, when your friends turn up.'

Across the road, Mrs Honeysuckle emerged from her house staring, handbag over her arm, red lips gathered as if for a big smackeroo. Rachel stared back.

Objectionable busy body, thought Rachel.

'Hello, Fran. Please don't apologise. You know I'm always insanely delighted to see you.'

Rachel's eyes gleamed with mischief as she then whispered in Fran's ear: 'I don't know if you've noticed my neighbour, but if she's so keen to look at us, how about we give her something to talk about?'

Without waiting for a response, she kissed Fran on the lips, her eyes smiling confidently over Fran's shoulder at Mrs. Honeysuckle as she did so. The kiss turned into more than mere show.

'Pity we don't have more time to ourselves, actually.'

Rachel made way for Fran to enter, glancing at Mrs Honeysuckle as she did so. Mrs H appeared to have frozen on the spot. Once Fran was safely over the threshold, Rachel cocked her head to one side, still grinning at her neighbour. Just before she shut the door she spotted Aggie holding up a rainbow scarf and appearing to fix it onto Mrs H's garden gate.

Rachel stifled a chuckle and turned to Fran.

'What can I get you?'

'Oh, just some water, thanks. Driving.'

Rachel had hoped Fran would come by taxi and join Jane and her in killing a few bottles of wine. She felt here heart sink a bit in her chest, and then her stomach tightened. Would Jane think Fran was boring? Oh well, at least Suzy would be good company for her.

No sooner had Rachel got back to the kitchen than the doorbell rang again. This time, both Jane and Suzy stood on the step, Jane waving a bottle of red wine and Suzy a bottle of sparkling water. Both were grinning from ear to ear.

'Saw that old – sorry, I'm gonna use a sexist word here Rachel – cow across the road, as I got out me car. Talk about throwing daggers in this direction. Who does she think she is? What IS her problem, eh?'

Suzy's solidarity was like the limestone pavement at Malham; it held Rachel up with a timelessness that meant she never had to question its presence. Rachel smiled warmly as she opened the door wider for Suzy to pass.

'I daresay she thinks we have a man in here and are about to perform some kind of castration ritual on him,' Jane muttered as she followed suit.

'Or maybe we are about to have an all-woman orgy,' came the voice from the back.

All three women fell silent.

'Hi, I'm Fran. I got here just before you.'

Nicely played. Well done, Fran.

'Which one is which?' Fran asked warmly, although Rachel knew she would have already guessed from the accents.

After introductions and drinks Rachel made her apologies and retreated to the kitchen, leaving the other three to get to know each other. She popped back into the living room every now and then to find that her life history had been bared, or rather some of it. Fran now knew how each of the women had met Rachel – Jane when they were both social workers, and Suzy when they were both training to be counsellors – and that they had met each other through Rachel. Thankfully, they appeared to have left out the bit about how they had supported her through the break-up of her first, abusive lesbian relationship – how they had brought her food and cajoled her into eating and drinking, picking up the pieces of her self-esteem and gluing them lovingly back together. Rachel wasn't quite ready for Fran to know the more painful details of her former love life.

She also noticed the two women left out some vital information about themselves, including the fact that Jane saw her work as a substitute family, and that Suzy was supporting her son through med school on a carer's wages. But there was plenty of time for Fran to get to know more – if, that is, they were to get serious one day. For now, Rachel told herself, it was still early days, and anything could happen.

Finally, dinner was served: a starter of crab meat on a bed of rocket on toasted seeded bread, with a very light homemade mayonnaise dip. Jane wolfed this down, but Suzy picked hers over, looking puzzled and eating the most miniscule mouthful before placing her knife and fork deliberately and neatly on the plate. Fran was given a vegetarian pâté made by Rachel from fresh ingredients.

This was followed by a goat's cheese and chutney tart served with roasted parsnips, sweet potato and butternut squash, together with steamed kale. Once again, Suzy grimaced.

'Any meat, Rachel?'

'No, my love. I thought we might try out something new. You don't have to eat it but do try. You never know – you might be surprised.' Rachel bit her lip; she knew she sounded patronising, as if encouraging a child to eat.

If Suzy was offended, she didn't show it. Instead, she tucked in, making hums of approval as she ate.

Finally, Rachel served a dessert of mango, strawberry and yoghurt fool topped with chopped nuts, which was met by Suzy with the same suspicion then surprised delight. After all this, coffee and mints, which everyone enjoyed.

As the dinner progressed, the wine flowed. Both Jane and Rachel's speech became increasingly slurred as their arm movements expanded with little attention to direction, or indeed who might be in the way. The four women sat one on each side of the table. Fran turned increasingly to Suzy on her right for conversation despite Suzy's coarse vocabulary and vocal volume, which seemed permanently set to maximum. They were discussing women's mental health over dessert, theorising about depression as a result of oppression, when Jane suddenly burst into their conversation.

'A woman after my own heart, Fran!' She stifled a burp. 'What a relief! I can szee you think like a feminist!'

Jane sat back with a self-congratulatory smile. Then, having seemingly realised she might need to explain herself, she sat forward to within eight inches of Fran's face as if conveying the secret to life, the universe and everything.

'You see, in my eggshperience, lezhbians are not always feminist. I have known some in my time that simply are lezhbians because of some biological need, and don't seem to szee the need for sisterhood, or for understanding the problems of women as a funcshshunn of patriarchy.'

There was silence.

Which Jane decided to fill.

'What about you, Fran? Which came first, the deshizun to sleep with women, or the dessizhun to support women?'

Fran's cheeks went the colour of ripe strawberries just as Rachel realised the room was now spinning. Rachel looked in alarm at her lover as she saw Fran pull herself upright. She had turned away from Suzy to face Jane sitting opposite her, and Rachel could see that her body had tensed as she prepared herself to respond.

'I have never fancied men at all. I have always loved women.'

There was a pause, as Fran carefully placed her knife and fork down either side of her plate. She continued, her hands calmly in her lap. 'Actually, I have more than one lover. I live in a communal house with three other women. We are in a committed, polyamorous set-up.'

She paused, glancing at Rachel without expression before turning back to her audience.

'Rachel is, as it were, the cat among the pigeons, shaking up our cosy little ménage-á-quatre. I have yet to tell them of my… infidelity.'

Rachel looked on, frozen.

Fran turned to address her now, her voice tightly clipped:

'Sorry Rachel. I was going to tell you at some point. The right time just didn't ever present itself.'

Rachel felt kicked in the guts. She was back there on the day she graduated with her PhD, being publicly shamed and abandoned by the senior lecturer with whom she had been in an abusive lesbian relationship for three years. She could hear the woman's voice saying she would never amount to much, that her research on domestic violence was pointless and that moreover she was a lousy lover. All Rachel could hear was cruelty – as if Fran was relishing the pain she was causing her. Rachel wanted to run and hide or sink through the floor and beyond, into obscurity. But all she could do was sit there paralysed, staring at Fran through increasingly foggy eyes, her body shaking. Fran smiled sweetly back at her, seemingly in control.

Suzy reached into her handbag, pulling out a pack of cigarettes. She reached again, retrieving her lighter and lit up to glares from both Jane and Rachel. Fran immediately started coughing.

'Sorry, Suzy. I'm asthmatic. Would you mind smoking elsewhere, or should I go?'

Jane and Suzy exchanged glances. Rachel knew they would jump to her defence. They would both be mad as hell at Fran for hurting her. But Rachel could also see in their speedy exchange the decision to limit any damage.

'No! Don't go!' came the chorus.

'Sorry. I wasn't thinking.' Suzy stubbed her cigarette out rhythmically on the back of the packet, then replaced it carefully inside.

Rachel remained silent, studying the tablecloth dispassionately. She felt as if she had been transported into a Chinese martial arts movie, with everything happening in slow-motion.

Jane was the one to break the spell, suddenly sounding sober.

'Fran, I'm sorry. That was crass of me, saying that about lesbians and feminism. I can imagine it hurt and upset you. I think we got off on the wrong footing. We've been dying to meet you, haven't we Suze?'

Jane looked at Suzy as she inhaled deeply. Suzy silently nodded. Jane breathed out hard and then in again, and continued:

'I need to say that I don't like the way you told Rachel about this, nor the fact that you have kept it from her for so long. You've misled a woman I love dearly by not telling her about your domestic arrangements.'

Jane's voice cracked a little as her arms moved to close round her stomach.

'But I was wrong to talk to you the way I did, and no doubt that was behind the way in which you did tell her, and us.'

Jane paused, looking round the table now. Suzy nodded again. Rachel felt light-headed as, feeling the support of her two friends she now searched Fran's face, finding it impossible to read. Jane continued.

'I don't sit in judgment on anyone for how they choose to live their life, so long as they aren't hurting anyone. I have no doubt that you hurt my friend tonight. I have no idea why you strung her along, but up to that point I quite liked you. And I could see you were making Rachel happy. Which is why this is all the more shocking and upsetting.'

Rachel felt an urgent need to head to the bathroom. Once there, despite feeling she might faint she locked the door before being violently sick. When she eventually emerged, still lightheaded and needing water, Suzy already had her coat on and her keys in her hand.

She put her arm round Jane, saying it was time they went. Rachel's eyes searched the room.

Suzy looked at her friend, her face full of regret.

'She's gone, love. I'm sorry.'

When she closed the door on the world and returned to her living room, Rachel saw Aggie sitting in one of her armchairs, her head in her hands.

'Fuck off!' was all Rachel could say as she turned to crawl up the stairs, her tears now flowing like water over a burst dam.

A Kind of Family

Richard

After the disastrous meal Rachel threw herself into her work and did not answer her phone other than to Jane and Suzy, who seemed to be taking it in turns to check on her daily. Jane was full of apologies about her drunken gaffe, while Suzy simultaneously defended both Jane and Fran.

'Rachel, Fran seemed lovely until that slightly unfortunate bit of the evening,' she observed on one occasion. 'Look, I know Jane likes a drink, but she isn't the only one to say the wrong thing after a glass or two.'

'I know, Suzy. It's OK. I've forgiven Jane. She's full of remorse. Though I've told her she's an idiot. And a drunken one at that.'

'Takes one to know one,' Suzy quipped, to which Rachel managed a laugh, of sorts.

Rachel decided the affair had been a nice interlude up until the meal, but it was time to move on. Except that a big bit of her wasn't convinced.

One day after a particularly tiresome staff meeting, she found herself walking behind Richard on her way out.

'Richard! Fancy a coffee?' Richard, she knew all too well, would always fancy a coffee with her, and so long as he was not either teaching or chairing a meeting, he would find time for one. Rachel felt a bit guilty, knowing that her own interest in Richard was purely platonic. But she valued his friendship, and right now she needed a friend she could trust – someone who would not judge.

A Kind of Family

He turned round, smiling. Richard's blue eyes twinkled at her in a way Rachel had never seen them twinkle when he looked at one of his students, or when he did his best to laugh at the Dean's jokes. His faded tan corduroy jacket hung off him looking as crumpled as if he had slept in it, the pockets misshapen from shoving felt tips, tissues, keys and other items into them over more than a decade. His shoes, once smart brogues, were similarly fraying. Rachel wondered what he spent his money on, but then she remembered that he supported various good causes which were far more important to him than buying a new pair of shoes when his own were still perfectly serviceable. However, his lack of attention to updating his wardrobe might also be explained she knew, by the fact that he also had a rather less than Quakerly love of whiskey and an equally un-Quakerly gas guzzling Porsche.

'I could really do with a coffee, as it happens Rachel. Shall we pop over to the students' union?'

'No. If it's all the same to you can we go somewhere a bit quieter? The senior common room, maybe?'

Richard's face showed momentary concern as he looked at his watch, but before Rachel could feel worried, he adjusted his expression to his usual indulgent smile.

'Sure. Love to.'

Rachel waited until Richard had taken a sip of his black coffee and she had taken a good gulp of cappuccino before she opened the conversation.

'Richard, how are you? I haven't had a chance to catch up with you in ages.'

'I'm fine, Rachel. Working on the new book. Takes ages, as you know! How are *you*?'

'Oh, gosh, Richard!' Rachel took another sip of her coffee, looking down so that she could gather herself.

'Something happened out of the blue, and I thought all my Christmases and birthdays had come at once. But I'm afraid to say, it all went pear shaped.'

She could tell that, despite her efforts to keep the enormity of how this had affected her under wraps, her voice hit tremolo as she completed her last sentence.

Richard said nothing. He just looked at Rachel, his face full of compassion. Waiting.

The ball's in your court! Just get on with it and put the poor sod out of his misery!

Thanks, best friend.

'It's a woman.'

Richard looked down into his coffee. Then he drew breath and looked again at Rachel with a well composed, wide-eyed smile.

'Well, that's good, isn't it? How many years has it been, Rachel?'

'A fuck of a long time, Richard,' Rachel rejoined, knowing what game they were playing now. The one in which they shared confidences, knowing each other inside out and upside down. Always benign. Always without making demands on each other. The unspoken rules emboldened her.

'Turns out, though, that my liberal politics had not prepared me for her polyamorous lifestyle!'

So now, it was said. Richard remained looking steadfastly at Rachel, his face a practised mix of concern and un-shockable support.

'That must be a hard one to take in.'

'Richard, have I ever told you that you would make a great counsellor?' Rachel quipped, not for the first time. Rachel knew she was taking part in a well-rehearsed dance, designed to keep a safe distance between them.

He smiled back. Rachel continued as if Richard had spoken.

'Yeah. I don't expect her to give up this lifestyle. Who would? She lives with three other women. They're totally committed to each other.

I'm the fly in the ointment. It was obviously a fling to her – a big mistake on my part.'

'Do you know that?'

Rachel thought. No, she did not know, but there was no way she was going to ask. 'I don't want to risk finding out that I'm surplus to requirements. Would you?'

Even as she asked this rhetorical question Rachel bit her tongue, wishing she could unsay what she had just said. But then, it was also the right question to ask Richard. He had never asked her out. He knew she would say no. Okay; she had had a male lover in the past, but that was a long time ago. The abusive affair with her first lesbian lover had nevertheless opened her eyes to the possibility of a fulfilling relationship with a woman.

Richard's eyes were visibly becoming moist, and in that moment, she felt an inexplicable connection to him that went way beyond being colleagues and friends. His openness touched her in the centre of her chest as he continued despite his vulnerability.

'I guess I can understand what's getting in the way, Rachel. But I also know that if you don't ask, you will never know for sure.'

As he spoke, Richard's gaze seemed to penetrate Rachel's soul. She knew he wanted to help her, even though he would never take his own advice, but her sense of connection had turned into discomfort.

Rachel stood up.

'Maybe you're right Richard. Thanks for the chat. I'd better go. I'm teaching in half an hour.'

Richard sat down in Meeting for Worship in his usual place opposite the clock. He liked to know what the time was – partly to avoid ministering too close to half past eleven when the Elders would shake hands to end the Meeting, and partly to reassure himself about how much time was left. It wasn't so much that he wanted the Meeting to be over, but that he knew he needed time to still his mind and become part of what Quakers call 'the gathered Meeting'.

Today was especially challenging. It was mild weather, and sunny. He felt restless, wishing he was walking in the hills, or even marking student work while sitting by the window. But it was important to him to keep turning up to Meeting, whatever state of mind he was in. And besides, today was his turn to make the tea and coffee. At least that meant getting out of sitting through notices that he could read online, which when spoken aloud always felt like an irritating waste of time that could be spent on more productive tasks – including that omnipresent marking.

He looked at the clock. Already 10.35, and his mind had been on other things for the past five minutes. He was brought back into the room by a particularly vocal baby whose mother was making futile attempts to shush him. He wanted to go over and reassure her, thank her, even, as her baby had brought him back to the present. Back from his distracted replaying of the moment Rachel had told him about her new love interest. He felt close to tears. Of course, he knew Rachel had had relationships with women, but he had lived in fantasy hope – until now.

He berated himself. Why had he not just asked her out, long ago? Why was he always the good male friend and never the lover? He blamed himself. He was a pushover, weak and ineffectual despite exercising regularly in an effort to feel more traditionally masculine.

Richard looked around the Meeting. Next to the central table on which sat a rather sad yellow rose in a glass of water, three of the older members of the meeting were deep in worship. Each one looked totally serene, with benign smiles on their faces. Richard made a mental note to ask each of them how they 'centred down' for meeting – and then immediately dismissed the idea. He knew how to do it. It just wasn't always that easy!

A Kind of Family

After what seemed like two more minutes but was actually ten, a couple of people stood up and looked around the room. The children all dumped their books and soft toys with parents, who whispered in their ears, and out the children eagerly trooped, for three quarters of an hour of fun. The older children would have a deep and meaningful discussion on some topic like modern-day slavery, while the younger ones would get out the glue and paints and make something that had a very loose connection to Quaker values, possibly after hearing a story.

The room re-adjusted as late-comers entered the room immediately after the children left, and the Meeting went into a new gear. Richard focussed on his breathing – watching it go in, and out – and then on his connection to and love for the other people in the room. He was aware that this Quakerly love was not universally easy. He guiltily noted a sense of irritation with the Friend in the corner who spoke quietly to his voices, and with another Friend who spoke at every meeting, often quoting from the Bible. That Friend had clearly prepared his ministry, despite the written advice to the contrary. Thanks to the mindfulness course he had undergone at the university Richard managed to compassionately move back to a sense of waiting and opening to the Light. Finally, he entered a deep place of oneness with himself and with all humanity, relieved to still be able to find this state of bliss.

At one point someone stood up and spoke about something that seemed to cut across Richard's fragile inner peace, but he had learned long ago that not all ministry 'spoke to his condition', while it might to someone else. This enabled him to 'hold in the Light' the person who was speaking, while not really focussing on the words. If asked about what had been said during Meeting Richard realised he probably would not be able to say. But it didn't matter; no-one was going to test him on it. Eventually, the Elders shook hands and Richard leaned over to shake hands with the people on either side of him, then he reached across the aisle between two sets of chairs to shake some more hands. And then, he stood up and made for the door, aware once more of a deep sadness within.

He was not looking forward to having to make conversation while serving the tea and coffee.

A Kind of Family

Strike that

Rachel threw her keys across the kitchen table and kicked off her shoes, then pulled on her favourite rainbow jumper. She walked into the living room and looked at the answering machine. Fifty messages. The message system was full. She considered deleting them all, but then there might just be something important in there. She decided to put it off for another day, and instead moved into the sanctuary of her study.

Today was not a day for having the doors open. She could feel a wintery nip in the air. She sank into her capacious jumper, willing the colours to give her some warmth. Despite the greyness outside, Rachel loved this view. Her study was her sanctuary. Rachel sighed as she gazed past her chipped ironwork patio furniture, towards the copper beech tree.

And then, a now familiar voice came from behind her.

'I fink you'll find she's been leaving you messages. It's time you listened to 'em.'

Rachel could see Aggie's reflection in the glass before her, a self-satisfied smile spreading across her face as she stood there, arms crossed. Rachel bristled.

'Why don't you just get lost, Aggie?'

'Um… because I care.' Aggie's voice sounded soft, unlike her usual self-assured bossiness. Despite herself, Rachel found she was warming to this strange woman who might or might not be the product of her own unconscious, but whom no one else could see or hear. This was so unlike her previous experience she felt as if the very ground on which she stood and sat had become unreliable. Had she really been listening to this woman for months? Taking notice of her? What possible explanation was there, if not that Aggie was a psychotic hallucination?

'Rachel, you're not mad.'

The bluntness with which Aggie broke into Rachel's reverie shocked her back into the present. She looked at Aggie with her mouth open. For once, no words would come out. Rachel stared at Aggie for several seconds then out to the garden as she let out a sigh and brought a fist to her mouth. Then she smoothed the hair back from her forehead, aware that tears were coming out of nowhere.

'Look, I'll leave you to cogitate.' That soft, tender voice again. 'Just listen to yer phone messages. I know you'll do the right fing. I'm off. But I'll be back. See ya.'

And Aggie was gone.

Rachel shook her head as she walked back into the kitchen, where she found a glass on the draining board and a half-drunk bottle of cabernet sauvignon on the work surface. If she was going to listen to these bloody messages, she would need a drink.

Once back in the living room she settled into her favourite armchair with Annie at her feet, doing her familiar circular dance before settling with her weight on Rachel's foot. The first message was from someone selling replacement windows.

Delete.

Then, the second one:

'Rachel, it's me. I guess I keep ringing at the wrong time. I just want to apologise for my outburst at the dinner table. It was wrong of me, to tell you in that way. Can we talk? Please?'

Delete.

'Hi Rachel. I know you must be angry with me. I was a shit. Look, I did intend to let you know, but it never seemed like the right time. I want to explain. Please call me?'

Delete.

'Have you had a non-fault accident in the last three years?'

Delete.

'Rachel, I guess you're ignoring me. I can't blame you. But Rachel, and this is really, really hard for me, I am telling them all about us tonight. I cannot live a lie. Please call me.'

Fran's voice sounded tearful. Rachel found her resolve weakening as wayward tears began to form in her own eyes. Annie shifted to look up at Rachel, tentatively wagging her tail. Rachel stared straight ahead. She felt dizzy.

She pressed save, and then waited for the next message.

'Rachel, I've told them all. They were shocked, but very supportive. They want to remain my friends. They love me, and don't want to lose me entirely, but they realise sometimes we have to move on from even the best of relationships. I know we haven't committed to anything, and I've probably fucked up royally what little chance we did have of a relationship, but I just want you to know I was wrong not to tell you before. And, well, it would be wrong of me now to continue with them as if nothing had happened. They say I can stay living here for the time being, while I sort myself out.'

Rachel could tell Fran was crying as she recorded her message. She forced herself to continue listening to Fran's words, just about audible between sobs.

'Rachel, I love you. I'm so, so sorry I didn't tell you before. I guess I knew I wasn't in a position to offer you anything until I'd got myself out of the mess I'd created. Rachel, I want you to know that if you'll have me back, I'm all yours. One hundred per cent. Of course, I can understand if you…'

Rachel began dialling, now sobbing herself, her heart swelling in her chest. As soon as the phone rang, it was answered.

'Rachel?'

'Fran. Would you like to come round?'

Fran opened the conversation:

'Rachel, I was totally out of order. I'm not excusing myself, but I confess I felt humiliated by Jane's questioning about my sexuality. Still, it was wrong of me on so many levels. And I should have told you from the outset about my situation. I guess I was scared you'd run a mile.'

'I know. And yes, I probably would have,' Rachel admitted. 'Jane does sometimes drink rather too much for her own good. Not that I can shout,' she added, aware that she did not want to place her friend entirely in the wrong.

'Yes, but I was still wrong,' Fran quickly added, touching Rachel's arm with feather-light reassurance. 'I felt humiliated, so I humiliated myself *and* you *and* Jane by coming out about my domestic arrangements in the most brutal way possible. I should not have told you like that, in front of your friends. Instead of waiting and working it out properly I waded in with my size ten wellies. Which is quite something for someone whose feet are a size four!'

Fran smiled at her own joke, in an obvious attempt to relieve some of the tension in the room. It worked. Rachel felt impressed by Fran's capacity for honest self-reflection, even if she did have a tendency towards too much honesty at times. Rachel also prized the capacity in others to apologise when they got things wrong – a capacity that had been sadly lacking from her previous relationships.

'Fran, thank you.' Rachel twizzled the wine glass she was holding. 'I admit I was shocked, hurt and humiliated. It reminded me of my last relationship, and – well – I never want to go there again. I've spent a lot of money on therapy, trying to get back my self-respect, and I won't let anyone demolish me ever again.'

Rachel paused. Her voice sounded hoarse. She placed her glass down carefully on the coffee table beside her. Then, looking into the distance she dug her nails into the cuticles on either hand.

Rachel's body collapsed in on itself as she breathed out. 'I've been avoiding you, in case you hadn't noticed. I… I don't know whether or not I can trust you now.'

'I know. Rachel, I wish there was something I could say to make things better between us.'

Rachel forced herself to look at Fran and saw eyes that were full of tears and puppy-like remorse. Her heart began to soften, but her unseen armour stayed firmly in place. This had to be resolved, and properly.

'I've known Jane more years than I care to mention. She's a good friend to me. And she has a heart of gold. I know she was mortified as soon as she said what she did. She's told me so. Please, Fran. Give her another chance.'

Fran looked at her shoes.

'OK. I can't say I'm looking forward to seeing her again, but… well, I want to make it work with us. After all, I'm giving up three women to be with you.'

'Actually, your phone message didn't quite sound like that.' Rachel felt clear-headed now despite Fran's growing smile which she felt was a deliberate attempt to disarm her. Instead, Rachel felt emboldened and angry, convinced that Fran was trying to guilt-trip her by bringing up what she had given up in this rather disingenuous way.

'It sounded like you were separating from them because you'd deceived them, not because you'd fallen out of love with polyamory. In fact, it seems to me you wanted your cake and eat it. How do I know you won't just start a new polyamorous set-up if we get back into seeing each other?'

Fran's smile had vanished.

'I see. Yes, I can see it must look that way. All I can say is, I'm not normally deceitful. In fact, honesty is my middle name. Ask— Anyway. Being with you, I experienced something far better than my polyamorous set-up. I realised I actually want an exclusive relationship. I'm trying to be honest here, Rachel. I'm not saying I don't ever want to see those women again. They're like my extended family, and I will probably always love them. But not in that way. I'm here. I'm yours if you'll have me.'

Rachel looked at Fran, her anger melting as she saw how wide-open Fran was being with her. In that instant, she remembered a friend of hers who had died of breast cancer in the previous year, after years of caring for her elderly mother and denying herself the chance of love. Here was *her* chance.

She reached out for Fran's hand. Wordlessly, she pulled Fran towards her. The two women hugged and cried then, and afterwards went to bed where they cuddled each other to sleep.

Rachel and Fran began seeing each other more often, including weekends. They visited a nearby jazz club, walked in the hills with Annie, and saw a play by a new local writer. On some of their dates they met up with Jane and Suzy who quickly decided they liked Fran. A lot. It was during a walk in the park that Jane deliberately moved to walk alongside Fran. Rachel felt curious, wondering what they might be talking about.

'What do you reckon Jane and Fran are talking about, Suze?'

'Ah, stop being paranoid, Rachel! I do happen to know Jane wants to let Fran know we like her, and I suspect she also wants her to know that when you thought you'd lost her you were an absolute pain in the arse.'

Rachel shoved her friend on the shoulder and they both laughed as they kicked up the fallen leaves. Rachel always felt when she was with Suzy that she had permission to play. She welcomed these little forays back into her childhood, when life was simple, and leaves were for kicking. She enjoyed the rustle of dry leaves under her feet, wishing they could always be like this and never get wet and soggy.

Later when they were alone in the kitchen preparing supper, Rachel could not resist asking Fran about her conversation with Jane.

'Um… well, she told me you had been alone and miserable for too long, and that when I came along you got your sparkle back. Basically, I seem to have filled a gap where something was missing.'

Fran looked askance at Rachel, ducking slightly.

'Bloody cheek!' Rachel exclaimed in mock self-defence. 'I was fine on my own, thank you very much! Though of course, I do rather like having you around. You're a good fuck, after all.'

Rachel glanced at her lover, wondering if she would take the bait.

'You're not so bad yourself, Dr Drake.' Fran rubbed her body up against Rachel's. But just as Rachel was beginning to think dinner could be served a little late:

'Come on, Drake! I'm starving. Pleasures of the flesh will have to wait.'

Rachel pouted in mock petulance before continuing the conversation started earlier.

'Not that either of my friends can shout about being alone and miserable. Mind you, I have my suspicions about Jane.'

'Meaning?'

'I dunno. I think she might fancy some man, but she's a closed book when it comes to her love life and, to be honest I know there isn't any actual action on that front. Suzy, bless her, is open about the fact that she can't countenance a sexual relationship with anyone. She's firmly heterosexual, mind. She just doesn't trust men.'

Over time, Fran and Rachel increasingly spent time in each other's company whenever they weren't working. Because they both worked odd hours, they sometimes spent an afternoon together mid-week, at other times they met in the evening and overnight, and more and more of their week-end time was spent together in a mixture of domestic chores, walks and cultural activities, and lovemaking. Aggie usually made a cameo appearance either before, during or after each date, but thankfully never appeared during sex. Rachel got used to having Aggie around but was firmly resolved never to talk about her to anyone else for fear of being thought deranged.

Christmas came and went, Fran spending it with her sister Joanne while Rachel ate at Jane's house and Suzy came over for drinks. Fran remained living in the same house as the three women, though Rachel knew that arrangement could not last forever. She was reluctant to simply slip into living together for reasons of convenience, but when she thought about it as New Year approached Rachel realised she was ready to share her space with Fran – if a little scared.

'You know, I would love it if you actually moved in and we made this thing official.' Rachel tried to sound casual as they sipped their champagne, having seen the New Year in with Big Ben and a tender kiss.

'I can't. At least not until I'm sure that my friends would be welcome in the house.'

'But, of course they would be. If this becomes your home, you can bring whoever you want into it.'

'Yes, but don't you see? I want them to come and see *us*, not just me. I don't want you to be hiding in your study when they come round.'

'OK, I get it. It's time I met the women you live with. I know I've been putting it off.' Rachel gulped and looked deep into her empty glass. 'I confess I'm just a teeny bit scared. I don't know what they'll think of me, and I... well, if I'm honest I feel a bit intimidated about the thought of meeting three women who have a prior claim on your love.'

Once said, Rachel allowed herself to fully experience the enormity of her feelings. She had to admit to herself that she felt jealous, knowing Fran was still living with these women. And a small part of her did not trust them, or Fran, to keep it platonic. She wanted Fran living with her so there was no doubt. It was a statement – to them, and to the world. But first, she must get over this hurdle.

'Let's all do something fun together, to avoid any awkwardness.'

The two women looked down at their glasses, then up at the television in synchrony. Rachel silently noted this, realising with some satisfaction how often they moved in synchrony now. Jules Holland was prancing around on the TV, introducing bands with his usual slightly self-congratulatory enthusiasm. Rachel wasn't really listening to the music but was grateful for the distraction.

'*I* know!' Fran bounced up and down, looking pleased with herself. 'They all love tenpin bowling! Let's go tenpin bowling!'

'Great idea! Wow! Why didn't I think of that?'

Rachel put her glass down next to Fran's, pulled her towards her, and this time the kiss moved rapidly from tender to passionate. Aggie, who had been beaming her approval from the corner of the room, swiftly disappeared.

Debra's hair was short and her body stocky, yet with a softness to her movements and her smile that made it impossible not to like her. She was easy to be with, laughing and joking with the man behind the counter as she gave him her doc martens and was handed her bowling shoes.

As Debra took her turn (and got a strike), Rachel became aware of the woman sitting next to her, so quiet as to not draw attention to herself. This effort not to be seen together with her very small frame and apologetic stance reminded Rachel of women she had seen as their therapist; women who had self-esteem issues and sometimes an eating disorder. Rachel learned the woman was called Feather. She seemed to be the exact opposite of Debra. When asked what order she wanted to be in for the game Feather refused to say, instead suggesting Rachel choose which left Rachel feeling uncomfortable. When it came to Feather's turn she chose the lightest ball, and seemed to struggle to hold it let alone throw it. Yet when she entered the area from which the throw was taken she was transformed. She steadied herself, looking poised and strong like a dancer as she aimed her ball with sniper-like accuracy.

It was only the lightness of the ball that prevented it from being a strike. Her first throw resulted in split pins.

Next up was Roxy. Roxy had pink hair and was teased by both Debra and Fran for the fact that last week her hair had been green. Roxy was the bass player in an otherwise all-male rock band, and had just that morning come back from touring Europe. She had got out of bed specially to meet Rachel. Rachel later learned that, while Roxy had decided some time ago to give up drugs and drink, her band members were Debra's drinking partners.

The four women did their best to make Rachel feel included despite the fact that they all knew each other – intimately. They played three games in all, interspersed with drinks and snacks and occasional banter. Each of the three women Fran was currently living with asked polite, safe questions of Rachel:

'So, how many students do you have on your training course?'

'Tell us about your house – do you have a garden? Interested in gardening?'

'What's your favourite record, ever?'

And so on. Debra won the night, predictably, but Rachel did not embarrass herself, coming a respectable second some distance behind Debra, and almost neck and neck with Roxy. Fran was not far behind, and Feather struggled some way behind Fran, in last place.

At the end of the night Rachel bravely extended an invitation to them all for a couple of weeks hence to come round to her house one evening for some drinks and snacks. She felt it would be too much effort to make dinner; the evening would be stressful enough without having to impress with her culinary skill, or lack of.

When the evening for their visit came, Rachel was delighted and relieved that the evening went off well. Feather was not nearly as frightened and unassuming as she had seemed when they first met, though she hardly ate or drank anything. Rachel noticed she did the classic thing of holding food in her hand as if she was about to eat it, then speaking so that she could not put it in her mouth. She also fed other people from her plate: 'Oh, you must try this! It's gorgeous!' Then, she said she was 'stuffed', thanking her hostess profusely. Debra was warm and funny. She showed her softer side by hugging everyone and expressing concern for whatever was going on in their lives. And Roxy was full of anecdotes from the latest tour, including tales about her efforts to find a clean toilet that wasn't a urinal and the time when she had met Slash, one of her guitar heroes, and had crumpled into an incoherent wreck.

At the end of the evening, as the three women got up to go, Debra asked Fran:

'So, you're staying here tonight, I guess?'

Rachel felt immediately embarrassed, wondering if Debra was getting at her, but then she noticed Debra's warm smile as she embraced Fran. While still holding Fran, she looked towards Rachel.

'She belongs here. It's obvious. This woman loves you to bits, Rachel. Don't you babe?' She held Fran at arm's length, a benevolent, big sisterly smile on her face. Then Debra planted an affectionate kiss on Fran's blushing cheek. Debra seemed oblivious to Fran's embarrassment. Instead, she let go and faced Rachel square on, her feet astride and hands in pockets.

'And you love her. I can see it in your eyes. Who could possibly come between you two gorgeous babes, eh?'

Debra's own eyes were a beacon for and to the assembled group. The other two nodded and mumbled their assent.

And so it was, that in late January Fran moved the rest of her things into Rachel's house. Aggie stood silently just inside the doorway, watching as each cardboard box arrived, a look of surprise and at times alarm on her face. Once it was all unloaded Rachel expected her to stay on and 'supervise' the unpacking, but instead she just said:

'Blimey! Good luck finding places for all that lot, duckie!'

And once again, she was gone.

A Kind of Family

PART TWO

Commitments

A Kind of Family

Home from home

Fran steeled herself to make the long car journey to visit her mother. She knew Rachel would not be able to come; she was always too busy with work. Fran could not help feeling slightly jealous of her partner's job. Since she had moved in with Rachel six months ago, they had seen precious little of each other's families. Rachel had met Fran's mother once, and at that briefly and only because she had to do some work nearby.

As she turned onto the M1 southbound Fran berated herself for resenting her partner's choice of career; it enabled them to live reasonably comfortably whereas Fran's community arts job was teetering on the edge and very likely to disappear in the next round of funding cuts. Still, she sometimes felt as if books and papers were the 'other woman'.

The motorway seemed long and boring today, but at least there was a clear blue sky. Fran drove past a field where a burst of yellow rapeseed crop brightened up an otherwise bland landscape, she had driven too many times, in sorrow or desperation.

Susan, Fran's mother, lived in a very ordinary residential care home in Kent. She and Fran's dad, Steve, had moved from Yorkshire to the north Kent coast and near to their roots in London, once the girls had left home. However, Fran's older sister Joanne did not see why their mother should continue living in the family home some distance away from her after their dad's death from pneumonia. He had been at sea when he died at the age of 62; an autopsy revealed he had lung cancer.

A Kind of Family

He had never sought treatment for his persistent cough. And so, Joanne persuaded Susan to move nearer to her, in the heart of Kent. Susan was unaware of her attachment to the place where she had spent some of the happiest years of her married life, until it was too late. She moved into a poky little cottage near Joanne, then initially into sheltered housing after a stroke altered her life forever. Soon after the move into sheltered accommodation she broke her hip, leaving her more disabled than ever. Now, she was in a care home at the age of 73, by far the youngest in the home.

Fran pulled into a service station to break up the monotony. As she sat down with her coffee by a window, she was struck by how dirty the glass was, and smiled to herself. She would never normally notice such things but thinking about her mother had somehow sensitized her to the sorts of things that were important to Susan. Susan used to clean her windows every week until the stroke. She still saw it as her job to pass judgement on everyone else's ability to clean to within an inch of their lives, including Joanne's.

Fran drank the last of her coffee and sighed. It was useless putting off the inevitable. The next challenge would be the M25, then the Dartford crossing (always a nightmare at weekends in the summer months, as endless families made for France), then walking through the door and having to hold herself tight. She never ceased to feel the impact of seeing her mother crumpled up in her chair. It felt like a boulder thrown at her chest.

As she drove, Fran found herself thinking about the present situation in relation to her past experiences of being mothered by Susan. Joanne now did most of the day to day visits, since she lived nearest. Fran felt guilty that she could visit only infrequently, but Joanne seemed to relish the control it gave her. Fran knew that both she and her sister were at times resentful carers. Despite the fact that Susan had been an emotionally distant mother, she had demanded absolute loyalty from her daughters. As they were growing up it seemed nothing they did could ever really please their mother. When Fran didn't marry and have children by the age of 25, she became a huge disappointment to Susan. Joanne did better, bagging both husband and children as required, but her house was never tidy enough, clean enough, warm enough, or boasting the latest gadgets. Both sisters lived with their own and each other's guilt that neither of them was able to be the perfect daughter their mother craved.

And so, by the time she arrived Fran wished she was still somewhere north of Watford Gap. She parked her car in the impossibly small car park, squeezing her Punto in between a Merc and a Beamer. She took longer than usual to gather up her shoulder bag and the flowers she had bought at the service station. Despite their guilty resentments, Fran knew it hurt her sister as much as it did her to see their mother so disabled. Susan had been feisty and independent in her day, walking miles with Steve until he could no longer walk without stopping every few yards to cough. After that, she walked alone but always had Steve to come home to and look after, unless he was at sea – and he always came back. Until he died. Then she seemed to lose her will to live. She carried on living as if in a silent movie, stilted and grey.

'Hello Mum.' Susan looked up from the romance she was reading – a welcome escape, Fran knew, from the reality of her own existence. Her face lit up as she placed the book carefully in her lap. It immediately fell to the floor. Fran walked over and picked it up before steeling herself to kiss her mother. The kiss was returned with a wetness that only afterwards was wiped from Susan's mouth with the tissue she permanently grasped in her hand.

A carer walked in with Susan's lunch and placed it cheerily on the walker, just out of reach. Fran watched and wondered whether this was what they always did, rather than clear space on the swivel table provided by her daughters for that very purpose. There was no way her mother would have reached the food placed so far away, without falling. Fran felt the bile rise in her throat and swallowed its bitter taste.

A Kind of Family

It seemed to her that the carers, overworked and underpaid, were cutting corners because she was here to help for once. She could do their job of ensuring her mother ate. Clenching her jaw, Fran cleared the tray that held all her mother's immediate needs: tissues, water, spectacles, TV remote. She carefully laid out her mother's food and cut it into pieces she knew Susan could manage, all the time wondering – knowing, she thought – what happened when no daughter was there to cut up her mother's food. Was this why her mother was losing so much weight?

Joanne had said she would try to meet up at the home but was notoriously late for everything. There was usually some crisis or other with her many children. Fran sat watching their mother as she struggled to eat and hold a conversation – or rather a monologue – at the same time. Fran noticed her mother's gnarled hands, hands which had once knitted booties and bonnets for all of Joanne's six children. Now, Susan's hands could hardly hold a fork. Fran watched, her stomach tightening as her mother reached over with her 'good' right hand to hold her left wrist, her whole-body listing as she did so. Her toes pointed up, her legs refusing to rest as if she still had jobs to do – as if the fact that she could hardly walk was a bad dream from which she would soon wake.

Fran knew Joanne had told Susan to try to use her bad but dominant arm. She looked on as her mother obligingly tried to make her errant limb behave, to hold the fork so that she could pick up the food Fran had just cut for her. So that she, the woman who had once told them both what to do, could now do what her oldest daughter wanted. Knowing she was breaking the code of sisters, Fran found herself saying 'Mum, if it's too difficult, don't worry. Use your right hand'.

Susan had once been left-handed. She had told Fran that as a child she was called cack-handed and 'the child of the devil', made to use her right hand and criticised for the standard of her handwriting. Fran wondered if she was grateful now that she had spent so many years being forced to use her non-dominant hand, as she picked up the fork in her right hand and started to eat. However, it seemed her appetite had given up on waiting for her as she slowly chewed each mouthful at the front of her mouth.

Fran noticed the small stains on her mother's ample but atrophied bosom, mercifully unseen by Susan. She had always been so proud of her appearance; in her heyday she had worn lipstick every day, formed into a careful cupid bow on her top lip. Even now, Fran knew Susan visited the hairdresser every week for a wash and blow dry, a poignant echo of her past. Her fastidiousness had been compromised by home rules of one bath a week until Fran had challenged the home manager at a review meeting and had it increased to two. Susan continued to clench her tissue in her one good fist to catch any spills of which she was aware. This made it even more awkward to hold the fork, but she was not about to let go of this one bit of dignity.

Susan grew silent as she concentrated on the technicalities of eating. As she watched her mother, Fran recalled what Rachel had said about the mindfulness training she had attended at work.

'It's all about making the simplest of actions – like walking or eating – conscious. You make a deliberate attempt to slow these daily activities down and notice each little action within them,' she had explained.

Fran wondered how Susan would view such an activity. She was pretty sure Susan would do anything right now not to have to focus on the minutiae of eating and walking, both activities being excruciatingly painful, slow and precarious.

Susan placed her fork down on a half-full plate and looked up as if noticing Fran for the first time. Once more her eyes lit up to see her daughter.

'How's Rachel these days, love? Still working too hard?'

A small crumb appeared at the corner of Susan's mouth. She dabbed at it with her crumpled tissue, just too late to prevent it falling into her lap. She seemed unperturbed as her face beamed delight to see her daughter. As she watched her mother, Fran was aware of Susan's beauty shining through laughter lines and worry lines, each one telling a different story of stoicism, pain and ambivalent love. In that moment Fran felt her heart soften towards her often difficult mother, grateful for her attempts at independence.

Fran remembered her mother's feisty proto-feminism back in the days when she herself was forming as a young woman. Susan had joined the Women's Institute where she had learned about world religions and women's issues. This helped her to develop an open mind that was at odds with her own traditional way of life. Despite her initial disappointment that Fran had not produced a husband and children by her mid-twenties the news that she was gay was treated as a badge of honour. Susan saw it as an opportunity to brag to other people of her generation, implying that her family was somehow better than theirs due to its exotic new domestic arrangements. She had always boasted about her daughters to others even when expressing disappointment directly to them. This applied to whether because they produced lots of kids, took up unconventional careers or came out as gay. It was all the same to her; more news to shock and be shocked by, to entertain and secretly be entertained.

The meal clearly over, Fran reached into her bag.

'I've brought you something, Mum. Do you remember when you were clearing out all those old photos and negatives that you thought must be useless? Well, I was hunting through them the other day. Rachel's bought this new-fangled thing that can turn negatives into electronic files, and you can print them out.'

She could see Susan had not quite taken all this in. Her hazel eyes glazed over as she listened politely. Susan seemed disinterested as Fran handed her the photograph in its rather expensive silver frame. Fran had not known what to buy her mother for her upcoming birthday and thought this might be best given to her in person even though it was still some weeks away. Susan looked at the photograph, her brow furrowed.

'Who's that?' she asked, like a child dutifully trying to figure out a puzzle she has been given yet not really wanting to play the game.

'Mum, it's you and Dad. You're about 15 there. Don't you remember? Dad used to have that picture in his bureau. I don't know what happened to the original.'

She suspected Joanne had secreted it away like so many things. It was equally possible that one of her brood had decided to tear it out of the album and ruined it.

The frown on her mother's face slowly eased and her face became lighter, but her eyes seemed to have trouble focussing. Fran noticed her mother's hands shaking ever so slightly as she held the photograph awkwardly in her left hand, her right forefinger hesitantly trying to trace its features. The picture, in black and white, showed a girl sitting on a hillside with her beau, each wearing their Sunday best and smiling at the photographer. The young man looked very dapper in his suit and tie, his shoes shining in the sunlight. He was clean shaven, his hair slicked close to his head. He had his arm protectively round the girl's shoulder. She was beautiful, her young face smiling with the look of a girl who has just been told she is the most special person in the whole world. She was leaning into him slightly. She wore what looked like a white dress over bare legs, and a bow was just visible at her back. Her hair, as now, was perfectly in place, if darker and more wavy than curly, and secured with another bow.

'Thank you dear. That's lovely.'

Susan looked up at the crowded shelf in front of her, her eyes searching.

'Would you like me to put it up on the wall for you, Mum?' Fran asked.

A look of relief came over Susan's face, 'Oh, yes, dear, that would be lovely. Thank you.' But she held onto the photograph, seemingly unaware of her daughter as she looked imploringly at the image of her youthful husband, dead now over a decade.

'Oh, Steve, if you could see me now. I bet you never thought I would come to this.'

Fran felt her stomach and jaw tighten. She wanted to bolt out of the tiny, overcrowded room and leave her mother to her grief. She didn't want to face Susan's relentless sadness all over again. She found herself wondering why she had been so stupid as to think it was a good idea to present her mother with the photograph.

A voice cut into her thoughts.

'Hello sis.'

Fran rose to hug her sister. Always one of the best huggers on God's earth, Joanne held onto her sister for as long as possible before going over to their mother and giving her a perfunctory peck on the cheek.

'Hello Mum', she said, with rather less enthusiasm than she had greeted her sister.

Joanne's hair remained at shoulder length, with gentle waves cascading over her shoulders despite the fact that she had now reached the magic four-O. Long since she sported her natural colour, her hair had remained a light golden brown.

Joanne sat near their mother but turned towards Fran so that her sister could not avoid her gaze. Her eyes were fixed in an attempt at a smile, crow's feet creased along with laughter lines, but this did not fool Fran. She could see the imploring for attention in her sister's body, which held the hope that someone would notice her suffering.

Fran knew Joanne would be relieved to be able to share the care of their mother for once. She frequently told Fran in phone conversations and long emails and texts how worn down she was by her carer responsibilities; worn down by having to shout because their mother's hearing aid was either mislaid, had not been put in that morning, or the batteries had gone. Worn down by witnessing their mother's pain day in and day out. Worn down by continually fighting the little battles for effective care. Worn down by their mother's self-centeredness that, despite her better self, demanded her daughter drop everything when she needed her for some trivial problem that once she would have faced all alone and solved without a moment's hesitation but was now a source of blind panic.

Joanne had sent a long e-mail to Fran just this week, when she had heard Fran was coming down to Kent. She had offered a bed, beginning the email with an attempt at empathy about Rachel's demanding work and then launching into her own tale of woe about money, and her six children's many 'traumas'. As if catching herself and wishing to cover up her transgression, she had ended the email with 'Please ring me any time you want to chat'. Fran knew if she had accepted the offer of the bed it was she who would be doing the listening over a bottle or two of red drunk largely by her sister, the monologue going on far into the early hours of the morning so that she would then wonder why she did not simply drive home through the night. She decided instead to stay with friends half way, politely declining her sister's 'generous' offer.

Fran understood some of her sister's need for attention. Their mother had always delighted in telling the world that Joanne had been a 'mistake', leaving the poor child desperate for love and reassurance – a desperation she continued to play out to this day. Joanne had been born when their father was in the merchant navy. In those days, wives stayed at home and men could be away for months at a time on ship. As a result, their dad had had very little to do with Joanne's upbringing whereas when Fran was born, their father was working nearby, having taken a land job for a few years. He had been there when his second daughter was born, witnessed the birth, and fell in love with her immediately. Fran recalled having a hands-on dad – not because of any modern ideas of what a dad should be but simply because he could do nothing else; to be aloof would have been to deprive himself of his new-found joy. But this gift was not to be Joanne's. She had been at the mercy of their mother's capriciousness and dramatic outbursts, witnessed later

A Kind of Family

by Fran but moderated by their father's gentleness. Susan was creative, lively and forward-thinking, but she was not a natural mother. Fran never remembered being cuddled by her mother, who would always rather be reading a novel than spending time with them. They were largely left to their own devices to play, spending long hours out of the home without supervision.

Fran watched as Joanne started to look round the room. She found herself feeling irritated as she saw that her sister could not give up the habits of trying to make up for the deficiencies in the home. She pushed down her impulse to shout at Joanne as she saw her pickup discarded tissues from the floor. Fran could see Joanne's mouth forming a tight 'O' as she did so, her tongue reaching towards her cheek as if to prop up a fragile retaining wall.

Fran could recall when Joanne's presence was a source of comfort to her. Once, when she lay in hospital with some childhood illness, she longed to see her sister, but hospital rules had meant she was forced to wave through a window. In those days Joanne had long plaits and while Fran did not want long hair for herself (she was content for their father to put a pudding basin round her head and cut her hair short) she loved to handle Joanne's hair, feeling the lumps and bumps and twists and turns as each smooth strand of hair seemed to play hide and seek with the others.

Joanne moved to the bed, puffing up pillows before finally and noisily progressing to the bathroom. Fran could hear her clunking around, the water running fast.

Susan looked towards Fran with a frown of rising confusion and panic.

'Where's Joanne gone?'

Before Fran could reassure their mother, Joanne muttered under her breath, her true feelings safe from Susan's failing ears:

'Cleaning up, mother, which they should have done. This home is an absolute bloody disgrace.'

Fran moved to her mother's side and stroked her bony hand.

'It's alright, Mum, she's just having a bit of a clean-up in the bathroom. She'll be back in a minute.'

Fran allowed herself to revisit the forbidden territory of wishing it had been her Dad who had survived his spouse. As a child, she had followed her dad around, copying his every move. He taught her to swim, and she helped him with the DIY. They were inseparable. One day, aged about four, Fran was playing in the living room all alone. She found a plug in its socket and, being inquisitive she wanted to see what happened when she pulled on it, hooking her hands underneath the Bakelite surround in order to get a better grip. The shock sent her flying across the room. Her dad was the first on the scene, and before long she was in his strong arms, the container they provided shutting out her terror and allowing her tears to flow freely as he softly spoke of people who have electric shocks to make them feel better. It was only years later she realised he must have been thinking of his own uncle, reduced to having ECT for his depression after the war. Despite her reassurance at hearing her father's words, Fran never made the same mistake again. She shadowed him even more after that – and developed a healthy respect for all things electrical. Later, she learned how to change a plug by watching her dad. He was her hero. She loved him with a fierceness that was never quelled even when she reached adulthood and became a feisty, independent and outspoken woman. The day he died, Fran howled from the pit of her stomach.

Fran spent all of Saturday with her mother. On the Monday morning she had to work in, of all places, an old folks' home. Her body felt drained, registering both physical exhaustion from the journey and emotional exhaustion at having seen her mother so frail. It would be so easy to hide away from it all and not visit. Susan rarely complained, preferring to be seen as understanding of the pulls on her daughters' time. As Fran drove to work, listening to a CD compilation of Sinead O'Connor that had been given to her by a grateful woman in one of her art groups, silent tears cascaded down her cheeks as she got to the track 'Nothing compares to you', which the singer had recorded shortly after the loss of her own mother. Fran thought about her once vibrant and feisty mother, reduced to dependence. Her sadness turned to anger that threatened to overwhelm her. She reached out and turned off the CD whose music was crashing into her like rogue waves onto rocks. Rocks that must not be eroded. Not now. Fran had to stay in one piece.

Arriving at the home, the staff took one look at Fran and said in unison:

'It's Fran! It must be Monday!'

They looked worn out, poor loves. Probably working all weekend. Fran discovered after she had started working in the home that in residential care the days tend to blur for both staff and residents. She also found out this meant the usual boundaries of time were not observed, including start and finish times for her sessions. At first, she found this frustrating. She spent some weeks carefully dancing around the staff to negotiate turning off the TV in the living room (the only space in which to work) prior to each session. Cautiously, and taking care to let the staff know she understood how hard it must be to get round everyone in the morning for meds and personal care, she asked what would be the best time for the session to take place so that residents would not be disturbed for routine tasks. They agreed a start time of 10 am. Nevertheless, during her first session a member of staff walked in without acknowledging Fran and loudly pronounced to one of her participants:

'We'd better go to the toilet. We don't want any accidents in Fran's class, do we Alice?'

Today, Fran arrived at the usual time of 9.30 am, placed her bag down in the centre of the room, and looked around her. She noticed Alice's chair was empty and hoped it was just because the staff were taking her to the toilet and not that Alice was unwell, or worse. She would ask, if she hadn't seen Alice by the time she needed to start the session.

Fran's body felt heavy, but she took a deep breath and set about arranging the chairs into a circle, positioning the shape around those residents who were already ensconced for the day so that they did not feel put out by who they might see as this young intruder. Fran had been coming to the home for the past six months, but most residents did not remember her from one week to the next. However, when the music started and she pulled out her long elasticated circle of material for them to hold onto, their faces usually registered recognition and innocent joy.

Once the chairs were arranged, Fran put her music on. She had chosen Beatles music today, knowing that for many of her residents this had been an important part of their home life, some with their baby boomer kids grooving away to it while others would have been young marrieds, listening to the wireless as they engaged in domestic chores. A few were young enough to have been those baby boomers, illness and disability hitting them at a cruelly young age. At the time of the Beatles, some of her participants had probably complained the music was too loud and those ruffians needed a haircut. Yet now, the residents looked back wistfully to times when their home was the centre of family life, with people coming and going and bringing their friends for tea, all of whom would praise each woman's cooking as if it were the best in the world.

As she pulled her elasticated circle from the voluminous bag she carried everywhere she went, Carole walked in. Little older than Fran's mum Carole was upright and physically very able. Were it not for the fact that her cardigan was always buttoned up unevenly and often inside out, and that despite her cut glass accent she was wont to fart loudly and pick her nose, it would have been hard to understand why Carole needed care. Fran looked up at Carole, smiling hopefully. She was met with an icy stare.

A Kind of Family

'What in heaven's name are *you* doing here, child? Haven't I told you to play out in the school playground? This is the staff room, and you are not allowed in it. Now, be gone!'

'Car— Miss Sutherland. I am so sorry to trouble you. It's just that I am preparing a new class in music and movement, and I wondered if you might help me?'

'Oh, well, why didn't you ask, silly? Sometimes, you new teachers look so young I mistook you for one of the gels.'

And at this, Carole sat down in one of the chairs, seemingly satisfied that she was in charge. Having established this, she set about picking her nose with particular thoroughness.

Slowly but with increasing enthusiasm, the residents completed the circle, with just one or two chairs left vacant. Hands reached with painstaking precision to hold onto the elasticated circle, as together the group found a shared and familiar dance rhythm. Bodies moved in ways they had not moved since the previous week, reaching further than either the individuals or staff caring for them thought possible. Smiles crept onto some faces, while other brows knitted in concentration. No one was left out. Even Paul, who sat slumped in his chair with his eyes closed was encouraged to join in when Fran positioned herself beside him. As she swayed from side she deliberately brushed his hand with the cloth in an effort to engage him. She spoke gently and quietly, just to him:

'Hello Paul. Can you hear the music? Do you remember this one?'
Then:
'Can you feel the cloth swaying? Do you want to hold it?'

When Paul's little finger twitched slightly towards the cloth, Fran enthused:

'Wow, brilliant! Thank you for helping, Paul. You're doing great.'

After the session was over Fran ran alongside one of the staff members who was rushing upstairs.

'Where's Alice?'

'Died last night.'

Fran felt a thud in her chest. She stopped running and held onto the stair rail, dizzy and nauseous as the staff member carried on upstairs at great speed.

So that was it. Death. So normal and every day in residential care that Alice doesn't even deserve a mention unless asked about. Life in the care home moves on.

Driving back home, she sobbed again. For her mother, for Alice, and for herself. Though why she was crying for herself she could not quite fathom.

A Kind of Family

Coming out with it

Fran lay with her arm round a sleeping Rachel, a feeling of contentment spreading with unhurried warmth throughout her body. She had never felt this content. In fact, she had never before believed contentment was hers for the taking.

As a young woman she had battled with the expectations of friends, family and society that she should find a man with whom to settle down. Being both petite and pretty, no one expected her to come out as someone who loved women. It had taken a lot of courage when she did tell her mother, and some time longer before she told anyone outside of the family.

As she lay there, Fran remembered how at the age of fourteen she had worked on press-ups and gone to a series of Aikido classes to build strength, only to learn that the kind of strength required in Aikido has nothing at all to do with muscles and everything to do with inner attitude. She was, in essence, already there. All that remained was for her to come out.

Fran first tried talking to her sister shortly after the Aikido classes. It did not go well. Joanne couldn't comprehend a life without a man to look after her. Her whole life was geared towards the goal of marriage and motherhood. She already had a 'bottom drawer' in which she was saving precious things, for the day when she would have a home of her own.

'Jo?'

A Kind of Family

'Mmmm.' Joanne had her nose deep in *Jane Eyre*, for what seemed like the hundredth time.

'Jo, I have something I need to tell Mum. I thought I'd tell you first.'

Joanne looked up reluctantly from her book, an air of forced interest on her face.

'Jo, there's no easy way of saying this. I know you can't wait to settle down with some man and have two point five kids, but... well... that isn't my ambition.'

Joanne let her book slip further into her lap and adopted an expression of benevolent condescension.

'I know, sweetie. We're very different, you and I. I can see you travelling the world!'

'No, it's not that. Well, I might want to travel and have a career and all that. It's the men. It's the man thing I can't do.'

'Well, my love...' Joanne sounded like a woman of the world, all-knowing and confident in her own imagined future while pouring pity on her deficient younger sister. 'Of course, not everyone is cut out for the love and marriage thing. It doesn't happen for everyone.'

Joanne herself had not yet found Mr. Right, but was certain she would. Fran on the other hand, while not actually wanting a Mr Right felt irritated by Joanne's apparent certainty that her sister was highly likely to end up in the inferior pile labelled 'spinster of this parish'.

Fran made an effort to remember what she had learned at Aikido class. She breathed very slowly and deliberately, gathering ki into her hara. Only once she knew she was in control of her emotions, centred and strong, would she answer her sister.

'No, Jo, you have it all wrong. You see, I don't actually want a man. I want a woman.'

The ensuing silence could have split walls. Joanne sat frozen to the spot, staring into space and occasionally blinking forcefully, as if this might help her wake from an unpleasant dream. Meanwhile, Fran got bored with waiting for any response and found her eyes beginning to droop, until woken by Joanne's shrill voice:

'You dirty little bitch! How could you do that to Mum? After all she's done for both of us?'

At which point, Jo stormed out of the room, slamming doors behind her.

Shortly after this, Susan popped her head round the door.

'Everything alright, sweetie?'

Fran was sitting with her knees curled up under her chin, her arms held tightly round them. She was rocking forwards and backwards, silent tears rolling slowly down both cheeks. Susan stood at the door, rooted to the spot.

Fran looked up at her mother. She felt no empathy for her mother's inability to know how to deal with her daughters' emotional lives. Instead, in that moment she felt utter contempt. And so, she was able to say what she needed to say.

'Your darling eldest daughter seems to object to the fact that I'm a lesbian!' She shouted, as if Susan was entirely responsible for both facts.

'Oh, that! She'll calm down, dear. No use crying about it. Go and find a tissue. Dinner will be ready in a bit. I don't want you crying into my chicken casserole and ruining it. Now. Dry your tears.'

And with that, Susan forced a smile onto her face before exiting the room.

And so, that was how Fran had come out to her family. To a mixture of overreaction and underreaction. After that, all the in-betweens of her friends would be easy to handle. It took twelve more years before she was ready to come out to the world.

Fran shifted to snuggle her face into Rachel's hair, breathing in the smell of her. For a while, it brought her back to the present. But today was a lazy Sunday and once again, she found her mind wandering back in time.

Apart from the heteronormative expectations of society, there were other reasons why Fran never felt she deserved contentment with just one woman. Fran now saw her polyamorous phase, long though it lasted, as just that; for her, unlike perhaps the other three, it had been a kind of late adolescence. She had been like the kid with the cookie jar once she no longer felt she had to pretend about her sexuality. She wanted it all then, and right away. But throughout her experimental hedonism she had never actually felt she deserved someone who could love her utterly, unreservedly, and exclusively. She had missed out on the deep sense of calm that having just one woman brought into her life. Until now.

When she first moved in with Rachel, Fran had felt awkward. An intruder. It wasn't that Rachel did anything to make her feel that way; she was at great pains to consult Fran about every little detail of their shared home, willing to move her own things out to make way for Fran's few precious possessions. But this did not stop Fran wondering when it was all going to come crashing down. She fully expected Rachel to get bored with her and chuck her out on the streets. At first, she realised now looking back she must have been horribly clingy, seeking reassurance that Rachel did love her and wasn't about to change her mind and decide she loved men after all. She had heard Rachel speak fondly about her colleague Richard and secretly wondered if they were meant to be together. She found herself engineering rows with Rachel.

'Fran, I know what you're doing,' Rachel interjected in the middle of one row. 'I can see now that you're feeling insecure. I truly am sorry we can't get a place together that isn't mine, but it doesn't make sense to move. I have this house, and you don't have property. I know it makes you feel anxious. And then, there's your Mum.'

Fran darted a look at Rachel at that point that said very clearly 'Don't come that close!' But Rachel persisted.

'Darling, I know your Mum wasn't very affectionate and demonstrative. You've told me that you had that classic thing of thinking you are adopted. I did too. But then, I've had a lot of therapy and come out the other side. Well, mostly. Fran, look at me.'

Fran was angrily folding washing, not wanting to meet Rachel's eye. She raised her head and squinted at Rachel, then dropped it again.

'I know you expect me to reject you, and I think it's because you've never fully believed you're loveable. Even when three other women loved you. They also loved each other. It's scary for you to be with just one woman, isn't it, my love?'

Fran hated that Rachel could see into her soul. She wanted to scream at her to stay away. But instead, silent tears rolled gently down her cheeks, as a clean blouse lay crumpled in her lap.

It was only with the passage of time, and the reassurance of spending time with their friends together as a couple that Fran gradually came to accept this relationship was for keeps, and Rachel wasn't going anywhere. Now, as summer gave way to autumn and their first anniversary had come and gone, she was finally able to admit to herself she was where she belonged.

Fran realised her arm was beginning to go to sleep. She felt Rachel stir.

'Rachel, are you awake?'

'Yes, my love. Never more so.'

'Good.' And at that, Fran eased her body out of bed. The autumn air jarred her body, and her teeth were chattering by the time she was positioned on one knee beside the bed, holding her lover's hand.

'Rachel Drake. I love you more than I have ever loved anyone. Will you marry me?'

The sight of Rachel's confused face made Fran's teeth chatter and her body tremble all the more. Her supporting leg began giving way.

'Darling, we can marry. It's 2014 and soon to be legal,' Fran continued, despite her fear of rejection.

'Oh my God! So it will be! And then, a smile crept over Rachel's face. A smile of love and delight. 'Yes! Yes, oh yes and yes again!'

And so, Fran bounced back into bed. Their lovemaking was slow, tearful and sensuous as they each indulged in luxurious thoughts of a whole lifetime ahead of them, together.

The next day, however, Rachel was less certain. She felt she had uncharacteristically been swept away on the tide of euphoria knowing that two women could finally, in 2014, marry each other. While it was undoubtedly a political act for them to marry this was also for keeps. And that thought made her brain seize up like a watch that had been dropped in water. She realised they had been so busy enjoying their life together they had hardly discussed anything of importance for the future. She still felt she hardly knew anything about what was deeply important to Fran. Yes, she knew Fran had principles, but beyond that? What if she turned out not to be the woman she seemed? Rachel could feel her palms becoming clammy as a hot prickling sensation crept up from her chest to her ears, and her stomach seemed to shrink to the size of a walnut.

She paced into the kitchen and put the kettle on. Just as she was grinding the coffee beans Aggie appeared out of the corner of her eye, making Rachel start. Aggie was wearing a head scarf over her rollers, and her now familiar stained all-over pinafore. Her feet were in newish slippers with a ridiculous bobble on the front, and in one hand was the cigarette whose ash never spilled.

'I'm in no mood to talk to you today, Aggie!'

'S'alright. I'm not stopping long. Look, I just wannna suggest that maybe you two need to spend some time getting to know each other, that's all. I fink you'll find she *is* very different from you personality-wise, but you go together like a 'orse 'n' cart. Or maybe the sun and the moon. Just try it. Please.' Aggie spent a couple of seconds looking at Rachel, then disappeared.

Rachel had to admit that Aggie was talking sense. And so, after she and Fran had each attended to some important emails Rachel suggested they have coffee together and chat about 'stuff'.

'Fran? We haven't talked that much at all, about stuff that's important to us, have we? I mean, we've been too busy either working hard or having rampant sex to find out much about each other, haven't we?'

Rachel saw a pained expression creep across Fran's eyes, and she thought for a moment she might cry.

'Rachel, are you having second thoughts?'

'No. No, silly,' Rachel lied.

Christ! Why did you lie, you coward? Shape up, Drake! Have you no spine?

Rachel decided not to pay attention to her best friend this time.

'And to prove it to you, how about I make you a cuppa? I'll put the kettle on.'

Before answering, Fran kicked off her shoes with uncharacteristic abandon – and then picked them up and took them out into the hall, where she placed them neatly together facing out away from the wall, as always. She returned to the living room and settled herself into one of the armchairs, tucking her stockinged feet under her and looking lovingly at Rachel.

'Do you mind if I have a hot chocolate, my love?' Fran grinned apologetically at Rachel, who stroked her hair in response.

'You can have whatever you want, my darling.'

But Rachel felt trapped by her own duplicity. How could she be honest now, about her fears? Fran was obviously reassured, but Rachel's fears were stronger than ever. What if once they did start talking about the big stuff they found little in common? What if Fran wasn't the right woman for her, or more likely *she* was not the right woman for Fran? After all, Fran's life used to be pretty unorthodox to say the least, whereas Rachel saw herself as just a boring old academic.

Rachel Drake, this is getting you nowhere. You know what you have to do.

For once, Rachel was glad of her bossy headmistress. She gathered herself as she made Fran a hot chocolate and herself a coffee, realising this was something best faced head on.

A little while later, the two women sat together in the living room; Rachel in one of the armchairs with her coffee, Fran in an armchair with her hot chocolate adorned with a marshmallow. The excitement with which Fran greeted this simple gift touched Rachel, though she herself could hardly wait until it was late enough to open a bottle of wine.

'So – where shall we start?'

Rachel opened the conversation after settling down into 'her' armchair and grabbed a cushion for her lap. She was immediately aware that while this offered some needed comfort and security, she might be seen as putting up barriers, so she deliberately placed the cushion back down beside her.

Fran took the lead: 'Well – what sorts of things are important to each of us? Maybe if we start there, the rest will follow.'

'OK.'

There was that knot again. Rachel knew there were things she needed to ask Fran about, but she was afraid of the answers. Oh well.

Feel the fear and do it anyway.

'Fran? How about we start with how each of us interprets feminism? I mean, I know we are both feminists, but... well... I guess there are lots of ways to be a feminist, just as there are lots of ways to be left wing.'

'Well, yes. I can see where you're coming from.' Fran laughed, then saw the tightness in Rachel's brow and stopped.

'Rachel, I know I used to be polyamorous. But that's all over, I promise. It all began at an impressionable age, when I knew I didn't want to buy into the patriarchy of possession. It was a rebellion against all that, but it never really worked. No one knew where she stood with anyone. We used to do a little dance around each other, trying to work out who was sleeping where each night. Sometimes – quite a lot of the time, actually – I would just slope off to my own room and make it clear I needed time alone. Other times, I admit, the excitement of knowing I was screwing a woman I loved, but who had recently screwed another woman I loved, was what kept me in it. And yes, sometimes we would have orgies, but they mostly disintegrated into giggles and chat. It was hard to keep it going for long, to be honest. It became boring. And above all, I realised some time ago I just wanted one person in my life, someone I could rely on, and who could rely on me. Not to possess in the way that men sometimes do, but to commit to. To be able to feel secure with. And that, my love—'

At this point, Fran slipped out of her chair and fell to the floor beside Rachel, grabbing both hands with her own, '—is when I fell head over heels in love with you.'

Rachel smiled, and the knot sidled away to hide under a nearby rock.

The women squeezed hands, and each kissed the knuckles of the other, before Fran walked back to her chair. There was a pause. Then Rachel spoke:

'What about spirituality? Or God?'

Fran's smile rose like the sunrise. She sipped her hot chocolate.

'Well, not the patriarchal version of that, for sure!'

'No. Me neither. So, what *do* you believe?'

'Um… I'm not sure, to be honest. I've read a bit about Quakerism. I like their idea of a piece of the Divine in everyone. Though what I mean by the Divine I'm not sure.' Fran frowned as she sipped.

'You see, I must confess I just think we're a bundle of atoms which happen to have been very neatly arranged.' Rachel was aware as she spoke this sounded very stark, but she continued.

Better out than in, Drake. Then, if she doesn't like it there's still time …

'I simply cannot believe that we carry on living after death,' she continued, aware even as she said this she wasn't as sure of herself as she once was. She ploughed on. 'Nor that there is an intelligence that somehow makes everything happen. I'm firmly Darwinian I suppose. It's hard to argue with the evidence of science.'

Fran looked down, examining her nails. Rachel sensed a gulf opening up between them. How could she believe that the two of them were just bundles of atoms, and live harmoniously with someone who seemed to have a sense of the Divine? Yet if this relationship was wrong, how come it felt so right?

'OK. I don't dispute that there's little evidence we live after death. I also find it hard to believe in God as a separate intelligence outside of all of us. I suppose I lean towards a more Eastern philosophy, in which we all contribute to this kind of ever-expanding pool of Love and Light. We can choose whether or not to be aware of that Light, and whether or not to become one with it – or at least aim to. I also think we help it to grow through our thoughts and actions. In that sense, I suppose you could say I believe we create God rather than the other way round.'

Fran stopped, cradling her hot chocolate as she looked at Rachel with disarming frankness. Rachel wasn't sure what Fran had just said. It sounded like a load of hippy made-up philosophy. The gulf grew. Rachel struggled for some common ground.

'Hmmm. Do you know what? I can see that all of that makes sense to you, though it's not what I believe. I just don't know where it comes from. I mean, what's the evidence? When people talk about Love and Light I find myself wondering whether they're talking about something real, or whether it's all just a load of bullshit made up to make people feel life's worth living.'

As soon as she said this, Rachel could see Fran's face change from serene to troubled.

'Sorry, Fran. I'm just an old cynic. The trouble is, I don't trust ideas unless they make sense within my experience. And I simply haven't ever experienced this Light you speak of. I haven't ever felt the Divine smiling benevolently on me. So I'll have to take your word for it.'

Fran was silent. Her face seemed to be searching Rachel's as if she might find her answer there. At last, her body relaxed as she took a deep breath in and out.

'Rachel, we don't have to believe the same things. Being challenged keeps me on my toes. It's fine.'

Despite Fran's seeming attempt at reassurance, Rachel was worried that their differences in belief could become a source of conflict, if not now then potentially at some point in the future.

Ignoring the palpable tension, Fran continued pushing.

'OK, so what else?'

Rachel wanted desperately to end the conversation and go get some wine, but it was obvious Fran wasn't having that.

OK. In for a penny, in for a pound, gal. You go for it.

That sounded like Aggie's voice, but this time Rachel could not see her. Instead, she was inside her head like the headmistress and the best friend. Rachel decided to listen to her.

'Babies. You're still quite young, and I…'

Rachel trailed off. She wasn't ready for sleepless nights while trying to hold down an academic job.

'I would like to have a child. And soon.'

Rachel's ears were ringing at this admission. She stared at Fran, her eyes wide as if she could keep some control of the turmoil inside her if she just held her fiancée's gaze.

'OK. I can see this is a big one. Let's leave it to another time.'

Coward, jeered her best friend.

Rachel placed her hands round the oversized cup of steaming coffee, enjoying the feeling of warmth that reached her hands as she looked at the screen. It was the day after bonfire night, when she and Fran had held hands on the deck at the back and watched fireworks as they exploded all over the hill opposite. Her ring finger now held a simple but beautiful pearl ring. She had bought Fran an emerald. It still felt very strange to have an engagement ring. The last time she had worn one, it was for a man – a man who ended up, in fact, going off with his best man. That was all a long time ago, but since her conversation with Fran a few months ago about the important things in life Rachel still felt a mixture of excitement and panic whenever she thought about marrying Fran. She knew she had been putting off any resolution to their differences, focussing instead on the positives in their relationship, but she was plagued by a vague unease whenever she looked at her left hand.

Annie lay asleep at her feet, seemingly enjoying the peace in her mistress's study after the frightening bangs and sudden lights of the previous night which, despite the fact that she had been safely indoors had set her twitching. Rachel wondered what she was dreaming as she sat and watched her. The evening had all been too exciting for a slightly elderly lady.

Annie pricked up one ear and growled a long, low kind of growl. Rachel sighed, knowing now what this must mean. Dogs were more sensitive than humans to presences unseen. Having now got used to the visits, she had long since begun seeing Aggie as something other than someone inside her head – someone belonging to another time when London accents were London accents. It was obvious that Aggie had never met anyone with an Estuary accent, with its upturned sentences that turned statements into questions and its 'nah-eee' instead of 'nah'. Rachel still had no words to explain Aggie and she certainly had no inclination to tell anyone else. She looked around, but could see nothing and no-one.

'You might as well bloody well come out, Aggie!'

And there she was, standing directly in Rachel's field of vision just behind her computer monitor, peering over the top. It was enough to make Rachel jump, which irritated her even more as she leaped up to deal with the sudden heat of coffee spilled in her lap. She made an effort to compose herself. Aggie might be an irritating old crone, but Rachel had come to know that her heart was in the right place. Rachel sat down again, calmly this time, and invited Aggie to come out from behind the screen.

'Aggie. Sorry I was a bit rude just now. It's just that I'm trying to work while Fran is out shopping for stuff to do with her work. I have to make tea later on, and I have about a thousand emails to attend to. Literally.'

'Emails? Ah, yes, I *'ave* 'eard of 'em, although of course even a telephone in a neighbour's 'ouse on my street was a big event when I was growing up. You'll forgive me if I smile and nod.'

Aggie looked stern, and Rachel knew she had offended her with her obvious wish to be doing something other than chatting to her. She also knew by now though, that it would not stop Aggie from saying what she had come to say. Aggie stood there, her arms folded and without the usual cigarette for once. She meant business and no mistake.

'That's fine, Aggie. You probably have rather speedier forms of communication these days, in any case – far superior to emails, in fact.'

'Yes, I suppose I do!' Aggie chuckled, her ample bosom bobbing up and down as she did so beneath her clean, starched pinafore.

I am forgiven. Good, Rachel reassured herself.

'So, Aggie, what brings you here?' Rachel took the opportunity to sit back in her office chair and take a large mouthful of welcome strong coffee.

'Ah, well. I 'eard about the fact that fings are goin' well now between you two, and I am pleased to tell you, that I'm very pleased.'

Rachel smiled a wry smile to herself as she looked down at her coffee mug, then still smiling looked up at Aggie.

'I really wasn't joking when I said you have better means of communication than I do.'

'Well, no. You weren't, duckie. No.' Aggie's gaze held Rachel's.

'And?'

'Well, I just wanna say that, really. Congratulations. A marriage made in 'eaven, you might say.'

Aggie grinned cheekily, showing a gap in her front teeth.

'So – what you're saying, Aggie, is just in case I had any doubts, don't! You've made up your mind we had better go through with this, now?'

'You will, sweetie. You will. No need for me to tell you that.'

At this, Rachel pondered for a while, knowing Aggie was not quite finished.

'Aggie?'

'Yes, Rachel?' Aggie feigned a look of pure innocence which, Rachel thought (unfairly, she later reflected) was about as convincing as David Cameron's concern for the ordinary British working person.

'Why exactly are you here? I mean, why do you visit me? And why me? Why are you interested in my marriage to Fran?'

Aggie shuffled from foot to foot, displaying a concerned interest in her slippers. There was silence for several seconds as Aggie rocked to and fro'.

'Um – let's just say Rachel - I would rather talk to you than to Fran, but I do care what 'appens wiv you two. I care a lot.'

'But *why?*'

Rachel was aware of sounding somewhat exasperated. Why did she have to put up with these intrusions? Why was Aggie interested in her and Fran? What did it matter to her, a woman who had obviously lived in the days when lesbianism was something unspoken about, that these two women were planning a marriage, of all things?

And then it dawned on her.

'Oh my God! Did you secretly desire women, in the time you came from, Aggie? Is that it? Were you forced to live a lie?'

At this, Aggie collapsed into giggles, holding the wobbling folds of her tummy as she laughed so loud it obviously hurt.

'No, duckie! No! I loved my man. 'E was the centre of my world. The centre.'

She became still, her glistening eyes looking far into the distance. Then she turned back to Rachel.

'No. I loved my man. None of that. Mind you, I knew women who were that way inclined, poor sods. They 'ad a field day when the men went to war while the rest of us pined – and grieved – but then of course when the men came back it was a different story.'

She pulled herself up. 'It was never talked about,' she said, with a tone of propriety. 'But I knew. I could tell.'

'So why? You still haven't told me why.'

Aggie looked benevolently down at her seated companion, a look of genuine regret in her face.

'Now that, lovey, I cannot tell you. Maybe one day, but not now. I'll see you at the wedding – if not before of course!'

And with that, she was gone. Annie, who had long since lost interest, pricked up her ears again and raised her head before settling back down into a contented sleep, free from bangs and whizzes.

Rachel turned back to her computer, and as she did so realised her doubts about marrying Fran had disappeared. Nothing had changed, but somehow it just felt right, like finding the right balance of ingredients to make a curry taste authentic.

A Kind of Family

Meetings

'So, Fran. My love.'

Rachel lay on the bed, exhausted but happy. Fran cleared her hair away from her left ear, the right being buried in her fiancée's breast. She looked as if she might disappear forever into a cloud of comfort.

Rachel waited.

'Rachel, do continue!'

'OK. I think it's time we started thinking about the wedding. Have you thought about what sort of ceremony you'd like?'

'No, actually. Register office? I can't see either of us wanting to hire somewhere grand like Fountains Abbey, with champagne flowing readily in the cloisters, can you?'

'Well, no. Simplicity would be good, but I do want it to be right, for both of us.'

The two women sank into a contented silence, but without relaxing deeply as they each turned over the question.

'I know!'

Fran leaped up, her dark strong hair flopping over flushed cheeks, eyes alight with a mixture of post-orgasmic clarity and excitement at the prospect of planning her wedding.

'Well come on then, spill the beans!'

'Richard!'

'Pardon?'

'Richard! He's a Quaker, isn't he? I told you I'd been reading about them. Well, Quakers will marry same sex couples. They're all about equality, aren't they? In fact, I've heard they've had to make very few changes to the wording of the vows. And they do a nice, simple job.' Fran sat back on her knees, a look of satisfaction on her face.

'Oh, gosh! I like the idea of a Quaker wedding.'

'I know you two only meet at work normally,' Fran continued. 'But I'm wondering if we could arrange to meet him socially, so that we can pick his brains.'

Fran had long since got over her unease about Richard, reassured that Rachel had never in fact been attracted to him.

'I'll call him.' Rachel sat up in bed.

'Ask him to come over! Now!'

Rachel looked lasciviously at her lover's naked body right before her.

'Are you sure you want him over now, my love? Because I could go again, you know …'

'Richard?'

'Hello, Rachel. What brings this pleasure at eight o'clock on a Sunday night?'

'Oh, gosh, is it that late? Richard, I'm sorry to bother you. It's just that—'

Rachel was belatedly aware that she didn't have a clue how to tell Richard about her marriage plans.

Oh, you insensitive bitch, Drake! You know he has the hots for you!

'Richard, Fran and I wondered if you would like to come round for some food. Sorry. Didn't realise it was so late. What are you doing tomorrow night?'

'Oh, how sweet of you to invite me. Um – sadly, tomorrow night I promised to go and watch one of my students in some sad bloody production of *Marat-Sade*. It'll be awful, of course, listening to them going on about what's the point of a revolution without general copulation as they gyrate in front of the audience, but I'd better go. She'll never talk to me again if I don't.'

Rachel tapped her fingers on the kitchen table.

'Ah. OK. Well maybe I can catch you for a coffee some time tomorrow? Shall I come and see you when teaching finishes, perhaps? And then you can come for supper Tuesday, maybe?'

'Yes, perfect. Rachel?'

'Mmm?'

'Is there something important you want to tell me?'

Rachel felt her cheeks flush, grateful that Richard was unable to see.

'Oh, nothing that won't wait until tomorrow.'

Rachel waited until 5.30 pm. She knew Richard would still be in his office. He rarely left before 7 and Rachel guessed correctly that he would just grab a wrap at lunchtime and eat it later on the hoof, en route to the performance in the university theatre.

Sure enough, she found him sitting in semi-darkness, his angle poise desk lamp the only lighting in the room. He was answering an email when she walked in, Beethoven's Moonlight Sonata playing on a tinny CD player in the corner of his room. The walls of his tiny office were full of bookshelves, each one crammed with books and files, but he had managed to squeeze in two easy chairs and a coffee table in addition to his desk and office chair. Both easy chairs and the coffee table were piled high with books and papers.

'Oh, sorry! Let me move something for you!'

Richard leaped up from his unfinished email, shifting a pile of papers from one chair which he transferred to his desk. He then removed the pile from the other chair and looked around, as if out of nowhere some new space would emerge. Apparently giving up on divine intervention, he put the papers down beside him as he sat to face Rachel.

'Coffee?'

A Kind of Family

Richard's smile was genuine enough, but when Rachel declined, he seemed unable to conceal his relief. There were three used mugs dotted around his office.

'So, what brings you to my palace?'

'I have some news, Richard, and I wanted to tell you in person.'

Richard's face betrayed his concern.

'Oh, gosh, it's nothing bad,' Rachel reassured him. 'Don't worry, I'm not ill or anything.'

He breathed out, his shoulders visibly dropping their weight.

'It's rather good news, really. I wanted to share it with you first, because you are such a good friend, Richard. Fran and I are to be married.'

If Richard's face at first showed pain it was quickly concealed as he leaped to his feet and gave Rachel a kind of sideways hug in which his face looked down over the back of her chair while his torso held the kind of frame that would keep a ballroom dance teacher happy. He sat down again almost as quickly, smiling benevolently.

'I really am so happy for you, Rachel. I look forward to meeting the lucky woman.'

'Well, yes. I want you two to meet, of course, but we also want to ask you about Quaker weddings, if that's OK?'

'Oh, delightful! Yes, well, of course I'm not a registering officer, but I do know a bit about them. I've been to one or two, and I would be more than happy to discuss it with you.'

'Oh, thank you, Richard! You are a sweetie!'

Rachel stood up, and gave Richard a kiss on the cheek, holding his shoulders with both hands.

After she had left his office, what Rachel didn't see was that Richard brushed his cheek with the back of one hand, smiling wistfully. She did not see him turn back to his computer and the unfinished email, and she did not hear him say 'Oh, go to hell!'

Richard knocked on the door. He knew Rachel had a perfectly serviceable bell, but he felt reassured by the weight of the brass door knocker in his hands. He slammed it against Rachel's wide, bottle green wooden door, looking around him in embarrassment at the noise he had created.

Rachel lived in an urban area that in the nineteenth and early twentieth century was grand, then went downhill at some point in the twentieth century when smaller and new houses became fashionable and was now very much gentrified. The houses were large Victorian terraced properties with deep back gardens. Rachel's house still had the original sash windows in the front, but she had installed secondary glazing to keep out the cold and noise. Not that it was noisy here. In a cul-de-sac, Rachel's house was near to the end. There were trees at regular intervals along the street and a small green in the centre of the wide turning circle. Many houses had also created a drive from the front garden, but despite this, cars were parked everywhere. Richard had cycled and was able to bring his bike up the drive. Before knocking on the door, he had already locked his bike and placed it under cover of a tree. He now stood with a bottle of wine in one hand and his helmet in the other, wishing he had a free hand with which to rub his perspiring neck.

The door opened, and there she stood. Richard's first sensory impression was of Rachel's perfume – a thing she never wore to work. It was musky – and bewitching. He imagined himself burying his face in the skin behind her ears.

'Er, hi Rachel. Sorry. A bit gormless. I've just cycled.'

'Oh! Do you want to bring it in? We could probably get it into the hall?'

'No, no. It'll be alright so long as it doesn't rain. I've locked it up. And it's under your tree, in any case. It'll be fine.' Richard hoped he now sounded a bit calmer and more collected.

'Oh, OK. Do come in, Richard.'

A Kind of Family

Rachel stood aside and Richard stepped into her hall. He recognised a Manrique print over the stairs, smiling his appreciation for Rachel's broad cultural tastes.

'Ah! I see you've been to Lanzarote!' Still clutching his wine bottle after placing his helmet on the hall table, Richard was relieved to find something about which he could make small talk.

'Yes. I love his work, actually. It's a print, of course.'

'Of course!'

At the top of the stairs stood a boyish figure in skinny jeans and an oversized sweatshirt, who looked as if she could easily be one of his undergrads.

'You must be Fran! How wonderful to meet the woman who has stolen Rachel's heart!'

Richard hoped he sounded suitably delighted to meet her. Indeed, he convinced himself he was.

'Oh, sorry!' Richard turned towards Rachel. 'I meant to give you this!' And so, wine delivered, the three moved into the living room.

The two women sat side by side on one of the soft, voluminous sofas while Richard sat alone on the other, avoiding the easy chairs both of which had spectacles on the arms.

Fran stood up. 'Can I get you something to drink now? Dinner will be ready in about a quarter of an hour.'

Richard wondered if the two women had discussed roles in advance of his arrival.

'Oh, lovely. Yes please. I'll have a glass of red. Thank you.'

Fran went out to the kitchen, leaving Richard and Rachel alone. Richard fidgeted in his seat.

'Lovely place you've got here, Rachel.'

'Yes. I bought it before the area became gentrified, of course.'

Richard stood up and went over to peer through the window. He couldn't see much now that the sun had set. Nevertheless, he was able to form an impression of inspired cultivation and simplicity.

'You've obviously done a lot to it. The garden looks inviting.'

Richard berated himself for thinking how much he would love to have a garden like this to look at while he worked. He remembered his office at work, and the piles of paper. He often thought of throwing things out, but never seemed to get round to it somehow, and his flat was poky, without a garden and with stained walls and carpets. He had never had the motivation to improve it despite having lived in it some ten years. There didn't seem to be any point, without someone to share it with.

Fran returned with Richard's wine and one for Rachel, then sat beside her fiancée, curling her feet under her. Beside her was a glass of water.

A timer pinged in the kitchen and Rachel got up to attend to the meal, leaving Richard alone this time with Fran.

'I hear you are an arts worker?' Richard was practised at making small talk. He took pride in being able to converse equally easily with the Vice Chancellor at university, and the cleaner who had worked there more years than him.

'Yes. I work in various community settings – an old folks' home, a mental health day centre, a project for kids who have been failed by our education system. I run workshops in everything from creative writing and rap music, to dance movement. It keeps me out of trouble.'

At this, Fran grinned. Such a winning smile. Richard could imagine the people she served must love her. He was struck by how neat Fran was, as compared with Rachel's wild sensuality, but he could see there was a match here – a chemistry between them he could not deny.

'How do you find living with an academic? We're a boring lot, you know.' Richard flashed her a cheeky smile as he took a generous gulp of wine.

'Oh, you know. I leave her to do her thing, she leaves me to do mine. She works far later than me, but then my work is anything but nine to five. It works quite well, actually. We aren't in each other's pockets. Which means that when we do come together, well…'

At this, Fran blushed, and fiddled with her feet. The words 'come together' rang in the air as an unintended *double entendre*.

The pair were saved by the call to dinner, a vegetarian lasagne with garlic bread and salad. A nice simple meal which went well with the wine Richard had brought, and with the one Rachel opened after this.

'So, you two are getting married! I'm terribly sorry. I'm rather belated in my felicitations. I should have congratulated you both as soon as I set foot over the threshold.'

It was Fran who responded.

'Thank you, Richard. That's very kind of you.'

Her smile was warm and genuine, and Richard found that despite himself he was beginning to like her. It would make his task easier if he could like her. How could he hold onto his jealousy when Rachel's chosen partner was so absolutely delightful?

'And you want to know about Quakers?'

'Yes, if that's OK?'

'Of course.'

Richard did his best to explain his faith:

'Um. You see there's no creed. If you ask two Quakers what their view is of God, for example, you will get two completely different answers. In fact, some of us are non-theist and certainly not everyone defines themselves as Christian, though of course we do arise out of that tradition. But we also come out of a radical re-interpretation of that tradition, dating back to the seventeenth century. Am I boring you?'

The two women eagerly reassured him that he was not, as Fran reached one hand across to hold Rachel's.

'OK. Well, what I can say we tend to agree on is what we call our Testimonies. These are variously expressed, but briefly they refer to an emphasis through our actions on: Equality, Justice and Community; Peace; Truth and Integrity; Simplicity; and Sustainability. What this means in practice is that we try to treat everyone equally, we work towards peace, we operate truthfully and with integrity in our business transactions and our personal relationships, we live as simply as possible – I have failed miserably on that one, by the way – and we see ourselves as stewards of our planet, aiming to reduce waste and so on.'

Richard paused.

'So, how does all of this translate into how you do weddings?'

Richard noticed that Fran was driving the agenda. He found himself warming even more to her, appreciating her focus.

'So, when it comes to weddings, we were right in there with our willingness to marry same sex couples, due to our emphasis on Equality. And because of our testimony to Simplicity as you can imagine they are pretty simple affairs. Each wedding is seen as a special Meeting for Worship. Oh, I forgot to explain how we do worship, sorry.'

'It's OK,' interrupted Fran. 'I've done my homework on that. You all sit around in silence, there is no vicar, and anyone can speak, basically.'

'Well, yes. Though some of us feel that some members of our meeting could do with being silent for rather more of our Meeting time than is currently the case.'

The three shared a chuckle.

'Anyway, in a wedding we do have to have a registering officer who is responsible for the legal bit and who usually welcomes everyone to the meeting, because of course there are usually loads of people who have never set foot inside a Meeting House before.'

'Oh, that's good.' Rachel looked visibly relieved to hear this.

'Though actually, you would also have to accept that the Meeting feels they have a stake in each marriage that takes place within our Area Meeting, and so you would have several members of that Meeting attending your wedding. It is, after all, a Meeting for Worship.' Richard looked from Fran to Rachel, checking for their reaction.

'OK.' The two women looked at each other, sharing concerned glances, then nodded at each other before turning back to Richard, who seeing their nod continued:

'So, at some point, the couple stands up, and they declare to each other some very simple words. I've brought them along so that you can hear what is said.'

Richard reached into his jacket pocket but was stopped by Rachel.

'It's OK, Richard. There's plenty of time for that.'

She turned to Fran with an inquiring look that was met with a nod.

'I think we're both agreed that we want a Quaker wedding. So, what next?'

'OK. Well, we meet at 10.30 every Sunday for an hour. I suggest that you come along to a few Meetings for Worship, to get a feel for how we do things. It would be important that at least one of you was committed to attending, before you ask for a wedding. We don't marry people just because they fancy a Quaker wedding. There needs to be a bit more of a commitment than that.

Fran immediately responded.

'I would love that, Richard. I'll come along this Sunday. I'm looking forward to it.'

Pudding was a shop bought chocolate mousse, for which Rachel apologised but which Richard accepted with glee. When Richard left the house, he found it had been raining. His cycle home was cold and unpleasant. When he arrived back at his cold flat, he hurriedly pulled off his sodden trousers, ran a bath, and poured himself a large whisky.

Fran decided to put on some pale pink lipstick to go to the Meeting. She dressed in her kilt, a retro affair held together with a large pin, together with a light-yellow blouse that had short sleeves and a small rounded collar. Her botany wool cardigan was in pale green matching her kilt, and she wore thick brown tights with well-polished brown leather shoes. The pearls around her neck matched the two pearl studs in her ears, and together with her bob and the duster coat and beret she wore over it she looked altogether as if she had stepped out of the sixties.

She had arranged to meet Richard at the door, of which she was glad although the woman who greeted Fran with a warm handshake immediately put her at her ease. This Welcoming Friend quickly realised Richard's purpose and let him get on with offering Fran some literature on Meeting for Worship. He also showed her where the toilets were and explained that after Meeting there would be notices for about 15 minutes followed by a cup of tea, and that he hoped she would stay. Fran, however, made her excuses and said she would not stay on this occasion. She told Richard that Rachel was making lunch, although in reality even on Sundays lunch was a help-yourself affair. They intended to go out for their evening meal.

When Richard excused himself to Fran and went off to talk to someone about what he described as 'Overseers business' she was grateful for a moment to herself. She looked around at the simple but beautiful Meeting House with its wooden beams and plain carpet. The furniture was functional, non-fussy, but of a good quality. She watched the other people trickling in, including an older man hunched over, his right-hand trembling on his stick, the skin translucent and pale with veins protruding. He wore an old tweed suit, and what little hair he had was flying this way and that. Someone spoke to him with the raised tones reserved for older people whose hearing is failing:

'Hello Geoffrey! How are you today?'

'Oh, very well, thank you.' The older man raised his head. His smile could only be described as beaming. He dabbed at one weeping eye with a large white handkerchief which he extracted from his pocket with his free hand.

'Bit windy out there, Geoffrey?'

'Yes, yes. Not too bad though.'

At this point Fran noticed that Richard approached Geoffrey, his hands clasped reverentially in front of him.

'Hello, Geoffrey. I need your thoughts on a matter, if that would be OK? Are you busy after Meeting? I just need to consult you on something. I would very much value your insights.'

'Oh, yes. Hello, Richard. I might need to ring my daughter to warn her that I'll be a bit late, but yes, let's go in room one after notices, and take our tea with us shall we?'

'Fabulous. I shall see you later.'

So, thought Fran. Geoffrey is a much-valued member of the Meeting, obviously. He must be in his nineties. How lovely that his opinion is so valued.

Fran thought of her own mother, and of the people she worked with in the care home whose active lives were caught in a time warp, unseen by those who care for them. It was as if they had never run homes or companies, never taught anyone anything, and never ever been wise.

Fran followed the general drift of people towards the meeting room. Richard had already explained that she could sit anywhere she liked on the concentric circles of chairs, but that the chairs nearest to the table in the middle were usually occupied at least in part by Elders. They were the people who would end the Meeting by shaking hands, swiftly followed by everyone doing the same with their neighbours. She decided to sit on a chair near the back, facing the wall clock. It was twenty-seven minutes past ten. She had been told by Richard that the Meeting was deemed to have started the moment anyone entered the meeting room. Again, she looked around as she took off her coat and lay it over the back of her chair. It seemed that most people were in a state of utter calm apart from the few children whispering to their parents, or parents whispering stories to them as they held books on their laps with titles like *The soul bird, The kuia and the spider,* and *Giraffes can't dance.*

Meekums

Fran settled down and shut her eyes. Immediately, a whole host of things began flooding into her brain – tasks to complete, little niggling worries. She became aware that her shoulders were tense and willed them to relax. She wasn't sure what she was meant to do. How was this different from meditation practice? In the absence of any answer to this internal question she set about simply following her breath in the hope that something would happen.

Fran was jolted awake by a voice coming from the other side of the room, directly opposite.

Oh, shit! Did I really fall asleep? Why didn't someone nudge me?

Fran shook herself and tried to focus on what the man was saying. It was Geoffrey, holding himself up with his stick. His body was still bent over but his voice was as clear as a mountain stream:

'I was listening to the news this morning. On it were some children, not much older than some of you here today. They were from a country far, far away. A group of islands called the Solomon Islands…'

Fran felt her heart melting for this man who was trying to make his ministry speak to the children in the room. The whole point of what he was saying, as far as Fran could make out, was that we are all equal in the eyes of the divine – that these children suffering post-earthquake and tsunami were just like them, except that we all have shelter to go home to and can see a doctor whenever we need to.

At the end of the Meeting and all notices, someone spoke to the collection. It was not Geoffrey, but it was for the World Vision appeal following the natural disaster in the Solomon Islands earlier that year; the need was apparently still great. Reflecting on Geoffrey's ministry, Fran wondered if he had known what the collection was to be that week, when he decided to speak. She sought him out in the queue for tea.

'Hi. I'm Fran. I think your name is Geoffrey?'

'Oh, yes! Delighted to meet you. Is this your first time in a Meeting?' Geoffrey turned his whole body to greet her with that same benevolent, happy smile, beaming love.

'Yes. I was interested in your ministry when the children were still in earlier.'

'Oh yes?'

There was an interlude, while Geoffrey picked up a cup of tea and moved slowly towards a table to place it down.

'I'm afraid I can't chat as long as I'd like. Someone wants me.'

'I know. Richard. I heard him ask you. It was Richard that introduced me to Quakers. This is my first time.'

'Oh, delightful! I thought I hadn't seen you here before, but I'm never sure whether that is the case, or whether it's just that I'm getting old!' Geoffrey chuckled, shaking his head almost imperceptibly as if he found ageing a source of both bemusement and amusement.

'I wanted to ask, Geoffrey – might I call you that?'

'Oh, of course! We don't stand on ceremony, you know.' That wonderful beam again, like a beacon of light.

'Did you know what the collection was for?'

Geoffrey laughed, open mouthed.

'Gosh, no! Though I might have guessed, if I had thought about it. No, no. I only speak if I am called to. I'm not called all that often these days. But – well, it's hard to explain. I just get a kind of tingling all over my body, and the only way I can get rid of it is to stand up and speak. I never know what's going to come out of my mouth until I start. It really does require a total leap of faith and my heart is usually racing when I do. But of course, it isn't coming from me. I've just had to learn to trust over the years, that some sense will come out of this stupid old mouth. Now, if you would excuse me – I can see Richard over there, beckoning me. I'd better go. It was delightful to meet you. What was your name?'

'Fran.'

'Fran. How lovely. Short for Frances, I expect?' He pronounced the 'e', showing that he knew how to spell the woman's name.

'Yes, that's right.'

Geoffrey's dark brown, velvety eyes looked straight into Fran's as he took hold of one of her hands in his bony appendages, clasped gently one on top and one underneath hers.

'It was lovely to meet you, Fran,' he said, squeezing her hand ever so slightly as he did so.

And he was gone, leaving Fran with a strange feeling of having been touched by an embodiment of pure humility and simplicity such as she had never before experienced.

Later, Fran learned from Richard that Geoffrey was a retired Professor of Philosophy, his works still famous throughout the world.

A Kind of Family

All work and no play

Rachel sat and stared at the complex forms she had downloaded from the web in order to apply for promotion to Associate Professor.

Bloody hell, it's like doing a bloody dissertation!

And where is Aggie the Wise when I need her?

Aggie had been notable by her absence during this process so far, which puzzled Rachel. Was she losing her muse? She really felt the need for some moral support right now. Rachel had been amassing evidence of her successes at work over several years, knowing that one day it might just come in handy if she needed to justify her position. It went against her principles to big herself up, but she had to admit the strategy had paid off when she had been successful in obtaining a Student Education Fellowship. Being able to quote from student feedback had been essential, even if it did stick in her craw. She got up from her office chair and paced, followed by the ever-faithful Annie who inappropriately wagged her tail as she looked up adoringly at her mistress.

Bloody men never have this problem.

But as soon as that thought crossed her mind, Rachel thought of Richard and knew she was wrong – well, at least only partially right. Richard had a self-deprecating manner and was the last person to assume any sense of superiority over her. Perhaps that was why she warmed to him, seeking him out for chats about all sorts of things. He always encouraged her and told her how wonderful she was. But then, he had a soft spot for her, of that she was sure. His opinion therefore meant less to her; his glasses were rose-tinted.

There were other men she knew in academia who arrived in the job with a natural ease and a pre-formed sense of entitlement. Often very personable and friendly, they had a self-assuredness that came from a background of privilege and the expectation that they would do well. They usually had a very genuine interest in other people, which extended naturally to those who were in positions of power. Power didn't frighten them like it did Rachel.

And so, back to the forms. She sat down again, determined to get to grips with the process. Annie circled at her feet to find just the right position – which turned out to be with her hind quarters on Rachel's right foot. Once there, she settled and began twitching.

Evidence of excellence in learning and teaching. About ten different criteria for this, then the same for leadership, and finally for research. Now there was the sticking point. How many people did she know who had brought in serious research money for counselling and psychotherapy research? Her shoulders collapsed in on her frame, like a hot air balloon in trouble. Time to take the dog for a walk.

'Annie?'

Annie looked up, immediately alert from her dream. Her floppy ears became less floppy at the top, her eyes intently focussed on Rachel and her body ready to heave itself up from the place where she had been keeping her mistress's feet warm.

Rachel moved off towards the hallway to grab her coat, hat and boots with Annie obediently by her side, waiting for the lead. They stepped outside into a bright but cold day, the sun low in the sky so that it made everything look fresh and beautiful. There was a light wind, which blew away all tension as Rachel and Annie stepped out onto the hills. Once away from the main paths Annie was let off the lead, bounding joyously off into the heather, bracken and blueberry plants.

She stopped for the obligatory wee then bounded off again, criss-crossing the path in front of her mistress.

When they returned, the forms didn't look so bad. Rachel remembered a small amount of research funding she had secured and wrote a sentence about the paucity of opportunities for funding together with plans for bringing in more. And then she put the task to bed, opening a long trail of emails.

By the time Fran came home Rachel had prepared a simple meal of stir-fried vegetables and cashew nuts which Fran gratefully demolished. They spent the evening by the fire discussing wedding plans, finally settling on a live ceilidh band in the local community centre which also provided a bar.

'What about catering?' Fran twiddled her emerald ring.

Rachel frowned. 'Oh, God, I don't know. I don't fancy doing it ourselves, do you?'

'No, but we are talking megabucks if we don't. And, that could be the sticking point in terms of deciding how many to invite.'

Rachel knew Fran didn't have a lot of money, and she would be feeling anxious until they had sorted this particular detail. There was silence while the two women considered options. They googled caterers, were alarmed at prices and dismayed at menus.

'I know this sounds unusual, Rachel,' Fran began, now fiddling with her toes as she sat with legs underneath her.

'Well, my love, you *are* unusual,' Rachel quipped, pulling Fran towards her and planting a kiss on her lips. Then she noticed Fran's taut body and let her go.

'OK. Spill the beans. What idea is brewing in that beautiful head of yours?'

'Um… well, my friends, as you know, are all into communal living, and communal this and that.' Fran began rubbing the sole of her foot. She continued: 'Not sure about yours – nor indeed our families' – but how about we suggest everyone brings a dish for a bring-and-share meal? The Quakers had one of those the other day, and it was fabulous!'

Rachel considered the idea. She tried to picture it. Richard would be fine with it even if he did go to Waitrose. Jane and Suzy would be glad of the chance to contribute something. Debs, Feather and Roxy would join in with gusto. Not sure about Joanne, but she would have to get over herself. A smile crept across her face.

'Oh, sod it. Why ever not? Let's do it! And while we're about it, let's make our own invitations. We can use that photo of us that we got a complete stranger to take the other day. It's rather nice, actually. And put some nice words with it, the date and time and so on. Then everyone who wants to come, can come – and we don't even have to know! What's more, we don't have to chase anyone. Genius!'

Fran looked relieved, but only for a moment.

'So, Rachel. Do you think you should come along to Meeting for Worship sometime soon? We need to meet with the Registering Officer, and it would be good if you've been along first, so that you know something about how it might all work?'

Rachel bristled. She hated being cajoled into anything. Fran had begun attending the Quaker Meeting on a regular basis, and she had to admit she had begun to look forward to Fran being out on Sunday mornings; it was time when she could catch up on work emails without Fran knowing what she was up to. If Fran knew she was working at weekends, it would start a 'conversation'.

Rachel remained silent. She had to admit Fran had a point; despite her reluctance to consider anything that smacked of religion no matter how liberal, she had better accompany Fran at least once so as not to appear to be using the Quakers for her own ends. She also knew that for her own sake, she needed to understand something of what they were about before being married there.

'OK. Next week?'

Fran's shoulders broadened as she smiled one of her open, guileless smiles that made Rachel's heart melt and her legs turn to jelly.

Annie wagged her tail, and Rachel could have sworn she saw a figure going past into the kitchen, wearing a paisley pinafore and singing *Here comes the bride*.

'...wish to avoid compulsory redundancies if at all possible... hope to be able to make the necessary savings through a combination of natural wastage and voluntary severance schemes...'

Rachel doodled on the notepad in front of her, blanking out the sound reverberating around the lecture theatre. She looked at the clock. This would all be over in five minutes, then she could get back to her desk, hoping not to catch anyone's eye on her way out.

She did not want to hear this news, especially given that she suspected once they were married Fran would most likely be wanting to open negotiations about a baby. The thought of the screaming, puking and shitting little things terrified her. Well, at least if her job was under threat, she had ammunition! But for how long? She contemplated the two equally horrific prospects: no job and no money but avoidance of parenthood; or the job she loved being ruined by sleepless nights and the seemingly endless needs of a new mother and baby. Her doodles got fiercer. Realising she might be attracting attention with the severity of her pencil strokes she looked furtively around and was relieved to see everyone either looking intently at the Dean or whispering to each other, seemingly deep in their own thoughts about the news.

Returning to her desk, Rachel sighed as she looked at the unread emails. It was ironic, she thought, to be training others in how to help the generally stressed and occasionally mentally unwell, when her own job meant she faced impossible deadlines each and every day. She had recently learned to file incoming mail into separate mail boxes, which meant she could avoid reading the endless mail from David Fisher who seemed to think it wise to copy her into his every congratulation to a student who had actually managed to turn up to a tutorial. More troubling were the emails from her line manager, each with an attachment and requiring a response by yesterday. She currently had one hundred and five emails flagged either for today or anything up to three weeks ago, and fifty new unread emails, not to mention the many she had allocated to some date hence in the vain hope that by then she would have caught up on herself. Her shoulders and jaw tightened as she began tapping away with eight of her ten digits.

Still, at least tonight, much as she loved Fran, she could look forward to a few hours alone in the house, this being Fran's Tai Chi night. Just these emails to get through, one failing student to see followed by a meeting of the Research Committee which she hoped would be mercifully short, and she would be on her way.

Rachel breathed out as she turned her key in the lock and felt her shoulders begin to ease. Stepping over the adoring Annie she went straight into the kitchen, threw her shoes under the table, chucked her bags and coat on the tabletop and let her keys slide over its surface. She could hear Fran's voice scolding inside her head, but she didn't care. Wine time. She opened the fridge door and pulled out an exquisitely chilled sauvignon blanc. She plonked the large bottle on her sturdy, large farmhouse kitchen table and reached for a delicate but large glass. The glug-glug sound was music to her ears. Grabbing her novel (which had been tidied away to the back of the table since she had abandoned it on the edge this morning before going to work), she moved into the lounge to catch the sun's dying rays over her garden and the hills beyond.

'Oh, bloody hell! What the fuck are *you* doing here?' Rachel shouted as she slumped onto her favourite sofa. Her rudeness did not appear to put off the raggedy old lady whose head was just in the way of the setting sun, so that she looked as if she had a halo around her be-scarfed head with its rollers poking out. She was seated on a kitchen chair which seemed to have somehow been shifted into the living room just in front of the window.

'I fought you might like a bit of company, duckie, after the 'ard day you've 'ad'.

Aggie smiled sweetly as her upper set of false teeth dropped. She shut her mouth to re-adjust them, then began again.

'Now, what you doin' drinkin' that filf again, eh? What you need is a nice cuppa tea, my lovely. I'd make you one, if I could.'

'Don't bother', Rachel muttered, looking down so as not to catch the old woman's eyes.

Aggie hardly ever appeared in shoes. Always the same old slippers with the silly bobbles on the front, and thick dark brown stockings that were obviously not held up by anything. She seemed incapable of sitting decorously, her knees just a bit too far apart, but thankfully her paisley overall was long enough to cover any embarrassment. Her right hand was poised at a paradoxically lady-like angle, a cigarette held as usual between her outstretched forefinger and middle finger. The ash, as always, was long and slightly curved, about to drop. But Rachel had learned, irritating though this was, that it never would in fact drop.

'Aggie, I needed you when I was working on those bloody forms, but right now I don't want you here. I've had a really long day and I just want to sit with a glass of wine in the peace and quiet of my own home, watching the sun go down.' Rachel sounded weary. Talking to Aggie was, Rachel knew, not in the same league as the headmistress or the best friend. At least she could predict the other two to some extent, and if she tried really hard, she could banish them – but Aggie played by different rules. Plus, Rachel was still reluctant to discuss any of her 'voices' with anyone. The last thing someone working in mental health needs, she argued wryly, is a mental health problem.

A Kind of Family

'I fought you might like a little chat, see, cos a little birdie told me they are workin' your fingers to the bone. A trouble shared is a trouble 'arved, I always say. Now, tell your Agnes all about it'.

Aggie was not budging. That much was obvious. Rachel looked up. The halo had slipped a bit, a sure sign that tonight's sunset was not to be had. She might as well resign herself to telling Aggie all about her day, even though she had a strong hunch that she knew it all already.

Rachel was glad it was a Friday. Friday was a day she had negotiated to work from home, and she protected it like a child might protect their collection of coins. This meant she could see clients in the morning and write in the afternoon – if she could resist logging into her emails.

Today, she was meeting a new client. They had talked briefly on the phone, but he had been reluctant to tell her too much. His name was Adam, and she knew he was in his forties because he had mentioned 'getting to forty and hitting a wall'.

Rachel sat in her consulting room and looked outside. It was a windy, rainy day and she wondered if Adam would turn up. She looked at her watch – a nice big round one with hands she could easily read without her glasses, and a second hand. He was already two minutes late. Not unusual for someone who was trying to find the place for the first time and park a car, despite advanced warning from her about the problems and possible solutions.

Adam's appointment had been for 9 am – the first of the day. At ten past nine, Rachel decided to text.

> *Hi Adam. Just checking to see if you have our 9 am in your diary. If you're driving, please don't stop to answer this. I will see you when you get here. If you no longer need the appointment though, a text would be much appreciated.*

She looked back over the text, wondering if the tone was appropriate. Did she sound as if she expected him not to turn up? Or too bossy? Would he become flustered, or exasperated, or nervous? She clicked send and sat back in her chair. She decided to do some mindfulness while waiting. She found the audio file on her phone, and clicked play:

> *Focus on your body. Adopt a relaxed, upright posture, seated slightly forward on the chair. Feel your contact with the chair through your buttocks and thighs, and with the floor through your feet.*
>
> *Now focus on your breathing. In. And out. In. And out. You don't have to change anything. There is no end goal. If you find your mind wandering, as minds do, just come back to your breath, leading yourself as you would a small child, with compassion…*

Rachel heard footsteps on the stairs. Adam was arriving. She hurriedly turned off her audio, got up from her chair and opened the door to the waiting room, preparing a welcoming smile on her face.

Adam was slightly built and below average height with thinning, wispy hair that had obviously blown about in the high winds. He wore a college scarf of some sort, over an old gabardine mac. On his feet Rachel noticed, were scuffed nondescript black shoes. He hesitated to take off his coat despite the warmth in the consulting room, but he did unbutton it to reveal a beige woollen jumper and green corduroy trousers. His socks did not match.

'I'm glad you could find your way here. Was it difficult at all?'

'Er… no.'

Pause. Adam looked down at his hands, then fiddled with his coat pockets as if searching for inspiration.

'It's OK. Take your time, Adam. This is a safe space. You can speak as much or as little as you want here. We'll work until the end of your session time, and then continue next week if you decide you would like to continue. There's no rush.'

Rachel had already sent him a statement about confidentiality, so there was no need to go over that. She knew she needed to do an assessment, but right now making Adam feel at ease was uppermost.

'Right. Yes. It's just that... well... it's just... someone I love...'

Adam looked up at Rachel as his voice trailed off, his eyes searching hers. And then he looked down and began shaking. His whole body shook. Rachel's instinct was to reach out and hold him, but she didn't want to confuse him.

Professional boundaries are there to protect the client. He needs to know I won't intrude on his space, she reminded herself.

'I can see this is really difficult for you, Adam. What do you need right now?'

Adam continued to shake.

'Adam, can you hear me?'

A small and indistinct sound emerged like a child who was far, far away through locked doors.

'Adam? I can't quite make out what you are trying to tell me. But first, I want to help you to feel safe. Would you like me to make you a cup of tea? Or maybe bring you a blanket?'

'Blanket,' came the whisper.

Rachel kept some blankets in a cupboard for those times when she knew the client needed to be held. She felt relief at being able to do something as she stood up and walked to the cupboard, keeping a concerned eye on Adam as she did so. She pulled out a nice, big, soft blanket and carefully handed it to Adam, then sat down again in her chair.

Adam wrapped himself in the blanket, like someone who had just been saved from drowning.

Perhaps he has, thought Rachel.

Gradually, the shakes stopped. Rachel looked at the clock. The time had passed mostly in silence; just five minutes to go to the end of the session time.

'Adam, we have five more minutes today. You have been so brave to come here. I do hope you want to come again, despite it having been really difficult for you. I promise it will get easier over time. There's no pressure to tell me what's troubling you. In fact, I don't suggest you try to do that today. I want to send you out of here able to function in the world. But if you would like me to make another appointment, I can see you at the same time next week?'

Adam nodded.

After Adam had peeled off the blanket and buttoned up his coat to buffer himself against the wind and Rachel knew not what, she slumped down in her chair and found she was now the one shaking. She looked at her watch. A blessed half an hour until the next client. Just time to grab a cappuccino and refocus.

A Kind of Family

Friends

When Rachel arrived with Fran at Meeting for Worship, it was as if an advance party (albeit a peaceful one) had been sent out to greet her. She lost count of the number of people who came to shake her hand vigorously, declaring 'You must be Rachel! I'm so pleased to meet you!' – and variations on this. What struck her though, was that this delight in her relationship with Fran was not confined to the younger members of the Meeting, nor to women alone. One of the people who shook her hand warmly was an older gentleman with glasses, a beard and thinning grey hair. He stood tall and straight, and when he held her hand his gaze, though warm was too direct for her. She found herself wanting to let go of his hand as quickly as manners would allow.

Despite being thrown by the welcome, Rachel was surprised both at how quickly she settled into a state of inner peace, and how meaningful she found most of the ministry. One woman irritated her, however – a woman of around sixty who insisted on talking about Jesus every other word, which meant Rachel didn't listen to the rest of what she was saying. But she was struck by what the person who spoke next had to offer – something about us all being precious. She found she could relate to that, it being close to her own values. As she listened, she noticed Aggie across the room, wearing a very fetching pale lilac sixties style wedding hat with veil over the face. This clashed, however, with Aggie's red coat over a black dress with white lacy collar. Her shoes were black patent with little kitten heels, and for once her stockings were somehow held up. There was no cigarette in her hand – instead, she clutched a sausage-shaped, cheap blue imitation-leather handbag. Rachel realised she must be staring but Aggie winked at her in conspiratorial fashion. Rachel hurriedly closed her eyes to prevent being seen in her response to this and settled back into reverie. By the end of the Meeting she noticed she had fallen into a state of bliss despite herself – which she rationalised as the result of neurones firing in different parts of her brain.

After the Meeting, Rachel wanted to slip off but both Fran and Richard insisted they must stay for a cup of tea. Rachel found it excruciating to sit round a table with her hot drink and answer endless questions about what she did for a living, how she and Fran had met, and had she ever been to a Quaker Meeting before? What's more, she was alarmed to discover that at least six people who had never met her before intended to turn up to her wedding.

On the way home, she shared her discomfort with Fran.

'Well, darling, we were told this is what they do. They take weddings very seriously. In fact, my understanding is that they see themselves as responsible for upholding the marriage afterwards too, so that either or both of us can go to them to discuss any problems we might be having.'

'No thanks. I am not discussing our relationship with total strangers who aren't trained counsellors. And I would prefer it if you didn't, either.' Rachel was in the passenger seat, clutching her Fair-Trade woven bag to her as if her life depended on it.

Indoors, Rachel had a debate with herself. If she had attended sooner, would she feel any better about Quakers? They had been both welcoming and generous in their support for the wedding. But she also knew from listening to Fran that, as in all groups of people there were some who irritated even the generous and accepting Fran. There was a particular middle-aged woman who had spoken today and Rachel suspected this was someone Fran had previously mentioned to her. Fran had said she seemed to speak every week despite the notice on the wall in the Meeting House to dissuade that sort of behaviour. Rachel had clocked the messages about the nature of ministry in this notice:

> *… ministry is not the place for intellectual exercise. It comes through us, not from us. Although we interpret the Spirit it is that Spirit which will lead us to minister. The Spirit will decide which experiences are relevant and which will speak to the condition of the meeting. If you have to decide whether it is right to speak, consider that it isn't. If your words are important the meeting will find them anyway. (QFP, 2.60)*

> *Each Friend who feels called upon to rise and deliver a lengthy discourse might question himself – and herself – most searchingly, as to whether the message could not be more lastingly given in the fewest possible words, or even through his or her personality alone, in entire and trustful silence… (QFP, 2.64)*

> *Ministry is what is on one's soul, and it can be in direct contradiction to what is on one's mind. It's what the Inner Light gently pushes you toward or suddenly dumps in your lap. It is rooted in the eternity, divinity, and selflessness of the Inner Light; not in the worldly, egoistic functions of the conscious mind. (QFP, 2.66)*

When she first read this, Rachel had felt shocked by the starkness in the language. She had made a beeline for Richard after the Meeting.

'Quakers don't mince their words, do they Richard?'

'Er… no. Some of us sometimes find it difficult to speak honestly…' He trailed off, looking into his mug, then collected himself. 'But no, we try to speak the truth, even to power. Especially to power!' This last thought seemed to invigorate him.

'So, what happens if you lot have an issue with someone in the Meeting?' Rachel was curious to know how they might deal with the woman who ministered too much.

'Ah. Yes, well, that does happen of course. There's conflict in any group of people.'

Rachel was only partly surprised to hear this admission, but she played along, not wanting to let him know what she had heard from Fran.

'Really? I thought you Quakers were a peaceful lot. That's what most people think of when they think of Quakers, I suppose.'

'No, no.' Richard looked sorrowfully at her, then seemed to make an effort to replace his sorrow with optimism. 'Well, that is, we do have conflict, because we're human. But we try to deal with it differently. We have ways of communicating that allow us, in theory at least, to open conversations and that encourage us all to listen to each other compassionately. And if that doesn't work, there is always the possibility of a threshing meeting.'

'Threshing meeting? Pardon?'

'Let's save that for another day, shall we?' Richard smiled benignly as he would at one of his students, and Rachel knew better than to push it.

The date for the wedding was set as August 4th, 2014, a Monday. Fran went back to her old house for the night before the wedding. Joanne had wanted her to go to her house, saying it was only right and proper that she should be with family before such a big day. But Fran could not bring herself to do it. She felt guilty for shunning her sister, but she knew she needed to be where she felt loved in a less complicated way, by people who had been a family of sorts for the past decade.

When she had asked Debra, Roxy and Feather they were all delighted. Feather had jumped up and down, clapping her skeletal hands together so much that Fran feared they might become dust. Debra had given her a slap on the back, then a big hug across the shoulders with one arm. And Roxy had just grinned at her then given her an enormous, slightly sensual hug which made Fran feel just for a moment that she missed this woman rather more than was comfortable. It was Debra who spoke for all three, legs astride and tears glistening in her eyes as she spoke:

'Of course you must come here the night before your wedding. This is your home. It will always be your home if and when you want it. We're your family. We'll have a little ceremony to send you off.'

And at that, there were more hugs all round accompanied by tears and then tea.

And so the evening before her wedding, Fran took a large suitcase to the old house. It was strange, sleeping in her old bed.

At the door, she was greeted with warm smiles and hugs from all three women. As soon as she was through the door, Feather offered to feed her:

'You must be starving! Let me take your case upstairs to your old room. I have chicken stir fry on the go. Yum, yum!'

Feather's eyes lit up. Fran looked sadly back, knowing that vicarious pleasure was all Feather would allow herself when it came to food. In bed she had at first been similar, giving far more than she allowed herself to receive, though with three other women lovingly coaching her over the years she was finally able to enjoy receiving the pleasure she had previously denied herself. Fran wondered how that was going now – had she gone back to square one, punishing herself for the loss of one of her lovers? She would never ask.

Debra chimed in:

'Let her get in the door, my love. Fran – can I get you a nice cup of tea, maybe?'

Debra's role in the house was to help everyone else feel safe. But it occurred to Fran to wonder now after months of living with a therapist – who kept Debra safe? Who thought about her needs? Fran struggled to remember a time when Debra had expressed any concern for herself. She only ever seemed to care for others, though in bed she could be demanding. Perhaps that was where she got what she needed. It had not previously occurred to Fran to compare her lovemaking with Rachel with any she had had before, but one of the things that made it so special was that it flowed. It was uncomplicated, and equal. Raunchy, yes, and they sometimes took turns to be either dominant or submissive to each other but there were also times when it was as if their lovemaking was the ultimate expression of their being – no-one was leading or receiving, giving or following. There was a kind of inevitability to it and occasionally an expression of what Fran now recognised as the Divine. When that happened there was no thought, no planning, no guile. Just being in the moment, as if led by some superior being towards a kind of Nirvana. She had never experienced anything like it before she met Rachel.

Roxy squeezed Fran's hand as she came through the door. After the initial hug she had been hanging back, beaming, and when Fran sat down in one of the assorted armchairs acquired from charity shops or other people's cast-offs, Roxy picked up a guitar as was her wont. She picked out a tune as she chatted, playing with the same kind of ease and absence of conscious deliberation that some women have when they knit as they talk. And in that moment, Fran knew she was home. This was where she needed to be, the night before her wedding. This was her family, and she would never lose touch with them. They loved her unconditionally – they had even let her go without so much as a whimper, because that's what you do when you love someone. You let them go when it's time.

Later that night, Fran lay in bed looking up at the ceiling. The fact that the three women had never tried to replace her meant that not only was she still special in their lives, but on a very prosaic level they were each now having to pay more to meet the rent and bills. She knew they would never complain to her about this, but she felt a pang of guilt that she had abandoned these three, wonderful women. Silent tears began trickling gently down her cheeks as she hugged the duvet up under her chin. She didn't know whether they were tears of guilt, of love, or of missing the freedom she once had to make love to several different women in one week.

Rachel decided to go to the wedding from her own house. This was, after all, where she had lived all alone for more than a decade. She considered asking her brother whether he might come over from Australia and stay with her, but with sadness decided against it. He had made his feelings very clear. In a way, it was a blessing; her sister-in-law was very traditional, possibly homophobic, and emotionally closed. Hugs with her were like cuddling a shop mannequin.

And so, the night before her wedding Rachel sat alone with only Annie for company. Even Aggie didn't show. She felt lonely; an emotion she had not experienced since Fran started living with her. It puzzled and frightened her – how could she, a woman who had lived alone for years before Fran, now dread a night alone in her own house?

She settled down to write, but no words came. She tried to read – nothing too demanding. A novel for a change. She read a page, then realised absolutely none of it had gone in. All she could think about was tomorrow, and the relief she sought in knowing that Fran and she would be married with the same rights as any couple whether woman and man, man and man or woman and woman. They would never have to be apart again unless they chose to – or one of them died. She shivered at the latter thought, and hurriedly parcelled it up in her mind. Despite her attempts to banish all negativity, Rachel began obsessing about what could go wrong. What if not enough people brought food? What if her voice froze during her declaration? What if…? In the end, she decided to put the television on whilst sitting up in bed. She watched one detective episode after another. They provided just enough to engage her interest whilst not being too intellectually demanding. Eventually, she fell asleep watching Amanda Redman boss three men about whilst solving a crime. She never did see who had committed the murder. She had just fallen into a deep sleep when the alarm rang.

'Oh, shit, shit shit!'

Annie, who had been allowed back into the bedroom just this once, growled beside her.

'Huh. You resent the intrusion too, old girl, do you?'

Rachel leaped out of bed. There was no way she was going to be late for her special day. But first, coffee! She had no appetite at all but decided she had better have at least one slice of toast to avoid fainting on the way to the Meeting House. Richard had kindly offered to pick her up. Fran, Rachel knew, would be brought by the posse and crammed into a beaten-up old car, while she would arrive in Richard's sports car.

Fran was woken with a warm lingering kiss on her cheek and a hot cup of tea. Roxy sat on the edge of her bed.

'Morning, love,' she said, stroking Fran's hair back from her face.

Roxy couldn't be asexual if she tried, thought Fran as she woke, feeling warm and snug in her old familiar bed.

'Hello, angel.' And then – 'Hang on a minute. I could swear your hair was green last night. It's red. When did you find time to do that?'

'Oh, you know me. I thought we should send you off with blazing colours. In fact, we all have a little special something in that department.'

Fran sat up in bed, intrigued, and grabbed her tea. It tasted delicious. Roxy seemed to have a knack for making the best cup of tea on the planet.

At this point, Feather poked her head round.

'Hello, sexy,' she said, with uncharacteristic forthrightness. Fran wondered whether Feather felt emboldened by the fact that Roxy was already sitting on Fran's bed, Roxy's fulsome breasts pouring out over a skimpy vest and displaying a delicate guitar tattoo on her right bosom. Feather stepped into Fran's room.

'Oh, my God! I absolutely fucking love it!' Fran didn't usually swear, but the rainbow tie-dyed dungarees Feather was wearing looked gorgeous on her, her bony bare feet poking out beneath them and sporting multi-coloured nail varnish.

'OK. Where's Debra, then?' The other two women looked at each other, grinning.

'Debs!' Feather called, excitedly.

Debra's head appeared at the door. She was already dressed for the wedding. Fran could hardly believe her eyes. Debra was wearing a dress! And what's more, it was two-tone, green and purple, made from flowing crêpe. Her short hair had been blow-dried and smoothed back behind her ears to look demure, and she was wearing soft brown eyeshadow together with a light pink lipstick. On her feet she wore sandals and once again her toenails were painted in multiple colours.

'Wow. Come here, you gorgeous pair!' Debra and Feather both willingly stepped forward, and all four women embraced.

'Sorry, babe. I'm a bit behind. But if you would like to step downstairs, I have pancakes waiting for you.' Roxy did her best to sound like the hostess with the mostest as she stood up, her right arm opening as if to make way for the princess to walk before her.

Fran felt like a spoiled little girl. She giggled, clutching her mug to her. Once out of bed she put on her furry slippers and followed her three best friends – her sisters by other mothers - downstairs to breakfast.

A Kind of Family

Once having feasted on pancakes, blueberries and bananas sweetened with agave nectar, it was time for them all to get ready. Feather did Fran's hair and make-up and Roxy helped her dress while Debra washed the dishes.

Just before they were due to leave the house Feather announced they had just one more thing to do. She told Fran to wait in the living room. The other three women left her alone, feeling excited and nervous. When Feather returned to collect her, she could hear one of her favourite Sarah McLachlan tracks *Angel* playing. On the doorstep, Debra and Feather were holding a structure over their heads that they had obviously made out of wire and died cloth (more rainbows). Feather told Fran to walk under the canopy, out to the car and she walked behind holding onto the hem of Fran's dress. Fran now cried openly with love for these women who had cherished her body and continued to cherish her heart and soul. Finally, they all piled into the house Astra estate, which was bedecked, unsurprisingly now for Fran, with rainbow ribbons.

When Rachel opened the door to Richard in his grey suit, she first noticed his aftershave, and his clean, spruced appearance. He had obviously gone to a special effort. She saw his warm, appreciative smile and misty eyes, and chose to respond to this as she might to a father-figure – or the loving older brother she no longer had. Rachel smiled warmly back and took his proffered arm.

'You look radiant,' he said softly.

And she did. Rachel had been lucky enough to find a dress in an antique shop that fitted her perfectly. Made of cream satin silk, it was a bargain at £150. It hugged her figure, being long and straight as was the fashion in the twenties and thirties. On her waist was a simple belt in the same material, with a diamanté clasp. She had swept her hair to one side with a comb she hoped would match the waist clasp. In her hands she carried a simple posy of vibrant purple cornflowers from her garden, tied with green ribbon. She held a white lace shawl round her shoulders, her shoes simple, low satin sling backs.

Richard had gone to the trouble of threading white ribbon through his window and bonnet, so that Rachel felt like a 'proper bride, which of course you are'. When they arrived at the Quaker Meeting House, Rachel spotted the Astra in the car park, more chaotically but she knew lovingly decked out. She felt her heart flutter as she knew this meant Fran was already waiting for her.

As Rachel and Richard entered the Meeting Room Rachel's heart stopped fluttering and began to melt. Fran looked gorgeous in a short, bright apple-green dress and jacket. The flared skirt of her dress was visibly plumped up with netting. She was wearing outrageous blue polka-dot heels. On her head was a sixties style hat also with netting, and in her hand, she carried a small handbag. She looked like Audrey Hepburn.

Richard led Rachel over to Fran, then sat down himself some distance away. The two women exchanged looks of love, amazement and excitement, then settled down into the silence. Rachel was surprised at how much she welcomed the quiet, almost forgetting what she was there for until Fran squeezed her hand.

Rachel's heart raced. This was the moment. She stood up, facing the woman she loved more than anyone in the world and clasped her hands so tightly she wondered if she might be hurting her. Fran's face was radiant. This was it, and it felt so right.

A Kind of Family

Fran spoke first:

'Friends, I take this, my friend Rachel Margaret Drake, to be my spouse, promising, through divine assistance, to be unto her a loving and faithful spouse, so long as we both on earth shall live.'

Rachel beamed pure joy at Fran, then looked down at the piece of paper on which she had written the words she must also speak. But then she realised she knew them. They came from the heart.

'Friends, I take this, my friend Frances Joy Baker, to be my spouse, promising, through divine assistance, to be unto her a loving and faithful spouse, so long as we both on earth shall live.'

The sense of relief that flooded Rachel's whole being as soon as these words were spoken was proof enough if she had needed any, that she had made the right decision in marrying Fran. Despite her avowed atheism she found herself inwardly noting that this Meeting for Worship for Marriage felt like the most holy of events. She became aware of a great swelling of love in her chest, not just for Fran but for the whole assembled Meeting, and for the whole of humanity.

Gosh! She thought. This must be what they mean when they speak of transpersonal experiences – a connection with something way beyond the self.

Rachel felt humbled. And as she kissed her bride, she couldn't help seeing over her shoulder that there was a woman sitting at the edge of the Meeting whom she had not previously noticed. She was dressed in a floral two-piece, her hair shoulder length, brown and wavy. Rachel couldn't help noticing the woman's hands were clasped over her stomach, her knees spread in a slightly unladylike fashion. And then Rachel realised, as she met the woman's beaming gaze; it was Aggie, spruced up for the occasion. No cigarette. No rollers in the hair. No pinafore. A matching outfit, and shoes! Rachel smiled back as she hugged Fran even more tightly, then the two women kissed gently on the lips before sitting down. Once seated, Rachel looked for Aggie, but she was gone.

PART THREE

Families

A Kind of Family

The call

'Jo? What is it?' Rachel woke to hear Fran talking into her phone, her voice tremulous. Rachel looked at the clock. Midnight.

Understanding the potential urgency though not yet understanding its cause, Rachel sprang out of bed. She pulled on yesterday's clothes as she saw Fran doing the same thing one-handed, the other hand clamping her phone to her ear.

'Which ward?' Fran's voice sounded urgent as Rachel forced her brain to catch up with what was happening. She resisted the urge to ask questions until Fran had finished talking.

'OK. I'm on my way.'

'What's happening, my love?'

Fran looked at Rachel as if only now registering her presence.

'It's Mum. She had a fall. They took her into hospital. Found her a bed straight away, thankfully. Ward 36. Medicine for older people.'

Rachel heard Fran's voice threatening to give way like a skater on melting ice. She could see her wife's hands shaking as she wrestled with the clasp on her belt. Tears started to form in Fran's eyes, but Rachel could see Fran push them back as she hunted round for her car keys.

'I'm driving you. You can't do this alone, Fran.'

'No! I can't wait! I have to get there!'

Rachel turned Fran around, holding both her shoulders squarely.

'Now, you listen to me! I am your wife. I will drive you. I want you there in one piece. Your Mum needs you there in one piece. I can be as quick as you, trust me.'

A Kind of Family

Within five minutes they were out of the door and in the car. Once safely on the road, Rachel could see Fran shivering despite a warm night and the car heater on full. The roads were clear. When they did pass the odd car, Rachel found herself wondering what those people were doing out so late. Were they on their way to sick loved ones too? What was their story? Time seemed suspended. More than once Rachel had to blink in order to work out what a shape was by the side or in the middle of the road. She was on high alert when she saw lonely wandering people in the night, until gradually they formed into shrubs or bollards and she breathed out her relief at not having to deal with madness, ghosts or worse. Small animals darted across their path. On one occasion, a fox nipped across, its back a level ledge as if trying not to spill someone's coffee. Eventually, the two women stopped at a service station for the bathroom. Rachel tried to get Fran to eat something.

'I can't. Sorry. I feel sick.' Fran's arms were wrapped around her torso.

Don't push her, Rachel Drake. Know when to back off.

Rachel decided to buy two bottles of water to keep them going and a couple of stale sandwiches, just in case.

It was still dark when Rachel parked the car in the deserted hospital car park. Fran ran to the hospital entrance and quickly located ward 36. Rachel was by her side in an instant, running with her along silent corridors, their footfall seeming to echo enough to wake the dead. They called a lift, but Fran lost patience and so they set off again, taking stairs two at a time.

When they got to the ward Rachel was surprised at how little out of breath Fran was, her own breath coming heavily and setting off a cough. They both reached for the hand sanitizer as Fran rang the bell, her eyes giving way once more to tears now that she was so close to her mother.

A nurse's voice sounded beside the door and Fran spoke her name. Abruptly, the door was released. They moved silently now, aware of how seriously ill other patients might be. They passed an old gentleman, white as the starched cotton linen in which he lay, oxygen cylinders by his side pumping into his nostrils. In another side room with open door lay an old woman curled up, her thin hair uncombed. Rachel could see large dark brown markings on her skin, visible despite her natural skin tone being brown. Rachel imagined that once this same skin was as beautiful as polished walnut, though now it was sallow, as if she was already flying away from her worn-out body.

As soon as they arrived at Susan's bedside Joanne jumped up and collapsed in tears on Fran, who suffered this outpouring of emotion stiffly whilst looking over her sister's shoulder at their mother.

Once Fran had managed to extricate herself, she and Joanne sat one either side of their mother, each holding a hand. Rachel thought Susan looked peaceful, her breathing easy, but then Fran squeezed her mother's hand and turned to Rachel.

'No response.'

Fran's face was expressionless as she said this. She seemed drained of all emotion. The curtains were drawn around Susan's bedside – a symbolic gesture of privacy. Rachel was acutely aware of a woman in a nearby bed who vomited repeatedly in the quiet of the night, her low moans suggesting resignation to a horrible fate.

The nurse entered their fragile sanctuary and looked straight at Fran.

'Hello. I'm Nurse O'Reilly. Are you the other sister, by any chance?'

Her voice sounded cheery. Rachel initially resented this, feeling the situation called for more reverence. But then she berated herself. The Irish accent always sounded chirpy to her, if not a little cheeky. Determining to overcome her preconceptions she faced the nurse and saw a face full of compassion and concern as she waited for Fran's answer. Fran also looked up, seeming to tear herself away from her mother in order to respond.

'Yes. Yes, I'm Fran.'

'Oh, OK. It's good that you managed to get here. I've asked the duty doctor to come and have a chat with you both. And you are?'

She had turned her gaze to Rachel, who answered simply, her hand already on Fran's lap for reassurance:

'My name's Rachel. I'm Fran's wife.'

'Oh, that's fine, then. You can all stay for the chat with the doctor. I just didn't want to assume anything – only family, you see.'

And with that, Nurse O'Reilly was gone, the curtains firmly closed.

Fran and Joanne exchanged urgent glances, then each looked down tearfully to their mother, adjusting their grips on their mother's hands in perfect synchrony as if they had rehearsed this dance many times before the performance.

Rachel excused herself from this private moment. She had to send a text to her client Adam, who was meant to be seeing her later today. She felt guilty for letting him down. Since the start of his therapy she had learned more about his past, which included the loss of his fiancée in a horrific car crash in which he was driving. He was very near the edge emotionally, and Rachel worried that her cancellation would feel like an abandonment. But she needed to be here with her wife, supporting her. For once, work was not going to come first.

'I'll go find where the toilets are.'

'Oh, that's easy! There's one right by the door as you come in.' Rachel could see that despite the gravity of their situation Joanne was enjoying being the older sister, in charge and in the know.

'Oh, OK. Thanks, Jo. But I think I'll look for water and coffee, too, so I might be a while. You OK, love?' Rachel turned to Fran, stroking her gently on the arm, shoulder and back. Fran looked up at Rachel and nodded, her face strangely peaceful.

Rachel wandered around the hospital corridors, partially deserted and yet strangely busy as if it were perfectly normal to be out at this time in the morning. A mother held her adult daughter, or so Rachel supposed. They were standing, the mother's eyes searching around presumably in search of a seat. The younger woman's legs were buckling under her, sobs echoing all along the dimmed walkway. Dishevelled doctors, their stethoscopes replacing recently discarded college scarves, shuffled purposively. Their bed hair looked strangely rakish as they hurried off to save a life or approve urgent pain relief. Rachel wondered how much sleep they had had since the last emergency.

She came across the eerily silent all-night cafeteria with its self-service coffee machines and cold drinks dispensers. A nurse was sitting on a sofa in one corner, munching on a chocolate bar. Rachel briefly considered buying crisps or chocolate, but somehow to have such a treat at a time like this seemed inappropriate so she settled on buying three bottles of water. Thankfully, the machine took notes, doling out change like a one-armed bandit hitting the jackpot. Rachel smiled ruefully as she gathered the coins and shoved them into her purse, weighing down her already overburdened shoulders. She wished she had brought a tote bag for the water as she balanced the three plastic bottles in her arms.

Rachel had clocked some toilets off the ward, on her way to the cafeteria. She decided she had better visit them now, even though she didn't really want to go. It was going to be a long night. Leaving the three water bottles by the sinks as she entered the cubicle, once inside and alone she felt a rush of relief to be unseen and unheard. Tears flowed freely, but when she heard the outer door open, she hurriedly gathered her clothing together. Whoever had entered the women's toilets had stopped near the three bottles of water. Rachel pictured the woman and imagined her puzzled expression. Before she could open her own cubicle door, she heard the other woman going into the one next door, adjusting her clothing, and sitting down.

Rachel hurriedly left her cubicle, washed her hands then grabbing the water became aware of an urgency to get back to Fran. She quickened her steps towards the ward, squirted the hand sanitizer and pushed the intercom button. As the door buzzed immediately, Rachel realised there was probably a camera in place.

As she approached the curtains, she berated herself for having dallied so long. A man's voice was speaking in soft tones, and then she heard her sister-in-law crying. Soon after this the man, a young South Asian doctor emerged from the curtains, looking downwards. He looked just about old enough to be leaving school. As he passed Rachel he looked up and nodded without expression. Rachel was at her wife's side in an instant.

'They say…' Joanne was the one to speak, forcing the words through her tears and looking back at her mother as if to reassure herself that it was OK to speak in front of her. 'They say that everything's packed up, basically. Her liver and kidneys, her bowels, and the bleed on her brain has flooded it. He said she might rally and look as if she is getting better but that will only be temporary. It's only a matter of time.'

And at this, Joanne sobbed long and hard. Rachel wished she had bought some tissues.

You're a bloody therapist, for Christ's sake, and you didn't think of tissues?

She looked around and seeing some on the bedside cabinet reached over and handed them to Joanne.

'Thank you,' smiled Joanne, looking as if she had just been given a very special, long-wished-for gift.

Rachel turned her attention to Fran, who was staring into an unseen distance. She placed her hands round her wife's shoulders, gently willing her to come back to her.

Fran turned to Rachel, her eyes hollow. 'I can't cry yet. She's still with us. I want to be strong for her.'

And with that, she looked down at her mother, her eyes filled with the love Susan was unable to express to her.

'I know, my love. I understand.' Rachel gently rubbed Fran's shoulder, then moved her hand to lightly squeeze Fran's knee as if to say, 'I'm here if you need me' before removing her hand.

'I brought us all some water.' Rachel nodded her head towards the table at the end of the bed, where she had placed the three bottles.

Fran looked vacantly towards the three bottles as if looking at something utterly foreign, then gazed back at her mother's face.

After a few minutes Fran turned first to Joanne, and then to Rachel. 'I'm not leaving her, no matter how long it takes. Just so that you know. I will go to the loo when I need to, but that's it. Other than that, I'm not leaving her side.'

Rachel knew Fran needed to do this one thing for her imperfect mother, to make this connection with her at last; to heal their past.

Joanne's brow furrowed. 'I can stay until about six, but then I need to get off to get the kids up and see that everyone gets out of the house on time. I'll be back later though. I'll just pop into work and let people know what's happening.'

Rachel could feel Fran stiffen beside her, and knew it was best to stay silent at this point. She herself would stay with Fran and take shifts.

Before the morning bustle of the ward started Joanne was gone, kissing her mother as if it was just a normal day and she would see her soon for all the usual gossip. Shortly after Joanne left daylight began to filter through the curtains.

'Fran? I didn't want to say this while Joanne was here in case it inflamed things. But I'm not going anywhere. Why don't you take the opportunity to go to the loo, and then when you come back, I'll go in search of breakfast for us both.'

Just as Rachel was finishing her speech, the curtain opened. It was the same nurse who had been on duty when they arrived.

'Can I get you ladies a cup of tea and some toast?' The Irish lilt in her voice sounded reassuring this time. It brought a faint smile of gratitude to Fran's lips, and Rachel could feel her relax ever so slightly.

A Kind of Family

It was Rachel who answered for both of them: 'That would be most welcome. Thank you.'

'OK. I will bring the toast now, and I'll let Joan know – our tea lady – to put her head round here when she gets to this part of the ward.'

The toast tasted heavenly, despite the white bread. Salty butter and plenty of it. The two women consumed it as if they had not eaten in weeks, Rachel quietly wishing there was more. When it came, the tea was lukewarm, milky and sweet despite both of them saying they wanted no sugar. Joan appeared to have been distracted by a handsome African-sounding doctor who happened to be passing by at the time. Joan looked to be in her mid-twenties though it was hard to tell, with ample hips and a uniform that barely stretched over her similarly large bosom. She chuckled constantly, bringing welcome if temporary relief from the seriousness of life on the ward.

Now that the ward was waking up Rachel began to notice the other patients, all of whom looked gravely ill. The woman opposite who had been vomiting in the night was curled up in a foetal position like the woman she had seen on her way in all those hours (it felt like weeks) ago, her sparse grey curls just poking out above the thin duvet. Next to her was a woman who when she heard Joan approach pulled herself up to sitting despite clutching her side. She was much younger, maybe in her thirties or forties, with lines in the back of both hands, a drip and monitors noisily recording various physiological processes. Rachel wondered what was wrong with all of them. Was anyone else dying? How many would ultimately get better? She wished she could get away from this stark reminder of her own mortality, despite her resolve to be there for Fran.

Fran looked down at her mother with the same soft look she had had all night. 'No breakfast for you, my love. No more breakfasts for you.' Her voice cracked. Rachel squeezed Fran's hand.

Joanne was good to her word and came back after seeing everyone off, but then she had to go again when the ward started serving lunch.

She popped back briefly in the evening but declared that her old bones could not cope without her bed for a second night. And so, she went. Rachel began to feel as if she now lived here. In these few intense hours she was already becoming institutionalised, recognising staff as they came and went and exchanging short but meaningful pleasantries with patients and their loved ones. The small space behind Susan's curtain held the illusion of being a home for them all - the ward their street in days gone by, when people knew each other's names and business.

As the ward hushed into night mode, a nurse poked her head round the curtains.

'Can I get you two ladies a mattress to put down beside the bed, and a couple of pillows? I'm afraid I can only run to one mattress between you, but maybe you can take shifts or go head to tail? I can give you a blanket each.'

It was a different nurse – one they had not seen before. For some bizarre reason Rachel noticed her lovely blonde plait to one side. She was young, maybe twenties, but sounded much older. She had obviously witnessed vigils like this before.

Rachel and Fran gratefully accepted, and before long Rachel was spooning behind Fran, her arms wrapped around her wife so that Fran could stay right by her mother's side. Rachel's backside trailed over the edge of the mattress as did one of Fran's knees on the other side, but at least they could lie down. Rachel was aware of Fran's alert body next to hers and wondered if she would sleep at all.

Rachel must have slipped into sleep herself, because she was awoken by Fran sitting up.

'Her breathing's changed,' Fran said in answer to the unasked question. In no time, the mattress was stowed under the bed and both women were beside Susan. Her breathing was heavier, noisier. The nurse must have noticed too, because she silently opened the curtain, looked at Susan as if making an assessment, then turned to Rachel and Fran.

'Yes. There's definitely a change. Probably time to gather the family.'

'OK.' Fran was alert and in coping mode. She rang her sister, quietly speaking into her mobile.

'Come,' Was all she said, and the phone call was over, Fran standing now above her mother's bed and gazing lovingly down at her with moist eyes.

Joanne arrived, taking off her coat and dropping it on the chair she had used the day before and the day before that as she rushed breathlessly to hold her mother's hand.

Once all three women were assembled the end came quickly. Rachel could hear Fran whispering things to her mother, relating tales from their childhood to send her mother on her way with, tears now falling readily as she continued to pour love into her.

Susan's body contracted as if attempting to sit up in some supreme last effort, and then she collapsed back onto the plump pillows, exhaling. There was a pause. Her body opened and closed a couple of times as if taking in air and breathing it out, but there was no noise. Finally, she was still, a look of utter calm on her face as her muscles relaxed at last.

Fran uttered a wail unlike any other Rachel had ever heard. Rachel just managed to catch her as her legs buckled. Joanne shushed from across the bed but was immediately silenced by an uncompromising look from Rachel. Rachel held Fran close to her, stroking her silky hair and whispering in her ear.

'It's OK, my love. You let it out. You've been so brave.'

The two women held onto each other and wept. As Rachel looked over her shoulder, she saw Aggie. For once, she wasn't looking at Rachel. She seemed focussed on Susan, holding her by the hand. Then Rachel had to stop herself from shouting out as she caught her breath, but Fran seemed not to notice. Rachel's vision clouded with colours: a bright fluorescent apple-green, purple and violet. In the middle of this colour Susan seemed to stand up and was led away by Aggie to the corners of Rachel's vision. They were both smiling. Rachel closed her eyes and when she opened them her vision was still cloudy, but colourless. She looked at the bed and there lay Susan's empty shell of a body.

A Kind of Family

Belongings

When it came to clearing out Susan's things there was very little to go through. Much of that had been done when the two daughters had moved her into the home in which she had spent the last few years. In the end, Fran was the one to do the deed as Joanne sank into a deep depression without her mother to care for. Fran became worried about her sister, wishing they lived nearer to each other. She tried speaking on the phone with her brother-in-law Roger, an ineffectual man who had spent his life working on one scheme after another designed to bring in millions, all of which had failed.

'Roger? I'm a bit concerned about Jo. Have you noticed any change in her since Mum died?'

'No, no. She seems fine, actually. Seems to have taken it better than I thought.'

Fran breathed in and stopped her breath, swallowing hard.

'It's just that she told me the children are now taking themselves to school. That's not like her. She was always so – well, mummyish.'

'Yeah, yeah. She seems to have woken up to the fact that they are getting older. It's a good thing, surely?'

Fran knew it was probably useless trying to get Roger to see what was going on – let alone to take any action. She would have to go and see them.

When she arrived, Roger sat at the kitchen table while Fran quizzed him about how things were. Joanne was upstairs, having a 'lie down'.

A Kind of Family

Roger scrolled through his iPad, bought with Joanne's earnings, and took large gulps of coffee in between offering sparse details.

'What am I to do, Fran? Look, I know I told you everything was OK. But she won't get out of bed. To be honest, it's taking its toll on me. I'm having to do all the getting kids' uniforms ready. And I'm having to send out for pizza every night 'cos she won't cook.' Roger smacked his palm against his chest. 'It's me you should be worried about!'

Fran could hardly believe what she was hearing. This man seemed perfectly happy for his wife to be the main breadwinner – a very twenty-first century phenomenon – yet he was stuck in the early twentieth century in terms of his assumptions that housework, cooking, shopping and childcare were women's work. Where did he get off? If he had helped out a bit more around the house in their twenty years of marriage things might be different now. For a moment, Fran wondered if Jo had taken to her bed as a way of punishing him. But no, she wasn't like that. Jo had always seen her role in life as taking care of others. Fran could see it now. As the younger sister she had had freedoms her older sister never had. Fran could afford to be adventurous, whereas her sister had been programmed from a very young age to accept her lot as a woman, and that lot must be taking care of others at all costs.

Fran gave up trying to galvanise her brother-in-law and climbed the stairs to see her sister. She knocked softly on the big wooden door, and on hearing a muffled groan of assent from the other side she lifted the metal latch, creeping inside.

'Hey, sis. Come to see you.'

Joanne hauled herself up onto her elbows as Fran moved to her side, plumping up her pillows in a rare expression of sisterly softness. Joanne smiled at her sister, a brief moment of gratitude and recognition in her eyes before they returned to their blank expression.

Fran frowned as it occurred to her that her sister probably hadn't eaten or drunk anything in some while, given the way Roger was.

'Can I get you something? A nice cup of tea, perhaps?'

Joanne stared into a corner of the room as if she might find inspiration there to tell her whether or not she was indeed thirsty.

'Tell you what, I'll get you one anyway, and then you can try it and see if you want it. No harm done if it goes to waste.'

Fran descended the stairs. Her stomach felt like a tangled ball of wool whose end was lost. Something else was troubling her besides her concern for her sister. Was Jo turning into their mother? Was Fran about to become a carer? She shuddered, then resolved to ensure that Jo would soon be on her feet, back to her old coping self.

In the kitchen she silently made tea, ignoring Roger's enthusiastic remarks about the latest business guru he had just found on Facebook. She deliberately didn't offer him a 'brew'[1].

Once back upstairs, she began in earnest.

'Jo, you can't go on like this. You have children who need their mother. You, and only you can be that person for them.'

Jo looked up at her sister as if only then noticing she was there in the room. A look of puzzlement followed by a flash of recognition passed over her face, and Fran knew in that instant that she had done the right thing in intervening so directly. Joanne looked around the room, her eyes searching for something.

'What is it, my love? What do you need?'

'My clothes. I've got to pick the kids up from school.'

The look on Joanne's face had turned to panic.

'It's OK. They're walking together. They'll be perfectly safe. That is one positive by-product of you being unwell, Jo. Roger refuses to take them or bring them back, so they've had to learn to do it using their own two feet, which can only be a good thing. Don't go back to mollycoddling them. Your youngest child is eight, and your oldest is sixteen. If they do it this year before Esme goes to high school, then

---

[1] A northern England expression meaning a hot drink, usually tea.

Charlotte will be able to do it next year after her sister is no longer able to walk with her. She'll find a friend to walk with, I daresay.'

Fran surprised herself. She knew she sounded bossy, but it had always been Joanne's role to boss her around. The role reversal paid off. Joanne sat up in bed looking down, nodded her head, then looked up at Fran.

'You're right. I've been too much of a pushover, haven't I? I'm not like you, Fran. Never was. Remember when we were kids and you would be off climbing trees? All I wanted to do was play house.'

Fran remembered this as if it were yesterday. She, climbing a big oak tree with Jo at the foot of it, not daring to put one foot up. She wondered how much had been genetics and how much to do with their mother's conditioning of her oldest daughter. But what was done was done, and here they were, like chalk and cheese as the aunties used to say yet bound together through an invisible thread stronger than graphene.

Joanne dressed, wobbling like someone who had just got over influenza. Then with the kind of strength reserved for mothers she straightened herself, announced she felt hungry and said she was going downstairs to make an omelette. Fran offered to make it for her, but Joanne insisted. When the two women came downstairs Roger already had his coat on.

'I'm off out now you're up,' he declared, without further explanation.

Fran felt hot with fury, but then relieved that she no longer had to deal with him being around.

Once Joanne was comfortably sitting at table with her omelette Fran broached the subject of their mother's belongings.

'Jo, I'm going to the home later today to begin clearing out their Mum's things.'

Fran watched and waited as Joanne slowly moved her food from plate to fork to mouth. She nodded almost imperceptibly.

Fran had been galvanised by a recent phone call from the home. They needed the room, and besides that she knew the rent was only paid to the end of the month.

'I know we got rid of a load of stuff when Mum moved in, but didn't she give you some things to look after, Jo? Not that I need anything. I've got all I want from Mum. You remember she gave us each something special a few years ago, so that we wouldn't have to deal with receiving it after her death?'

As she said this Fran was reminded of their mother's thoughtful act. She might not be able to show love in the usual ways, but she had moments like this of absolute clarity about the future in which she also demonstrated her ability to put herself in her daughters' shoes. She had given them each a significant piece of jewellery: Fran had a charm bracelet with little blue silver clogs and a St. Christopher's medal and suchlike hanging from the links of its sturdy chain. Each charm, Fran knew, symbolised an untold story. Fran imagined her own stories into existence: her mother visiting the Netherlands and coming back with the silver clogs; being given the St Christopher by an aunt before going on her first long train journey to Cornwall or Scotland; and the *commedia dell'arte* faces because she harboured a secret love of the stage. Joanne was given her mother's engagement ring, a diamond solitaire. She had protested at the time, saying their Mum should still wear it, but Susan had been stoical in her insistence.

Joanne was silent for several seconds as she considered what their mother had given her to look after, then raised her eyebrows and opened her mouth, looking upwards as she did so:

'Oh my God! I'd completely forgotten the little trunk she gave me to look after. It's up in our attic. If only I could remember where the key is...' She got up from the table leaving half her omelette and began wandering round the kitchen, as if looking would assist her memory.

'Eat!' Fran repeated her new-found sternness with her sister. 'It'll wait. I have too much to do today, anyway.'

When it came to it, Fran couldn't bear to visit the home that day. She was exhausted from caring for her sister, dealing with her obnoxious brother-in-law, and her own grief. Instead, she drove home to collapse in the arms of the one person she knew would demand nothing of her.

A few days later, Fran received another phone call.

'Hi sis'. Fran's heart danced to hear her sister sounding like her old self again.

'Well hello, stranger!' She grinned into the mouthpiece.

'I've got it.'

'Pardon?'

'The trunk. I sent Roger into the loft to get it down. It's sitting here, waiting for you to open it. The only trouble is the key. I have no idea where it is. I'm sorry…'

Her voice trailed off into a choked sob.

'It's OK, sis. I'll come and get it. I know you aren't up to dealing with this. We're in this together, remember. You did most of the care while Mum was alive. This is the least I can do. I'll come down next week some time. I just need to shift a couple of things around in my diary.'

Rachel sat opposite Adam. His shirt sleeves were rolled up to just above the wrist, exposing dark hairs on his forearms. He was leaning forward, his head in his hands. She became aware of a sexual charge in the room, momentarily horrified at the thought she might fancy one of her male clients. She put it to the back of her mind, logging it as something to talk to her supervisor about.

'So, Adam, I can see this is raw. How come it has come down to you, to go through your fiancée's possessions? She has a mother and father, right?'

Rachel wondered if she sounded resentful. She was cross with Joanne for leaving so much to Fran but had not breathed a word of this to her wife. Once again, she consciously laid her own life to one side, determined to be present to whatever Adam might bring to therapy.

'Um… well, we *were* living together. And about to be—'

Adam collapsed into sobs. He didn't need to complete the sentence. Their wedding date had been just six weeks away when she died. Once again, Rachel – or rather her best friend – kicked herself mentally in the shins.

Oh Christ, Rachel! Their wedding day was to have been today!!!! You stupid, stupid girl!

'It was today, wasn't it?' Rachel spoke quietly, like someone treading over bare floorboards in someone else's house in the dead of night.

The sobs deepened as Adam nodded his head vigorously, reaching for the tissues with snot pouring from his nose. His eyes were red, his cheeks flushed, but despite the way he looked Rachel once again felt a throbbing in her groin.

Jesus, Drake!

OK. Time to take note of this. Rachel knew that erotic countertransference as it was called usually had meaning of some sort, but she wasn't ready to share this with Adam.

And then he looked up, composed. His blue eyes met Rachel's.

'She looked a bit like you, actually.'

His voice sounded calm, and the redness seemed to vanish.

So that was it. Now Rachel knew what she needed to focus on. 'Tell me about the things you need to go through – what stories they hold.'

'My love?'

'Mmm?' Fran had her head in a book about Dance Movement Therapy. She carefully marked the page with a clip-on bookmark and looked up at Rachel.

'I'm coming with you when you go down to go through Susan's things. I know you think you can do this alone, but I want to be there for you just in case.'

Fran frowned.

'It's OK. I've got someone else to teach my sessions. My diary is clear.'

Fran draped her arms round Rachel's shoulders, gently kissing her on the cheek.

'I don't deserve you.'

'Don't be silly,' Rachel chided, colouring slightly. Rachel knew the task of going through Susan's personal possessions would end up being more painful for Fran than she seemed to think it would be. But she would not take over – she would allow Fran to take it at her own pace.

They decided to go to the home before going on to Joanne's house. They arrived shortly after lunch, having left home around nine to avoid traffic. They had to ring a bell to be let in, having agreed in advance they would say as little as possible to the concerned staff member who opened the door. After signing in they climbed the stairs to Susan's room. The first thing Rachel noticed was the closed door, which she knew from listening to Fran talk about her visits was so unlike the days when Susan used to sit in her chair with her door open in hopeful waiting. When Rachel tried the door, she found it unlocked. She mumbled crossly something about the fact that things could have gone missing, but Fran didn't seem to care. She hurried inside and shut the door again. They did not escape notice though; a woman shouted along the corridor:

'Will you make me a cup of tea? I've had nothing to drink all day!'

Rachel took control.

'I'm sure they'll be along with the trolley soon enough. Keep a look-out for us, will you?'

'Who are you to be ordering me about?' came the haughty reply. Rachel shut the door before she could get embroiled, hoping the woman wouldn't follow them. She did not.

Fran's eyes filled with tears as she looked around the room, seeing ten years of memories.

'I just want to keep it all just as it was,' she whispered. 'Then maybe she won't actually be dead.' Rachel placed one hand on Fran's back and whispered gently to her:

'How would you like to do this Fran? Shall we start with the easy bits? Maybe in the bathroom?'

Fran nodded her assent.

'Shall I do that bit while you have a sit down and just take it all in?'

Another nod, and Rachel guided her to the upright chair – which she knew Fran had sat in many, many times to listen to her mother's tales about people Fran knew not at all and cared about even less, or to watch her eat with painstaking concentration.

Once Fran was safely seated Rachel got to work throwing Susan's various creams and potions into a large bin bag which she announced she would take to landfill. She looked round the door from the poky en suite toilet to check with Fran:

'Darling? I'm just throwing all your Mum's old pills and potions. They aren't any good to anyone. Her toilet bag is very grubby. Would you like me to do the same with that?'

A vacant nod.

'And her toothbrush, flannel and hairbrush?'

Another vacant nod.

Once that job was done Rachel decided someone else could clean for once – Joanne and Fran each used to clean whenever they visited despite the fact that the home employed a cleaner. Fran had told her there were always tissues on the floor, the sink always had bits in it, and Susan's toothbrush was usually caked solid with old toothpaste. It was a relief even to Rachel to know those days were over. She found herself wondering if either of the daughters had yet allowed herself feelings of relief and made a mental note to remind Fran not to feel guilty if she did.

'Now. How about you stay there while I go through all of Susan's clothes? I've brought a case, and I suggest we simply take them all to a charity shop. I can do that for you.'

Fran seemed to be coming to her senses.

'Yes. Yes, I'm sure neither of us will want anything in that wardrobe.'

And then:

'Thanks, Rachel. I don't know what I would do without you.'

Fran's eyes filled with tears, her voice like a radio that needed tuning.

Good. That's better than being a zombie, thought Rachel.

Once the clothes were done it was the turn of Susan's books, an endless supply of romances in which the doctor (pilot, business executive) woos the young feisty woman after first managing to make her very angry. All the stories ended the same way; after first hating each other they fell in love and the young woman was taken care of as women should be, by a powerful and rich man. They were to be donated to the home's little library. Boxes of unopened tissues were taken for Rachel's psychotherapy practice. Rachel knew, though, that she was leaving the difficult things until last – Susan's few pieces of jewellery, photographs on the wall, her handbag and purse, and whatever was in her bedside cabinet, which was never opened in front of anyone.

In the end it was easy to deal with the photos as they were mostly of Joanne's children and so it was decided to take them to her. Similarly, Fran suggested Jo might want the handbag and purse, though she kept the chequebook so that she could save Joanne the job of alerting the bank. There was little jewellery, but Fran said she needed to take it all to Jo and divide it out there, so this too was packed away in a smaller suitcase for later.

It was time to open the drawer. As Rachel looked towards it, she saw Aggie standing guard by the bedside cabinet. She had a look of patient officiousness, the cigarette back in her hand but this time in a cigarette holder which gave her an air of 1930s decorum – and status. She was wearing her pinafore, this being messy domestic work, but her hair was out of rollers, a clean scarf covering her locks with the exception of her fringe. She looked quite the domestic services manager.

Once opened, the two women saw that all that was inside the secret drawer was a solitary photograph, and a key. The photograph was of Fran's father, taken in the 1970s judging by the long sideburns. The key, they presumed, would open the trunk. Once the key was firmly in Rachel's hand Aggie nodded at Rachel and disappeared. She had not uttered a word.

When they got to Joanne's house, she readily accepted the handbag and purse together with the photographs of her children. The jewellery box and the photograph of their dad were left at Jo's house for decision another time.

Much later that evening, Rachel drove Fran back home through the dark. The trunk lay unopened on the back seat. It was made of dark wood, with metal strips and a large lock. Measuring roughly two feet wide, and about one foot both in height and depth it struck Rachel as more of a novelty treasure chest than a proper, secure trunk.

They arrived home around midnight. When the two women got inside the house Fran, who had carried the trunk as if it was more precious than the crown jewels, laid it on the kitchen table, the key poised in her hand and Rachel by her side, a hand tenderly resting on her back.

'Is this the right time, Fran? There's no rush, you know. No one and nothing is depending on you opening this now. You've already done so much today, you poor lamb.'

At this point, Fran seemed to feel the weight of her body. She folded over forwards towards the trunk, and the key dropped noisily from her hand onto the kitchen floor. Before Rachel could register this change, Fran was sobbing in her arms.

'Why don't I run you a nice bath and light some candles, and then you can relax in it?' Rachel whispered tenderly into her beloved's ear.

Fran nodded through her sobs.

After checking she was OK and lying her down on one of the sofas, Rachel went upstairs to prepare the bath. When she came down Fran was dozing but when she heard Rachel she got up and, clutching her jumper to her like a tired, obedient child she walked towards the stairs.

'Take as long as you like, my love,' Rachel called after her, mentally making a note to check on her in five minutes so that she could reassure herself that Fran hadn't fallen asleep in the bath and drowned.

Buried treasure

Fran was alone in the house, as ready as she would ever be to begin the task of going through her mother's most treasured possessions. The key worked easily in the old-fashioned lock. She opened the lid with the care and precision of a bomb specialist.

The first thing she saw was a photograph of her mother and father on their wedding day. Her mother wore a lacy white mini dress, a short veil on her head. Her father was sporting a new suit. They both looked hopelessly in love though Fran knew they had been together for a long time before this. She turned over the black and white photograph. The only inscription on the back was the date 12th June 1965. An early summer wedding. Fran put the photograph to one side, forming the beginning of a pile to keep. She would give the original to Joanne, who had never mastered digital technology, and she would scan it so that she could put it on her screen save.

Fran pored through old programmes and tickets, finding one for the famous 1970 Leeds University Who concert and a trip to London in 1969 to see Ravi Shankar on the South Bank. Then there were various other items about which she knew nothing, including a swimming medal, a piece of coal, and then a random collection of old coins contained in a tin box.

And then she found a bundle of letters. She unfolded them carefully, laying them out in the order in which they had been stored.

The first one was written in bright blue ink. Fran imagined the writer having to dip the nib repeatedly into an ink bottle, blotting paper

A Kind of Family

in hand. The writing was neat, with no crossings-out and almost no splodges.

> 2, Bush Crescent,
>
> Garforth,
>
> Leeds
>
> 10th May 1965

My love,

It's still not too late to change your mind. I would not mind your Ma being there, even though I have never met her. I just fear you might regret your decision in years to come.

I come from a big family as you know, and I feel bad that I am taking up most of the places at the church and afterwards. You and I have both saved for this wedding, and I want it to be your Day. I can hardly wait to see you at the aisle, my darling. Just over a month now.

I love you more than ever.

Looking forward to the day when I can call you my wife – Mrs Steve Baker. It is just such a shame that I have to go to sea so soon after our wedding.

Your ever-loving,

Steve

The letter was signed in a surprising scrawl. Fran imagined her father practising his signature, to make it more flamboyant than his otherwise neat hand.

The next one was from an earlier date, the writing more old-fashioned and scrawling, but the spelling was perfect which surprised Fran. She knew her grandmother had been brought up in a working-class family in the days when no matter how bright you were, if there was not enough money for books and uniforms children were unable to progress to the grammar school and simply stayed on in their first school until the age of fourteen before being sent out to work very long days.

3 The Meadows

Skipton

North Yorkshire

March 3rd, 1965

Dear Susan,

I hope you are enjoying your flat in Leeds, and that you are getting along OK with the other girls. I ~~love~~ do think of you, often.

I heard from one of my friends – her daughter ~~is friends with~~ knows you I think. Maureen Fields, is it? – Anyway, this friend ~~embar~~ of course thought I must know and would be coming to your wedding to Steve. I could have ~~er~~fallen through the ground, but I kept up appearances I am glad to say. Who would want to tell the world that her daughter isn't speaking to her and hasn't invited her to her own wedding?

Anyway, if you can be bothered to reply, do let me know when the wedding is so that I can send you a card at least. I don't expect an invite. You always were a strong-headed girl. One day you will thank me though, for making you wait. I just hope you don't regret marrying a merchant seaman, but it is your choice. You are a big girl now and I can't stand in your way.

Mum.

Fran felt the force of the anger simmering under the surface in this letter, like a knife twisting in her guts. She knew her mother was estranged from her own mother, but she had previously had no idea of the strength of feeling that had been expressed by the grandmother she had never met.

The next letter was in the same hand, with no crossings out. Both letters had several ink splodges on them and the ink was brown and faded which made it difficult to make out the words.

3 The Meadows
Skipton
North Yorkshire
May 6th, 1965

Dear Susan,

I know you don't want to talk to me. Clearly, my last letter didn't touch your heart as I had hoped it might. Now, I am reduced to pleading with you. You are my daughter. My only daughter, in fact because as you know you had four brothers. I longed for a daughter and was over the moon when you were born after war broke out. Your father died at sea soon after this as you know, leaving me to bring up my children on my own. Life was hard. There wasn't the help in those days, but we managed.

I didn't want you to marry Steve, I grant you. Not because I didn't like him – I hardly know him, really – but because I did not want to see my daughter go through the same as me. There, I've said it. That is why I made you wait. Maybe I was right, maybe I was wrong, but Susan if you have a heart at least contact your brothers and invite them. Even if you won't have me there, have your brothers. They don't deserve this. And come to that, neither do you. I know you blame them for siding with me, but in cutting us all off, you are left with nothing other than Steve's family. Don't do that to yourself. Or to any kids you might have.

I hope one day to meet my grandchildren, if you have any.

Have a nice wedding.

Your Mum.

Fran sat cross-legged in front of the trunk, unsure what to think or feel. The knowledge that she had four uncles and God alone knew how many cousins was mind boggling. But how to start about finding them all? Did she even want to? She decided that was too much to take on right now, so soon after losing her mother. Maybe one day. But what if they were not nice people? Blood isn't always thicker than water…

Fran hid thoughts of contacting her long-lost uncles away with the contents of the trunk. She turned the key, placed the trunk under the kitchen table and turned to other more mundane tasks. The repetitive physical act of cleaning and chopping vegetables calmed her at first as she focussed on each scrape of a carrot, each slice of an onion. She felt grateful that she had already prepared her upcoming workshop for teachers on using the arts with children who show behavioural problems at school. What she needed now was something she could use as a movement meditation – nothing that demanded actual thought. There were enough thoughts beneath the surface of her mind, all noisily clamouring to get out. As she chopped and scraped and washed her vegetables, she allowed herself to reach in and pull one of these wayward thoughts out. She turned it over to examine it. The anger and distress in her grandmother's letters were tangible. Susan's mother had tried to make amends, but she couldn't stop herself from using passive aggression in an attempt to let her daughter know just how much she had hurt her. Did she not see that this would only inflame Susan's emotions even further?

A sudden pain of realisation hit her – she could never now ask her mother about what had happened. Susan's silence about her family throughout the years Fran was growing up now made perfect sense, as if lost story fragments had emerged from the letters to find each other and complete their narrative – or at least, to form a more recognisable if still incomplete one. There were still so many unanswered questions. Why didn't she see that her mother was just trying to protect her, even if she had gone about it in the wrong way? The sudden realisation that her grandmother was also right – that Fran's dad did die at sea, just as her grandfather had – hit her straight between the eyes. If he hadn't been a merchant seaman, might he have sought help? Might his breathing distress have been dealt with in a timelier manner? She was aware of grief for this grandmother seeping through, confused with her own grief and anger at losing both her father and her mother.

By the time Rachel walked through the door, all that was left of this chaos of emotions was anger.

'Where the hell have *you* been? I've been waiting for you!'

Rachel put her keys and bag down carefully. Fran knew this was an attempt to be sensitive to her own need for neatness, but any softening of her anger was halted when she saw Rachel kicking off her shoes and letting them land wherever they would as usual.

'Whoa, whoa! What is this about, Fran? Has something happened, my love?'

The softness in Rachel's voice wasn't what Fran expected. She felt herself crumple inside as she grabbed hold of her sweaty T shirt and pulled at it with both hands. And then she howled, almost inaudibly:

'I opened the trunk.'

Pause.

'I found letters.'

Another pause while Rachel simply looked on, listening.

'Mum wouldn't have her mother at the wedding because she didn't approve of my dad being a merchant seaman.'

'Right.'

'I have four uncles somewhere Rachel! And God alone knows who else!'

At this, Fran slumped into one of the armchairs, sobbing uncontrollably.

Rachel walked over to her and began stroking her head from behind, leaning down to kiss her hair.

'OK. Well, we have work to do here. For a start, let's do a search for your mother's maiden name. She was brought up in South-East London, wasn't she? Around Greenwich? Plumstead was it? That was in the borough of Woolwich at the time. So – this bit I don't recall – what was your mother's maiden name?'

'I dunno.' It had never occurred to Fran to ask her mother about her life before marriage. It was an off-limits topic. Fran stopped sobbing and, rubbing her eyes sat up in the chair, a look of inspiration forcing its way through the tears.

'Jo might know. I guess I'd better give her a ring.'

But when she called Joanne, she was left feeling even more puzzled. She emerged from the bedroom where she had made the call and Rachel was waiting for her, peering at her face.

'Hello? Earth to Fran!'

'Oh, sorry Rache. I guess I'm feeling I can't take many more surprises today. Um… well, Jo says we knew about the four uncles. And get this! Her maiden name was Drake! You don't suppose we're related, do you?'

'Blimey! I hope not! At least, not too closely! That would be weird.'

The two women laughed nervously, relieved to have something to lighten the mood.

Despite their tiredness, Fran and Rachel decided there was no time like the present to do some research. They were soon both sitting at Rachel's computer; Fran in Rachel's comfy office chair, and Rachel on a hard kitchen chair.

They began with the free-to-access 1901 census, where they found a Lilian and Frank Drake, newly married by the looks of it at the ages of 20 and 22 respectively, residing at Southport Road, Plumstead. In 1911 they were still living at the same address and childless.

A few days later, Fran decided to pay for access to further census records. By now she had become so curious about her past she felt unable to stop until she knew the truth. In 1921, the Drakes had moved to a property in Tuam Road, still in Plumstead – Fran assumed this was a larger house because by now they had two children: David, born just a year after the previous census, in 1912, and Frances whose age indicated that she was in fact born a year before the 1911 census, probably in 1910, and was thus older than her brother. But where was she when the 1911 census was taken?

Rachel suggested perhaps Frances had been staying with family members in 1911, which Fran agreed was plausible, but said she felt was unlikely. And then a penny seemed to drop for Rachel.

'Oh my God! My grandfather was called David Drake, and – it's just coming back to me - he was from Plumstead! Let's search the next one!'

The 1931 census showed David Drake now grown up, aged 19 and still living at home but working as a butchery apprentice. Frances, however, had apparently married a sailor called Stanley Cockroft and was now living in Woolwich, a few miles away from her parents.

'Hang on. Cockroft is a Northern English name, isn't it?' Asked Fran.

'Yes, it is. Which might explain why your Mum wanted to come to Yorkshire in the first place. Your dad might have come from here. It's a shame she ever went back down south.'

Fran knew Rachel blamed Joanne for the fact that Susan had moved to Kent from Yorkshire, necessitating long drives and time out from work every time she wanted to see her mother. However, she said nothing more at this point, for which Fran was grateful. They carried on searching.

There was no 1941 census due to the war years, and by 1951 things had changed considerably. By now, Frances was a widow with children to bring up on her own including Susan, born in 1941. Fran and Rachel held each other tight as they wondered whether Susan's father had ever managed to meet his little daughter before he died.

David was now married to someone called Sheila – who turned out to be the grandmother Rachel had spoken about, much younger than her grandfather and very glamorous. In 1951 they had a five-year old son - Rachel's father, also called David.

'So – hang on a minute.' Fran stared at the screen as if willing it to answer her unasked question.

'We are second cousins, I think. My grandfather and your grandmother – the one you never met but whose letters we found – were brother and sister,' Rachel concluded.

'So that means…' Fran continued, a smile creeping across her face 'that any child we have will be biologically related to both of us.'

Rachel remained silent for a few seconds, her body visibly stiffening.

'I think it's time I made us some coffee, don't you?'

Where past and future are gathered

'But darling, you don't have to do anything for this baby, I promise. I will get pregnant, I will give birth, and I will be the one to stay at home for several months after the birth. It's true I'll lose a lot of money because of the fact that I work on hourly rates for most of what I do, but with your pay we'll be fine. And if you get the Associate Professorship you've been working so hard on, we'll be quids in!'

Rachel's heart sank. Fran sounded so excited by the prospect of making a baby. How could she deny her? Before she could answer, Fran delivered her next attempt at persuasion:

'And with all that attachment theory you teach your students, you can make sure we will both be ace parents!'

Fran settled her head back onto the pillow, a dreamy look in her eyes. She was already imagining an idyllic life for the three of them. Rachel looked at her beautiful, youthful and exuberant wife. She could see that the thought of motherhood had brought a kind of glow to Fran's being, and her heart softened. She knew better than to buy into Fran's ridiculously optimistic view of the world herself, yet she felt drawn into Fran's plans despite herself – and despite the university budget and staffing cuts which Fran had conveniently left out of her perfect scenario, not to mention the fact that promotion was by no means guaranteed. She suspected, in fact, that she didn't stand a cat in hell's chance – most people moved on to other universities for promotion; the university had made it nigh-on impossible for its own staff to progress.

Despite all this, her mouth opened with a will of its own, and before she knew it she was speaking.

'OK. We'll try. You can use some of your inheritance to pay for the treatment. I'm not convinced by your perfect life scenario, mind. But I love you, and life is to be lived adventurously, or so Richard keeps telling me. Bloody Quakers!'

Fran bounced up onto her knees, then leaned over and planted a kiss on Rachel's lips.

'Oh, God I love you! You are one hell of a woman, Rachel Drake! And we are going to be the best parents!'

Rachel pulled back.

'But whose sperm are we going to use, Fran? Do we ask a friend, or do we rely on the clinic to provide that?'

'Hmmm. Hadn't thought that far ahead. Who do we know that we both like, and whose genetics we wouldn't mind our child having? And, crucially, who would do it for us and not expect any reward, and especially any parenting rights?'

They both spoke at once – Fran with excitement in her voice as she clapped her hands together and bounced up and down on the bed; Rachel in low tones, as if she had just heard very bad but inevitable news:

'Richard.'

Richard sat with his cappuccino in his hands. He seemed to be pondering the patterns in the chocolate sprinkles, reading them like tea leaves.

'Richard, you don't have to make a decision right now. I can give you a week or two to think. There really is no rush. We haven't yet started the process, though of course we're keen.'

Rachel hoped she had struck just the right tone, both understanding and yet letting Richard know they would need an answer fairly soon. She knew Richard wasn't prone to procrastination, however.

He looked up from his coffee and faced Rachel square on. She suddenly found him rather attractive, as his eyes met hers with a piercing bright blue honesty.

For fuck's sake, Drake! This is not the time to start fancying a colleague who clearly has the hots for you, and whose sperm you are trying to get in order to fertilise your wife's eggs!

The bizarre nature of the situation made the corners of her mouth turn slightly upwards, causing Richard to frown. He kept his eyes squarely on hers.

'Yes.'

And there it was. Settled. He would provide the sperm to the clinic direct. The two women would not have to handle it, and the clinic would manage the fertilisation. As she got up to leave, Rachel thought she saw Aggie out of the corner of her eye clapping her hands, but when she turned to look no-one was there.

Richard wandered round the clinic waiting room picking up leaflets to avoid sitting down. He tried talking to himself:

'What you have to do here has been done by countless men before. Think of it as a good deed. That's all it is.'

It didn't help. What if he as overheard? What if he couldn't get an erection, or took too long? Or was extremely quick?

Eventually, he was shown into a small room and provided with a plastic container. Lads' mags were scattered around the room – and some with male pinups. He was reassured that he could lock the door from the inside and would not be bothered. He could take as long as he liked and leave the container behind in the room when he left – all he had to do was announce he was leaving. The jar was already marked with a code which identified it as his, destined to make Rachel and Fran's baby.

He unzipped his trousers and took them off, sat on the uninviting plastic clad armchair with disposable paper linking, then flicked through the mags. He was enticed by some of the pictures, but all he could think about was Rachel. In the end, he decided if he was going to ejaculate for her, he could bloody well think about her, just this once.

He pictured Rachel on a beach, in the moonlight, with nothing on. She was lying in the sand on her back, the waves lapping over her body. His mouth reached down to taste her saltiness and she moaned. He moaned. He carried on as her back arched, and then he moved up to kiss her full on the lips, his chest rubbing against her pert breasts as he did so. It was obvious she wanted him.

Before he could get to the good bit, Richard ejaculated hard and fast, some of it into the jar and much of it over the floor. He felt suddenly ashamed, not just because he had made a mess and had been fantasising about the woman who hoped to use his sperm to have a baby with her wife, but because he hoped there would be enough in the jar. Amidst the shame, there was also a deep sadness and regret, that his transgression had been only a fantasy – could only ever be a fantasy. Rachel would never groan in pleasure at his touch. She loved Fran, and they would be having this baby using his donor sperm. Without him. He slammed the door on his way out.

A few days later, Rachel and Fran sat in the waiting room, flicking through women's magazines with storylines like: 'My husband loves another man', and 'My best friend went off with my Dad'.

Finally, the door opened.

'Ms Drake and Ms Baker?' The nurse looked inquiringly round the room, despite the fact that the only other couple there were a middle-aged woman and man.

They stood up and followed obediently to where the doctor was waiting; a congenial man with a slight paunch who looked up from his notes and over his glasses at them, smiling and gesturing for them to sit on two upright plastic chairs.

'Welcome, welcome,' he said, in a sing-song accent Rachel recognised from her days of volunteering in Ghana as possibly Ga. Only then did she notice the tribal markings on both cheeks.

'Now, I have some news,' he began, then paused for effect, smiling and laughing as if he had just made a really good joke.

Yes. Bloody get on with it then.

'You see, it is like this. It is actually really surprising.' Another chuckle. 'I am afraid, Ms Baker, that your eggs are not plentiful. Your hormone levels are quite low, and I do not think you can conceive easily. But don't worry. You will be a mother, of that I am almost one hundred percent sure. Because, you see Ms Baker, your wife here can supply the eggs for you.'

'What? Excuse me?' Rachel leaned forward to insert herself into Dr Afutu's line of vision. He turned to her.

'Yes,' he smiled benevolently at Rachel. 'Yes, you will provide the eggs for us to fertilise in a test tube, and then we will insert one of these fertilised eggs into your wife's body. Then, hopefully, you will have a son. Or daughter. It is in the lap of the gods, so to speak.'

At this point the doctor sat back, still smiling as if he and they had just won the lottery together.

Rachel's throat went dry. She looked at Fran, whose colour had drained out of her face so that instead of her usual natural tan she looked a faint yellow. Rachel reached out her hand to her wife, who looked at her with bewilderment, tears welling up in the corners of her eyes. Rachel's heart went out to Fran. The idea of having a baby meant so much to her. What a blow to hear she could not conceive naturally! And then it dawned on her.

Oh, no! They are going to bloody put me through hell to get those eggs! She looked down at the floor, inadvertently letting go of Fran's hand as she did so. And then came the next bombshell.

'If you donate 50% of your eggs, the fee gets reduced. But you have to make that decision before you know the quality of them, how many of them there are and so on. I should warn you that it is possible if you decide to donate, that you will not have a child, whereas another couple might, using your eggs. I will leave you to think about it.'

Once home, it was Fran who spoke first.

'I'm not putting you through the harvesting process more than once, Rachel. Which means we don't sell half of your eggs. They're too precious. I'm paying for this, so discussion closed.'

Rachel opened her mouth to speak. They both knew if they didn't donate, someone else would be missing out. However, once they had fertilised embryos there was another chance to help someone, at least theoretically, though they wondered if they could ever bring themselves to offer help to another couple using full sibling embryos to their own child. But that was to be crossed later.

The next few weeks and months were spent in a state of perpetual upheaval, as Rachel first had to suppress her cycle with daily injections, then after two weeks a further daily injection of Follicle Stimulating Hormone. The injections had to be at certain times of day, come what may. On one occasion she had to leave a class to fend for themselves, nip to the toilets, and inject. At the end of it her skin felt as battered as she imagined it might feel if she had been an addict who had been shooting up, a particularly hormonal addict.

Then there were the frequent trips to the clinic, often with a few days' notice, to have scans to check how things were progressing. They had to travel some distance to these appointments, timing the litre of water Rachel had to drink so that she would not be absolutely desperate for a wee but would have a full bladder for the scan. A day and a half before D-day she had to administer one final injection to mature the eggs.

Finally, the day came when her eggs were to be harvested. Rachel knew she would be given an injection to sedate her, but she was shaking with terror as she and Fran arrived at the clinic, Fran's face betraying her concern.

Thankfully, the sedative meant that Rachel remembered almost nothing of the long needle inserted inside her to harvest the eggs, although later when they got home she felt the need to curl up with a hot water bottle as cramps wracked her womb and she bled steadily onto her sanitary towel. Fran was solicitous, bringing hot drinks and whisky and gently suggesting an early night.

There was then a wait of about a week, during which the eggs would be fertilised and the best one or two embryos would be chosen for implantation. Fran was instructed to use a pessary to prepare her womb for receiving the embryo, in order to give her the best chance of pregnancy.

When the two women arrived for embryo implantation Fran was insanely happy, radiant even, as if she were already pregnant. She refused to countenance Dr Afutu's warnings that the implantation does not always take first time. When they arrived, they were told that there were multiple suitable embryos, and so only one would be inserted on this occasion, the others being frozen for future attempts.

During implantation Fran lay with her legs in stirrups as a catheter was passed into her womb. Rachel held Fran's hand and watched in awe as an arc of light danced across the monitor. She must have looked as if she had seen a miracle, because the doctor spoke up.

'Yes, that is the embryo leaping into its new home,' Dr Afutu pronounced.

Fran opened the passenger door in Rachel's car, giving her wife one last kiss before she left. Rachel watched as Fran walked towards the school where she was running another training session for teachers. She was laden down with art materials, some carried in a bag while the smaller items were in a backpack. Rachel could see how the uneven weight pulled on Fran's shoulder, and she worried about Fran doing that in a few months' time, when she might be pregnant with their daughter or son.

As Fran slipped into the school entrance and disappeared from view, Rachel turned to look over her right shoulder, signalled, and pulled out. She fell into a reverie, imagining the gorgeous little bundle she and Fran might have, how she would care for her wife throughout the pregnancy, and how she would love to hold her newborn. Their baby.

'So, 'ow does it 'appen, then?'

The voice from her left jolted Rachel out of her daydream and firmly into the present. Hardly a present reality shared by anyone else, but her present reality nevertheless. Rapidly correcting her steering to avoid hitting a cyclist who had crept up on her nearside Rachel stole a quick look at Aggie, who was ensconced in the passenger seat. Her legs were in an unladylike posture, knees apart, revealing rather whiter flabby thigh than was warranted. Her support stockings were, as usual, gathered around her ankles just above a pair of ragged old slippers with once-dainty bobbles on the top. Rachel found herself wondering why the hell Aggie always appeared in this rather unsightly manner. Why couldn't she have a wise woman that was a priestess from an ancient matriarchal civilisation? Or a wise, wrinkled but proudly dressed old African woman, complete with headdress? Why did she have to have a working-class cockney from the 1960s who never quite seemed to have got the hang of stockings and shoes?

She decided to keep her eyes on the road.

'What do you mean, Aggie?'

'Well, 'ow do two women get a baby togevva? I don't geddit.'

'Ah. I see.'

It never occurred to Rachel to wonder why Aggie was asking such seemingly naïve questions. She knew from listening to clients that by the 1960s any mature woman had probably learned the hard way about where babies came from. Mothers didn't always have 'the talk' in the early twentieth century and the idea of two women having a baby together was literally impossible. She would have to be gentle, without being patronising. Time to pull over.

Having stopped the car in a side street and turned off the engine Rachel turned to Aggie, who was sitting bolt upright in the car. It was as if even getting into a car had taken Aggie out of her comfort zone. Rachel now saw that although Aggie still wore an old paisley pinafore, underneath this was a clean white blouse with long, wide sleeves gathered at the wrist, the collar carefully draped over the outside of her workaday dress. This was, however, her one concession to being 'out of the house'. Her hair was still in the same rollers, underneath a tightly tied headscarf.

Rachel did her best to explain IVF. Aggie listened silently and with sage-like stillness, but Rachel could see her eyes glazing over. At the end of Rachel's explanation Aggie looked down at her worn slippers and said, almost inaudibly:

'Don't be surprised if it doesn't take first time. Don't give up though. Please.'

Rachel was just about to ask her what she meant, but Aggie was gone. She was all alone. A woman walked by with her toddler on reins. She noticed Rachel staring in her direction and yanked the toddler towards her.

The following two weeks were an anxious time. Rachel noticed that Fran had suffered a sense of humour breakdown, no longer sharing a joke or laughing at their favourite Friday night Radio Four comedy programme. The clinic did offer access to counselling during this period, but Fran declined. Instead, she quietly went off to work each day, ate the food lovingly prepared by Rachel each evening, read her novel curled up in 'her' armchair, and went early to bed.

A Kind of Family

Finally, the day came for a pregnancy test. The two women watched and waited for a blue line to appear in the window, tracing the second hand as it dragged round Rachel's watch. No blue line appeared. Eventually, they accepted that no pregnancy had occurred. That night, Fran helped Rachel prepare the meal, washed up, and unusually helped Rachel drink a bottle of Cabernet Sauvignon, afterwards opening the nice Marlborough Sauvignon Blanc Rachel had been saving for good news day. Her 'sod it' air warned Rachel not to question her decision.

'I'm not bloody going through that again!' Fran pronounced, her words slurring.

'OK my love. I understand,' was all Rachel could say. She knew better than to argue with someone who was that drunk.

Soon after this, Fran was snoring on the sofa.

'Fran, darling?'

Fran opened her eyes in alarm, then darted venom at Rachel.

'WHAT?'

'Sweetie, you fell asleep. It's been a hard day. Let's get to bed.'

Fran looked away, her eyes changing as she remembered the pregnancy test and the lost embryo which could have been a baby – their baby. Her face crumpled and she curled up in a foetal position, sobbing.

Rachel eventually got Fran to bed, and the next morning persuaded her not to go into work but rest in bed with the radio on and a novel beside her. She was reading *The Secret Life of Bees* and was sufficiently engrossed for it to provide some distraction. But Fran was still adamant she would not be going for another implantation.

'It's just too stressful, Rachel,' she declared through panda eyes.

'But you wanted this baby so much, Fran.'

'I know, I know. And I put you through so much, to harvest those eggs. I am sorry.'

Rachel decided not to push it and went downstairs to make a coffee.

She was immediately greeted by Aggie, who was pacing up and down with her cigarette in the air, the ash precariously long. Aggie was in business mode, her hair in rollers under her trademark scarf and her paisley pinafore on, complete with slippers and saggy stockings.

'You've *got* to get 'er to see sense!'

'I take it you mean about the baby?'

'Yes! I've kept out of it until now, as you might've gavvered. It was all goin' OK. But that one wasn't meant to be.'

'I see. And there is one that *is* meant to be, I suppose?'

'Yes! And 'e's very impatient to be born! I've got 'im tuggin' at my sleeve, 'ere!'

'Right. Well thanks for letting me know, Aggie. And what do you suggest I do about it?'

'*I* don't know! You live wiv 'er. She's a stubborn one, that one!'

'Great. Thanks for the advice, Aggie. Coffee?'

And with that, Rachel moved off into the kitchen. When she returned to the living room, Aggie had gone.

The next day, Fran had got things into perspective.

'OK, it wasn't even a miscarriage, was it? It just didn't happen. Let's have one more go. We have several healthy embryos after all. And us being second cousins and all, there is a golden opportunity here for us to make a baby that's ours.'

Rachel beamed at her brave little wife, then planted a kiss on her cheek. There were still plenty of embryos, so it was just a question of having one implanted.

Fran was not elated this time as they arrived at the clinic; her characteristic optimism seemed to elude her as she slid up onto the table and offered her feet for the stirrups. She winced this time as the catheter entered her vagina and then her womb. Afterwards, she pulled her underwear on slowly, her movements leaden. When they got home,

Fran suggested that she should do the next pregnancy test when Rachel was at work, so as not to build it up into anything big.

'But darling, I don't want you to face that on your own – what if it's negative again? I'll feel such a heel, just carrying on with my work and unaware of what you're going through.'

Rachel could see Fran's jaw set. Her little dynamite of a wife was impassable.

'Rachel, it's better this way.'

And with that, the case was closed.

Fran decided it was time to take the trunk and its contents to her sister. Despite possibly being pregnant and thus vulnerable she decided to make the journey there and back in a day, having cleared her diary on a day that Joanne said would be best for her. She initially felt resentful that it had to be to Joanne's timing. Her sister never seemed to understand that given Fran's self-employed status clearing a day of work meant the loss of a lot of money. Joanne worked part-time and was paid for holidays and sickness, but she always seemed to assume the position of senior sister – and so it was on Joanne's day off that Fran drove through the Kentish countryside on a crisp winter's day. Small villages were putting up Christmas trees. The low sun made the grass and crops sparkle and so by the time she arrived at her sister's house Fran's resentment was gone.

They emptied the contents of the trunk onto Joanne's dining room table, where Joanne had spread a sturdy tablecloth to prevent marks. She instantly claimed various items including the photograph of their parents and the Who concert programme, helpfully explaining that Fran could have the Ravi Shankar programme and swimming medal (whose significance they did not know). Fran was glad that she had digitised the photograph. They decided to dump or burn the piece of coal and various other items of no obvious value, and Joanne agreed she would keep the trunk itself. Joanne was standing over it, lovingly stroking the inside of it when she stopped, her hand tracing a bump in the lining.

'What's up, sis?' Fran inquired.

'I don't know. You have a feel.' Joanne stood aside to let her sister feel the bottom of the trunk. Fran noticed that the bump was in fact an opening in the bottom of the trunk – a secret chamber! She carefully hooked her fingernails under one edge and lifted to find what looked like several official papers and newspaper cut-outs. The two sisters looked at each other, Fran seeing her own shock mirrored in her sister's wide-eyed visage.

'I suggest we sit down and do this methodically,' Fran said at last. She let Joanne do the handling of the papers, knowing she would want full control. As each one was carefully lifted out Joanne spread it onto the table in front of them.

One of the newspaper cut-outs from the Yorkshire Post, dated 10.8.1914 showed a photograph of a couple holding a small, dark-skinned child. The headline read:

'GOOD NEWS IN TIMES OF WAR: DESTITUTE CHILD GIVEN NEW HOME ACROSS THE WORLD'

The article went on to state that the couple in the photograph, Lilian and Frank Drake, had adopted the little girl who sat on Lilian's lap, from New Zealand. They had heard through their church about the plight of unmarried mothers of Māori origin and were moved to help. They felt it was their Christian duty to adopt one of these children and bring her up in a loving Christian household. The couple already had one son, a two-year-old called David. The adoptee, who had been named Frances Agnes Drake by the couple, arrived coincidentally in London on the day that the War was declared: the fourth of August 1914.

Fran instantly felt empathy for the small brown girl in the photograph, and anger at the couple whose misguided religious fervour had separated a Māori child from her mother and from her whole culture. She instinctively reached down for her belly, as if to protect her own imagined child as she searched the photograph for untold stories. She saw the little girl's shoulders hunched over, her dark eyes staring straight at the camera. Her curly black hair was held in place with a slide, but it looked to Fran as if that hair didn't want to be tamed. Lilian, the adoptive mother, held her new daughter's little body away from her own. She sat stock still, a stern expression on her face as was the custom of the day. Photography was a solemn business in 1914 Fran knew; no-one seemed to smile or laugh for the camera. Lilian's husband stood behind the chair, his right hand on a pocket watch and his left hand on his wife's shoulder. He, too, was clearly aware of the seriousness of their situation. Not many of the families in their neighbourhood would have been photographed by a newspaper man.

Having taken in these details Fran looked at her sister as the reality slowly dawned.

'Blimey! Our grandmother Frances was adopted!' Joanne exclaimed, a look of utter shock on her face.

'But Rachel's grandfather – their existing child, David – was not,' Fran replied, almost inaudibly.

There were several similar cut-out newspaper articles, all praising the couple who had taken in this poor, Māori child.

Then they came across an Order of Adoption, handwritten on ordinary paper. It read:

Order of Adoption Under Section 16

In the matter of Part III of the Infants Act 1908 and in the matter of an application by Frank Drake of London, Carpenter and his wife to adopt Ahurewa Clifford

The order went on to give the date, which was about three months before the newspaper article appeared.

The next day, after getting in from work Fran did a computer search and found a copy of the 1908 Infants Act in New Zealand. She found that section sixteen referred to who might make an application for adoption. Reading on, she discovered in section eighteen that all that was required of the adoptive parents was that they should be:

> …of good repute, and a fit and proper person to have the care and custody thereof, and of sufficient ability to bring up, maintain, and educate the child; that the welfare and interests of the child will be promoted by the adoption; and that the consents required by this Act have been duly signed and filed.

So, the adoptive parents did not have to be Māori, obviously. In terms of consent, The Act went on to state that the Judge required the usual parental consent, and that unmarried mothers could according to section sixteen give consent for adoption. Fran wondered how real any such consent was; what choice did an unmarried mother have? To keep her child meant being unable to work, in all probability, unless one's employer was particularly understanding. To leave a child unattended was to leave oneself open to accusations of desertion (in which case the need for consent was waived) – and not to work would mean no food for either herself or her child. A Hobson's choice.

Fran sat on the edge of the bed, her laptop beside her, stunned by a potent mixture of rage, sadness and pain for that poor little girl, her grandmother whose haunted look stood before her like a ghost. No doubt the Drakes thought they were doing the right thing - their Christian duty. But in this moment, Fran could only feel utter contempt for them.

A Kind of Family

About a week after Fran and Joanne had found the secret chamber in their mother's trunk, Rachel arrived home to find Fran had laid the table specially using the candlestick she had been given by her mother and which was the one possession Fran remembered her mother having that she said had belonged to Fran's grandmother.

Sensing there might be some news Rachel obediently sat down, smiling up at Fran who had already poured herself a glass of sparkling water and was busy pouring Rachel some wine. Fran put the bottle down, sat demurely upright with her hands in her lap, and looked at Rachel, a half-smile on her face.

'I'm pregnant.'

Her voice didn't sound as elated as Rachel felt it should, given this news.

'Sweetie, thank you for going to all this trouble with a special meal and everything. But – well, forgive me for saying this but you don't sound all that happy. I thought you would be over the moon.'

'I *am* glad to be pregnant, obviously. But don't you see? This isn't genetically my baby anymore. I'm carrying an embryo made up of a donor egg and donor sperm, which has no genetic connection to me at all. I can't even get that bit right.'

Rachel understood now. Fran had felt inadequate when she realised her own eggs were of poor quality, but she had felt that having to use Rachel's eggs was OK because they were second cousins. This had seemed to soften the blow associated with her own fertility problems. Now having finally got pregnant, she still felt inadequate because none of the genes were hers.

'My darling wife, I know this embryo doesn't carry your genes, but you are the one that got pregnant. You're contributing your body for the pregnancy. That's huge, and it gives you a biological connection to our baby.' Rachel was thinking on her feet, but her argument clearly hit home as Fran sat and pondered her words. Gradually, her face lifted somewhat.

'You're right. You contribute the DNA, and I contribute the womb. We each contribute something.'

She seemed only partially convinced by her own words, but that was enough for now. Rachel reached across the table to Fran, who crept her own hand towards Rachel's. The two women squeezed hands, tears rolling now unhindered down Fran's cheeks. Rachel's heart felt swollen with love for Fran. But inside was a nagging worry. She just hoped that this pregnancy was going to work out.

The next day, Rachel had her usual session with Adam. She had spent several sessions wondering if she was actually helping him at all. He was a lovely, vulnerable man; he did not seem to have any trouble talking, but he spent much of every session silently crying. This time he walked in with an air of determination, threw his jacket on the sofa and slumped down, then looked up at Rachel. His eyes seemed to tell her he wasn't bottling out this time.

'She was pregnant.'

A smile crept across his face.

'She was pregnant. When she died. She was carrying my baby.'

Rachel steadied herself, determined not to let on that this news sent her reeling.

'So – I noticed you smiled as you said that.'

'We thought we couldn't have babies. We had been trying, you see. When it didn't happen, we decided we would get married. I know it sounds daft, doing things that way round, but it kind of deepened our love for each other. We had got to a place of acceptance about not being parents. But we had us. I had no idea, until the doctors told me. She was actually fucking pregnant. I *am* fertile.'

Rachel banished any thoughts that Adam's fiancée might have been unfaithful. Instead, she observed:

'So this means you can be a daddy.' She was aware that she might be moving things along a bit too fast.

'Yes.' Adam was smiling, but he was wringing his hands.

Rachel bit her lip. She *had* pushed him to move towards the positives too soon. He still had a lot of grieving to do. And besides, he still hadn't told her the story of the crash.

Swings and roundabouts

'Hi, Molly!' Fran watched as Molly shuffled into the big communal room, carefully studying her feet to make sure they didn't do anything wayward. Molly stopped and looked up, then a smile of recognition crept over her face.

'Hello, dear. How are *you* doing?'

Molly always greeted everyone the same way. She didn't know whether or not she had met them before, but Fran had heard from the staff (who presumably heard this from Molly's devoted daughter) that when Molly first received the diagnosis of Alzheimer's she decided, being the sensible woman she was, to treat everyone in the same way, come what may. She figured if she started doing this while she still had her faculties it would become a nice habit that might persist even after she had forgotten who most people were. Never having been good with names even before the diagnosis, calling them all 'dear' was also a convenient way out of that particular embarrassment.

'I'm fine, Molly, thank you. And yourself?' Fran continued their familiar exchange.

'Oh, not so dusty, well brushed,' said Molly, straightening herself ever so slightly before once more looking down at her feet to complete her walk towards a vacant chair.

Fran counted ten people in the room; eight women and two men.

'Where's Phil today, Joyce?' She asked of a woman sitting opposite her. Joyce had early dementia and could still remember who was who.

A Kind of Family

In fact, if you wanted to know anything about anybody including their most recent bowel movement, you asked Joyce.

'He's *dead*', she said, in a tone of voice that implied Fran should have known this.

'Oh, I'm so sorry,' replied Fran, with genuine sadness. Phil had been a lovely old man. Prone to walking round with his trousers and underpants round his ankles, but never complaining and not given to angry outbursts despite his advanced condition.

Part of the job, Fran reminded herself, secretly wondering if she would ever get used to it.

'Well, you gonna start, or what? What are we bloody well here for, anyway?' Wendy made her presence felt from Fran's left, prompting her to start the music and hand out the long circle of elastic for everyone to hold onto.

After the session, as she gathered up the elastic and was musing on how lively and chatty Nora had seemed today compared to usual, Fran felt a distinct tightening in her belly. It didn't hurt at first, only lasting a few seconds, but when she got into her car it happened again, and this time it hurt. She reached for her phone but then realised Rachel was invigilating an exam and could not be disturbed. She would just have to sit this one out on her own.

At home, she felt a familiar cramping that seemed to spread as pain throughout her pelvis. She hoped she was wrong, but once in the bathroom she saw a spot of blood on her underpants and her heart sank. In a desperate attempt to keep hold of her special state she reminded herself of women she had known who continued menstruating throughout pregnancy, or who had a spot of blood but continued with a live foetus to term. As the cramping continued in a regular rhythm, she reassured herself with practicalities; if she was going to miscarry there was nothing that could be done. She decided to go to bed and rest with a hot water bottle, inserting a sanitary towel into her underpants 'just in case'.

When she woke, Rachel was standing over her, looking concerned. Fran instinctively reached down into her underpants, then withdrew her fingers to examine them. Blood. Lots of it. At the same time she was aware of her womb being taken over by a force bent on twisting the life out of it. She instinctively curled inwards, clutching her hot water bottle for comfort as sobs shook her body. Rachel looked on, her face seemingly searching for something – anything she could do.

'I'll get some painkillers.'

Rachel rushed out of the bedroom then reappeared with a glass of water and two paracetamol. Fran remained in a foetal position, sobbing. Rachel looked on, the hand holding the pills going limp as she placed the glass down by the side of the bed.

'Fran, I'm so sorry. There are more embryos.' Then, with a note of determination: 'We're not giving up.'

Fran wished Rachel wouldn't try to reassure her. Why did she try to fix things? She was supposed to be a therapist! This was the worst moment ever of Fran's life, and she didn't need fixing. She needed holding, goddammit! But she wasn't about to show that!

'It's my body, Rache. I can't bloody make eggs and I can't keep a baby.' Fran's voice bolted like a pea out of a peashooter.

'Nonsense!' Rachel sounded stupidly confident to Fran's ears. 'You heard the doctor, and you've read the stuff online. This is very normal.'

Fran felt lonely, abandoned and in pain that went far beyond the physical clamping in her belly. She was tumbling in the dark, but Rachel was on a roll. She didn't stop there.

'Why don't we go together, to see one of the fertility counsellors?'

Fran's body closed up even further, but it made the pain worse. She entered into a silence, willing herself to find comfort there. But Rachel didn't go away. She knelt by the bed and stroked Fran's hair. Damn you, Rachel Drake! Sobs now added to the pain in her belly.

A Kind of Family

A long while later when she had cried enough to clear a path towards clarity and her womb seemed to have emptied enough to give her some respite, Fran spoke.

'OK. I don't know what else to do, other than give up. But yes, OK. One last chance. But you make the appointment. I can't bear to talk to anyone right now.'

Fran shifted in her seat.

'You look a little uncomfortable, Fran.'

Fran wanted the counsellor's eyes off her. She wanted to say 'Look at Rachel, not at me. She knows what this is all about.' But she kept her head bowed and wriggled in her chair, which felt as if it had a million ants in it.

'It seemed to be when Rachel mentioned sex that you started looking uncomfortable,' Kirsty persisted.

'I just haven't felt like it, that's all!' Fran curled up over her belly, as if to protect the child that was *not* growing inside her. The movement did not escape Kirsty's notice.

'I get it, Fran. I get it. Your body has been through a lot.' Kirsty glanced at Rachel.

Fran thought back to this morning…

She had lain with Rachel's arm round her, staring at a spider who was creeping slowly and determinedly to a spot just above her face. She contemplated standing up on the mattress to grab it, but the odds were it would then fall and scuttle into the folds of their duvet. She decided procrastination was a better option.

Their lovemaking had deteriorated of late into one of two kinds: in the evening, a lazy grope and a kiss which seemed to have a sedative effect on them both or, in the morning, mutual masturbation without the trimmings.

When they decided to have a baby together Fran knew Rachel had hoped it would give them both a renewed passion for their life together, but lately Fran just hadn't felt like it. She knew it was time to talk, but she also resented it – as with the spider, they might just start something Fran would rather not face up to – something that felt dangerous, intrusive, frightening.

That morning, despite her fears Fran had sighed, crawled out of bed, pulled on a dress and gone to open the window before catching the spider and throwing it out. Out of sight, out of mind.

'I can't bear to do it again.' Fran's voice surprised herself. Where did *that* come from?

'OK.' Kirsty sounded patient, understanding. 'What might happen if you did, Fran?'

'I might fail - again!' Fran's tears hung on to the precipice of her eyelashes, daring to drip despite her attempts to hold them in.

'So, what might failure at having a child mean to you?' Kirsty prompted, gently.

Fran could see the alarm on Rachel's face out of the corner of her eye. Fran looked up at Kirsty, then away. If she didn't look, maybe this would go away.

'Let me put it another way. What does having a child mean to you? And maybe, what does having a child using Rachel's eggs mean to you?'

'I feel like an utter failure!' Fran blurted these words out readily, and then paused. Still holding her belly, she continued, 'Right. I'm a lesbian. I've always been a lesbian.' She glared at Kirsty, angry at what she assumed to be the counsellor's heterosexuality.

'Can you imagine what it's like, growing up amongst girls whose sole ambition in life is to become a wife – to a man, of course – and mother, when you assume these things are never ever going to be available to you? That is the image of "perfection"-' Fran sounded the quotation marks with a note of sarcasm in her voice- 'we are sold as women. And the message is, if you aren't one of those women, you're an utter failure. So here comes a woman who loves me, and I love her, and we get MARRIED! And then, she loves me enough to go through that bloody awful process of egg harvesting and I CAN'T EVEN MANAGE TO KEEP HER EGGS INSIDE ME! It's like hearing those voices telling me all over again, what a rotten lousy excuse for a woman I am!'

Fran crumpled over, whimpering like an injured animal. So that was Kirsty's game! Get her angry so she blurted it out! Fran felt even more angry, sensing she had somehow been manipulated into revealing the real cause of her distress. Bloody therapists!

And then, there she was. Rachel had disregarded the implicit rules of engagement and was crouched down by Fran holding her, containing her in her arms.

'Oh, my love! You're not a failure, do you hear me? You are the most wonderful, sexy, funny, loving, creative woman I have ever known. And I love you, no matter what!'

There was a respectful silence before Kirsty spoke again.

'OK Fran. What I'm hearing is that you feel you've failed at being a woman. But I'm also hearing that the stories about what it means to be a woman that you – and we all – were sold as a girl might not be the ones you actually want to buy into. I might be wrong, of course, but help me out here – what do *you* think it means, then, to be a woman?'

Fran looked up in shock and surprise, her tears drying as she became engaged in this relatively intellectual and frankly novel exercise.

'Well – a woman can be anything she wants to be, provided she has the wherewithal and the resources necessary.'

'OK. So, am I right in thinking that you *don't* buy into limiting stories about what women can be?'

'Yeeeep.'

'Not all women choose to be wives or mothers, right?'

'Right.' Fran pulled herself upright, warming just a teeny bit towards Kirsty. 'OK. I can see where you're going with this. Despite my feminism, and despite the unorthodox arrangements, I have bought into the patriarchal narrative, right? Women should be able to give birth, or basically they are the most colossal failures?'

Fran looked at Rachel who was grinning back, her eyes moist. Then she looked back at Kirsty who nodded, her face more serious and inquiring.

'Jesus. What an embarrassment to sisterhood I am!' Fran clutched her head, then brought her hands down into her lap. She looked first at Rachel then Kirsty, and let out a laugh, initially as fragile as a preterm infant's cry. The laugh went on for minutes, turning from laugh to cry to laugh again. The other two women remained respectfully silent throughout.

At last, her energies spent, Fran stopped and looked at Rachel and Kirsty, her eyes flitting between them. She felt calmer now, less liable to fracture into a million pieces.

'OK.' Kirsty broke the silence. 'That's about all we have time for today. Thank you both for coming. Thank you for being so brave, Fran. And thank you both for working really hard in our session today. Let me know if you would like to book another.'

As they walked to Rachel's car, both women fell silent. Once inside, Rachel sat with her hand poised on the ignition. She turned to look at Fran, but Fran kept her gaze straight ahead. She could feel Rachel's eyes burning holes in her brain.

'One last go,' was all she said.

Rachel woke in a sweat. Her stomach had that sinking feeling she associated with a weird combination of sadness and apprehension. She forced herself back to sleep. The next time she woke, it was from a dream. She had been in London, cleaning the houses in a very well-to-do area. This involved cleaning the windows and doors, including a very serious black door with brass knocker. She had been using a broom and water in a bucket, aware that this would take her longer, but she was pleasantly surprised at how clean the houses looked after she had worked on them. Her friends arrived, apologising for how late they were. Rachel was secretly pleased they were late. She hadn't noticed the time, and still had much to do. They told her where they were going but she only half heard. Then she looked round, and they were gone. She had been left behind. She went to her basement flat, no way as pleasant as the houses she had been cleaning. Some students were going past. They were being posers, pretending to survey their lands. They were coming towards her flat where she knew they would comment. She thought of drawing the curtains but instead hid in the shadows as she looked up the phone number of one of the friends who had come to meet her. She pressed the numbers and waited. She heard the ringing, then voicemail kicked in. She rang Fran, who came immediately and tried to help her find them, poring over maps. But the maps were of London, and they needed Manchester. All was lost. Rachel had been left behind and could only work on, never to play out with her friends. Finally, she woke once more, still sweating profusely.

It was Rachel's first Exam Board in the role of Chair - a role she had reluctantly taken on to improve her chances of promotion despite the fact that the level of responsibility was above and beyond the grade for which she was currently paid. She had never before worked with the rather officious and somewhat gin-soaked Hilary Merryweather, Senior School Administrator. Hilary refused to 'do' I.T.; sending her emails was a useless exercise that resulted in a resounding silence. Rachel wondered how Hilary managed to hold onto her job – but then she had been there longer than Abdul the cleaner, and that was saying something. Hilary belonged to the days of sending paper memos to colleagues, a practice which she still upheld today.

The tone of the memo Rachel now held in her hands belonged to the Old School, I'll-show-her-who's-really-boss tradition. It read:

Rachel. Don't forget to bring all printouts of exam results, agenda and minutes with you. See you at 2 pm sharp. Tom should be able to arrange tea and coffee if you ask him. Hilary.

Surely, it was Hilary's job to bring the paperwork? But then, that would mean opening a computer. Hilary, like all other staff, had a recently upgraded computer on her desk. The keyboard remained in pristine condition while Rachel's was already sticking in places where crumbs from her lunch had dropped between the keys.

Rachel sighed. Resistance was useless. She searched through her file tree, found the necessary documents, and printed off one copy of each ready for the photocopying room. Then, she rang Tom in the postgraduate office.

'Hello?' he barked.

'Erm, Tom, I was wondering…'

Rachel knew her hesitation would only add to his annoyance. She tried a different tack.

'Tom, could you please provide tea and coffee in room 3.16 for the Exam Board this afternoon? Fifteen people, 2 pm.'

She knew her voice sounded officious, but at least she was being brief and to the point. Tom sighed.

'Right! Some *notice* would have been good, Rachel!'

The line went dead. Had he just slammed the phone down on her?

Half an hour later, after spending twenty minutes with a tearful third year, Rachel was cramped inside the tiny photocopying-cum-mail room feeling hot and decidedly bothered. She had intended to be waiting calmly in room 3.16 for her colleagues to arrive, but now she was in danger of being last in. Eventually, she gathered up all the papers, carefully arranged so that one set crossed over the other for ease of distribution and made her way to the Exam Board meeting room.

On arrival, she found the door shut. She caught Hilary's eye through the glass in the vain hope that her colleague would have a rare bout of magnanimity and open the door for her. Instead, Hilary looked at her with a mixture of curiosity and disgust then turned towards the new, expensively dressed senior lecturer in educational philosophy, coquettishly pushing back her wayward but alluring hair and throwing back her head in laughter to expose the naked flesh of her throat along with her ample bosom. Rachel, far from finding this display appealing felt slightly nauseous.

'Shall I help you, Rachel?'

The quiet, unassuming voice of Professor Harry Short made her startle as he reached apologetically across her body and turned the handle, deftly catching some mutinous papers and replacing them the wrong way round in her pack.

Rachel felt a sense of relief that at least one person in the Exam Board would be there to support her. As she took her place, she heard him say almost inaudibly:

'Good luck, Dr Drake.'

She settled into her seat. There, facing her at the table was a woman she at first did not recognise. She looked slightly out of place – somewhat old fashioned, with her grey hair looking as if it had just been taken out of rollers but not combed at all. Her lipstick was applied in a pillar-box red shaped to accentuate the rosebud on her upper lip. She had on a white blouse, but the top buttons were done up incorrectly so that one button showed above the others, unfastened because its corresponding buttonhole had been used for the one below. The result was rather more bosom than is usual at a formal university meeting. And then Rachel noticed the beaming smile directed straight at her, and the thumbs up that accompanied it. Rachel didn't know whether to be cross or touched by Aggie's appearance. She decided on the latter.

'Good morning colleagues,' she began.

And once having begun she found she knew the routine so well she was able to command authority. When she looked once more across the table there was a vacant chair where Aggie had sat.

A new member of staff walked in after the start of the meeting, without apology. When Rachel asked his name for the purposes of the minutes, she recognised it as the chap who had recently been appointed as part of a School-wide initiative to improve the research ratings. Rachel knew he had come from a rival university, and by the look of him she guessed he was also immediately post-PhD. Dr Woosnam was probably mid-twenties – she guessed he had had a scholarship to study full-time for his PhD. He was lean, and casually but expensively dressed. He had an easy, confident way both in his movements and speech that suggested a background of privilege. When they came to discussing one student's borderline marks he spoke with the kind of accent that could cut diamonds, breathing in slightly before commencing so that all eyes turned to him:

'I see that some of his modules have been passed at much higher marks than others. I wonder…' His unhurried speech irritated Rachel. His pause in the middle of a sentence denied anyone else the possibility of interruption, keeping the focus on him.

'…is there something here about different modes of assessment?'

His challenge was posed with such an air of authority despite his junior status within the School, that the programme leader was forced to respond.

'Um… thank you. That is certainly worth investigating…'

'…but it's beyond the remit of this Board. Thank you for your comments,' Rachel finished the programme leader's comments before she could enter into further discussion. The new staff member smirked, settling back into his chair with one arm casually draped over the back of the vacant chair next to him.

When she got back to her office after the Board, Rachel's phone rang.

'Hello, love.' Fran's voice at the other end sounded tremulous. Rachel immediately felt a panic rising in her chest as she wondered what bad news she might be about to hear. It must have showed in her voice, as she attempted to answer in a way that showed delight rather than concern.

'Hi Fran! What brings you to ring me at work, my love?'

'It's OK, Rache. I'm ringing with good news. Well, I hope it's good news. Best not to get too excited just yet.'

Rachel's heart pounded.

'Did you do a test?'

'Yep. Blue line. Like I say, best not to get too excited yet.'

Something made Rachel look up from her desk towards her office door. There, at the window she just caught sight of Aggie, still looking demure (for her). She was grinning from ear to ear.

Rachel watched as Fran hauled herself onto one elbow to peer at her laptop. She was meant to be planning a drama workshop for 12- to 16-year-old kids living on a nearby social housing estate, but Rachel could see Fran's body felt like lead. She was also cradling her nipples underneath her sweater as she lay on one side on the sofa.

'Painful, love?'

'Yep. I looked it up. One of the joys of early pregnancy during the colder months. It'll pass.'

'I'll turn the heating on.' Fran's eyes followed Rachel without protest as she left the room.

The dog followed Rachel out to the kitchen where the central heating controls were. Rachel heard her sigh heavily and Rachel looked down at her with a mix of pity and camaraderie. The poor bitch, rather like Rachel herself, would never know what pregnancy felt like. She was still musing on this when she returned to sit beside Fran and gathered Fran's feet up onto her lap. Fran smiled gratitude at her and allowed her eyes to close, giving in to the weight of sleep.

Rachel picked up her own laptop. She was desperate to get the wording for a research funding bid down to two pages now that she had finished writing her application for promotion and submitted it.

She sipped her cabernet sauvignon, silently thanking her parents for sending her to a school that taught précis as she reduced a six-word sentence to three. She then extracted her wife's laptop from beneath her body and laid it gently on the floor, carefully re-positioning Fran's now cold cup of tea so as not to cause any electrical malfunctions.

As she fought with the document in front of her, and with Fran now snoring heavily beside her, Rachel became aware of a presence in the room.

'*What* are you doing here, Agnes?' Rachel half spat, half whispered her inquisition.

''S alright, Duckie, I promise not to get in the way. Just thought I'd pop in to see 'ow you're getting on, wiv your little boy finally deciding to hang on this time, like.'

'Oh, thanks. Brilliant. I suppose you did *know* we'd decided not to find out?'

'Oops. Sorry, Duckie. I didn't fink. Now don't be *too* cross. Just remember, I'm your elder and I deserve some respect. I only mean well.'

Rachel looked at Aggie, her hair once again in rollers under a bright blue paisley headscarf, the usual brown-and-gold paisley overall (not matching the scarf, of course, and with a big tea stain down the left side), and the ever-present fag held delicately between forefinger and middle finger of her right hand. She looked an absolute sight. The ash, as usual, threatened to fall at any minute but never did. Aggie began shifting from foot to foot.

'Spit it out, Aggie.' Rachel didn't want to have to pay attention to Aggie's nervousness this evening. She had a research bid to finish, and a pregnant wife to think about.

'Um…' Aggie looked towards the kitchen. 'Just to let you know, there's a letter that went to the wrong 'ouse. It's on its way.'

And she was gone. Despite a mild curiosity about the promised letter Rachel was relieved to be left to get on with her research bid. She settled back into working.

A Kind of Family

At the sound of mail dropping on her doorstep Rachel carefully lifted Fran's legs off her. Fran moaned and shifted but didn't wake up. Rachel bent down at her front door. On the mat was a brown envelope with her name on it, and a university postmark. Her hands trembled as she opened it and read the words inside.

> *Dear Dr Drake,*
>
> *The committee has considered your application for promotion to Associate Professor.*
>
> *I am sorry to inform you that on this occasion you were unsuccessful. I realise this news will come as a disappointment. If you would like to receive feedback on your application, please contact your Head of School who will be happy to discuss the committee's decision.*
>
> *Sincerely,*
> *Professor David Schore*
> *Dean of the Faculty of Humanities*

Rachel read the letter twice just in case she had misread it, then slowly returned to the living room, dropping the letter onto the kitchen table as she did so. She looked at Fran, who had felt such a failure when she had miscarried. But she was now pregnant. At least she was making it in a traditional women's world. Rachel, on the other hand, was unable to compete in a predominantly man's world. She realised she was never going to be good enough for the world of academia. Having chosen a subject like counselling for domestic violence to research she had immediately marginalised herself. She poured another glass of cabernet sauvignon, moved to her armchair, and opened her novel. At least *The Colour Purple* had a sort of happy ending.

Christmas joy

God, you look terrible!

Richard examined his smoky image in the shaving mirror, an inevitable cut threatening to redden his white shirt.

Better face the music.

Larry the Labrador lumbered round his feet, doing his best to add encouragement.

Time to man up.

Richard ran downstairs, grabbed his jacket and keys before he could change his mind, and leaped into his red Porsche. Each time he turned the key in this symbol of masculine competitiveness not to mention disregard for the planet, he felt a mixture of excitement and Quaker guilt, the latter only serving to increase his pleasure. He parked up as near as he could to the School of Education and entered through its imposing door. Bypassing the Christmas tree bedecked with a cheap set of lights and some very sad tinsel, he ran up the stone steps two at a time to the third floor, pushing open the double doors.

The party was already in full swing. Richard made straight for the drinks, then held onto his slightly inferior glass of red by its long stem, not daring to take a sip in case he wanted more. He did not need his colleagues seeing him make an idiot of himself. He scoured the room, wondering who might not bore him, and vice versa.

Richard's heart missed a beat when he spotted Rachel talking to the Dean. Her body was against the wall, the Dean blocking her way out with his corpulent body as her eyes wandered beyond him. Richard swallowed hard, then like a knight in shining armour he dodged his way towards her, exchanging excruciating pleasantries with nameless faces on the way.

As Richard approached, he guessed that both the Dean and Rachel had been knocking back the free booze. They were now laughing loudly at something and Richard began to wonder if his good deed was misplaced. Before he could gracefully retreat Rachel called him, her face shining with simple pleasure. Richard's heart jumped up like an excited puppy, but he pushed it down.

Don't get any big ideas, dickhead, Richard reminded himself. She is in a same sex relationship, and you're a boring old fart. She's just drunk, idiot.

Then, like a wayward youth he paid no attention to himself whatsoever. He returned Rachel's smile, looking for all the world like a spotty sixteen-year-old infatuated with an unattainable older woman.

Rachel took a couple of steps towards him as the Dean looked around for someone else to talk at, his back to Richard. Richard felt momentarily spurned, but the pain of the Dean's rejection lasted only an instant. His heart was on fire.

Should I stay or should I go began blaring from the i-dock in the corner. Rachel and Richard smiled at each other like a couple of kids let out of school and wordlessly began to dance. Richard noticed with longing the way Rachel moved her hips in intimate time to the iconically sexy Clash guitar riffs. He sang along, full of sympathy:

> *If I go there will be trouble*
>
> *If I stay it will be double*
>
> *So c'mon and let me kno-ow ....*

Time for some air guitar. He looked like a complete pillock and he didn't care. He was enjoying himself. He was with the only woman in the room worth a second look.

At the end of the song, they made a pantomime of being exhausted. Then Richard heard the beginning bars of the much slower and melancholy *Nothing compares to you*. He seized his opportunity, putting his glass down with feigned nonchalant inebriation.

'Come on, Rache! I know this is your favourite. You won't find anyone else here that can put one foot in front of another. In Fran's absence, I know I come a poor second, but' – and here he mimed an eighteenth-century flourish – 'would you care to dance?'

Rachel almost collapsed into his arms, an innocent lamb to his horny ram. She leaned into him, burying her face in his chest. He could feel the softness of her cheek and the silky tickle of her hair against the hardness of his own breast bone, muscle and ribs. The smell of her fresh sweat was intoxicating. He breathed in long and hard to get as much as he could of her then boldly folded her hand into his, holding her close. He never wanted this moment to end. He could feel the eyes of the room on the two of them but this time, instead of wanting to hide he felt an insane pride.

And then, he became aware of his growing erection.

Damn!

Richard forced his bum out like an ostrich and concentrated hard on thoughts of endless School meetings and essay marking.

And then the song was over. Rachel peeled herself away.

'Gosh, I was almost asleep,' she murmured, smiling with heart-melting innocence. 'I'd better get back to Fran, poor love. The pregnancy sickness has been really bad lately. No let up. I need to go and tuck her up.'

'Of course,' Richard reassured her with a gentlemanly smile. Then he leaned towards her and gave her a chaste peck on the cheek.

'Love to Fran and the baby,' he cooed, despite himself.

A Kind of Family

Rachel picked up her coat and bag, then looked over her shoulder as she headed for the door:

'Tell you what, Richard,' she called. 'We're having a party on Christmas Eve. Why don't you come?'

Richard was thrown by this rare invitation into Rachel's private life. Since being consulted about wedding plans he had not received a further invitation to her house.

'Um... yes. Thank you.' Even as he said these words and watched Rachel sprint out of the door he berated himself inwardly for sounding pathetically grateful.

Richard stood looking at the door for several seconds, as if by looking he could still feel and smell the woman he was besotted with. Then he picked up his still full glass and drank the wine down in one.

Richard rang the doorbell, a bottle of Chateauneuf cradled in one arm.

He was surprised to see Fran answer the door. For a moment he had stupidly forgotten she lived there. She had on a light blue chiffon blouse that came down beyond her hips and black leggings with bare feet. He thought he could see the beginnings of a bump under these cleverly concealing clothes. Perhaps she wasn't yet ready to tell the world.

After a smiley, seemingly genuine welcome from Fran, Richard kissed her on one cheek and made his way immediately to the kitchen. He would have loved to open the bottle he had brought with him but decided this was bad form and dutifully poured himself a glass from the wine box.

He felt a hand on his shoulder as someone squeezed past him, and a shock of electricity went through his body. He glanced up at the woman who had had this unexpected effect on him. She had dark hair, a genuine smile, and curves. He also couldn't help noticing the fluid way in which she moved.

'Sorry to push past. I'm Jane, by the way.'

Richard took the offered hand in his own, resisting the temptation to kiss the back of it and declare 'Enchanté!' Instead, he politely introduced himself. Then, thinking he owed an explanation for his presence he told Jane of his work association with Rachel.

'Not in the same bit of the School – I'm in adult education, whereas she's in counselling and psychotherapy. But we have been known to share a coffee and ideas from time to time. I'm an educationalist. Into Paulo Freire. Not that you needed to know that,' he added, with a smile and a note of self-deprecation.

Richard's neck became hot as he realised he'd probably said too much and may well be boring this lovely woman.

'Interesting! No, really. I'm one of those insane liberals who has read everything from Karl Marx to Freire to – dare I say it – Susie Orbach.'

Richard was intrigued. This woman knew something of liberation politics. He found it strangely intoxicating to hear her speak. Intellectual prowess in women had always been a turn-on for Richard. He was surprised to find that he wanted to ravish her there and then.

Don't be a dickhead! He chastised himself. She's only being polite. You can't go propositioning the first woman you meet at a party.

Squashing his desire but not wishing to let go of Jane, Richard suggested they find somewhere to sit down so that they could continue talking.

'Sure. But hey, weren't you at the wedding?'

'Wedding?' For a moment, stalled in his efforts to get to know this woman he had forgotten about Rachel's marriage to Fran – and that he was at *their* party. His heart sank as he remembered, but he determined to make the best of the evening.

'Oh, yes. Silly me. For a moment there I wasn't sure which wedding you were talking about. Of course. You're one of Rachel's friends, aren't you?'

A Kind of Family

The word 'Rachel' caught in his throat. He unbuttoned the top of his shirt and noticed Jane glancing momentarily towards the top of his chest as he did so.

As they made their way across the room their bodies bumped into each other. Richard felt his body go hot as he gently placed one hand on Jane's back to guide her towards two empty seats. He wondered if this might be seen as a sexist gesture, but the feel of her back was just too delightful. It had been a long time since he had actually been physically close to a woman.

They chatted about politics and social justice, Richard fired up by Jane's brain as much as her body, but he couldn't help noticing her breasts and wondering what it would be like to feel them in his hands and in his mouth. The skin of her cheek looked so soft and kissable. The conversation paused a couple of times for each of them to talk to other people. Richard found he recognised several from the wedding. He also exchanged simple gifts with Rachel and Fran, but he kept his eyes on Jane. He was determined to go home with her, carefully refilling her drink whilst holding back on his own. The wine he had grabbed on arrival tasted unpalatable, so he decided to visit the kitchen and hope no-one saw him as he poured it down the sink. But when he got there his bottle had disappeared. After that it was easy to stay relatively sober.

Around eleven pm Jane announced it was time she rang for a taxi. This was the moment Richard had been waiting for.

'I can give you a lift. I have my car outside. I wasn't sure if I would drive home or not, but I have only had literally two small glasses all night.'

'Oh, gosh! Thank you. Yes, that would be wonderful!'

Jane sounded keen. Was he misreading her? He hoped not, but she was probably just grateful not to have to bother ringing a taxi. Still, Richard felt attractive in this woman's company. Before leaving he visited the bathroom and took a look in the mirror at his open necked shirt and unbuttoned waistcoat over very well-fitting jeans.

'Hmmm. You look pretty hot, old man.'

Oh my God! Did I just say that out loud?

Richard unlocked the door, keen to get to Jane before she changed her mind. Luckily, no-one was waiting outside the bathroom when he emerged. Phew!

When he got back downstairs, he couldn't see her and his bravado vanished as quickly as it had appeared. But when he spotted Rachel at the door to her study he saw Jane too.

Oh no! Jane will have told Rachel.

Richard felt stupidly embarrassed, knowing that Rachel would know he was giving Jane and lift. He figured Jane was bound also to tell her friend about the frisson that had been apparent between them – or had he imagined it?

Richard decided not to go up to Rachel or Fran to announce his departure. The two women were busy enough in any case as several people seemed to have decided to go at the same time. Despite guessing that Jane had told Rachel about the lift, Richard hoped not to be seen leaving with Jane, though he didn't quite know why. He stepped out of the door ahead of her, saying he needed to move some papers off the passenger seat – which was no lie.

Once they arrived at Jane's modest terraced house, she inevitably invited him in for coffee. Richard sensed that Jane would do this for anyone, but then he argued she probably felt she owed him for the ride and there was not necessarily any sexual intent. Nevertheless, he leaped at the chance.

Once inside, he wasted no time. As Jane was taking off her coat, he helped her, knowing this was an excuse to get close to her. He stroked her hair as he did so, murmuring something about it being beautiful. Lame adjective, he told himself, but he was determined. He kissed the back of her neck and felt a shock through his body. Jane turned, a look of surprise on her face, and Richard planted a second kiss on her lips.

A Kind of Family

'You really are rather beautiful, young lady,' he said as he pulled away, his hand caressing the back of her neck underneath her hair.

Jane laughed, a look of disbelief on her face that spoke volumes about how she saw herself, but then she stopped short and looked into Richard's eyes. Richard could see her mood change as her facial expression turned to one of mischief.

'You're not so bad yourself. In fact…'

Jane's voice was cut off by another strong kiss on the lips, Richard's tongue searching in her mouth. This time he could feel her response. He loved the warm velvety feel of their tongues entwining as he could feel the impact of his desire. He deliberately bent his knees so that she could feel it too, in all the right places.

Jane stopped, pulling back, a look of frank honesty on her face. Then she looked him up and down, her focus resting boldly on his bulge as she took hold of one of his hands and led him silently upstairs.

Once in Jane's bedroom Richard again kissed the back of her neck. He could feel her softening under his kiss, her knees buckling. Then he turned her round and began kissing her oh so tenderly on the lips. She was melting in his arms and it felt good to have this effect on a woman.

Richard deftly slipped her blouse off her shoulders, then unsnapped her bra fastening to reveal the two juicy, ample breasts about which he had fantasised earlier. Voraciously, he took first one and then the next into his mouth, sucking each one and playing each nipple with his tongue. As he did so he looked up at Jane's face. Her eyes were sparkling, and she was clearly enjoying it. He felt emboldened as he dispensed with her skirt, leaving her standing in just her panties. Before she could feel embarrassed, he knelt before her, tracing his mouth down her body and licking first her belly and then the inside of each thigh. Once he had done this, he stood up. He pressed himself into her, his member hard against her naked skin.

Then it was her turn. She removed his waistcoat and then his hand-dyed Indian shirt by unbuttoning it and lifting it over his head to reveal his muscular arms and hairy chest. He knew that at this point she would notice his usually unseen and very tasteful tattoo on his right upper arm. To his delight she traced it with her fingers before leaning down to catch each nipple in her teeth, forcing Richard to throw his head back and groan with a mixture of pleasure and pain. Then it was her turn to remove his trousers. She looked shocked when she discovered he had gone to the party commando. And then she froze.

'What is it?' Richard asked, breathless.

'Condoms. Mine are a bit old.'

'Back of my trousers. I was a boy scout,' Richard grinned, his peacock-blue eyes flashing wickedly at her.

Jane was about to go down on her knees, but Richard prevented her, instead going down on his once again to tease her underpants with his teeth. His face brushed against her sex through her underwear, as she made a kind of pleading groan. Before she could get too used to this Richard lifted her up and laid her carefully on her bed, showing just how strong he was. He sensed that this woman probably believed she was far too heavy for any man, but he found it easy to lift her which gave him a heady sense of potency.

Richard hoped to strike just the right balance between macho strength and consideration. He knew many women had been put off sex by men who were obsessed with getting blow jobs and didn't know jack about how to give a woman pleasure, caring still less. He wanted to show her that he did care. But a blow job would be nice. Very nice.

When he could bear the suspense no longer, he kissed Jane passionately on the lips before once again kissing and now biting the back of her neck and shoulders. She seemed to become lost in pleasure. Unable to contain himself he tore a condom open with his teeth, slipped it on the shaft, and suddenly he was entering her. She gasped. It felt so good to be inside her. He moved slowly, confidently, his breath on her ear and his strong arms supporting himself as he stroked her hair.

Then, he was overcome. His body was taken over by its own power, against his will. He found himself thrusting urgently, faster and harder. And then, one last thrust as his whole body tensed and he heard a voice shout:

'Oh my God! Rachel!'

He stopped thrusting as his body went into involuntary contractions. He could feel Jane's body tense beneath him. Richard was stunned into paralysis as he realised what had happened. He looked down into the pillow, wishing himself anywhere but here.

After what seemed an age Jane seemed to gather her energy together and pushed him off, then rushed into the bathroom and locked the door. Richard could hear sobs coming from behind the door.

He gathered up his scattered clothes, hurriedly dressing. He removed the flaccid condom with its contents, looking round and wondering where he should put it. Too ashamed to wait until Jane got out of the bathroom, he found a used tissue in one of his trouser pockets, wrapped it up as best he could, and placed it carefully in her bedroom bin.

Whānau

'My love, I want to go to New Zealand.'

Rachel was stunned to hear this news, not least because they had just had one of the best lovemaking sessions of their marriage; she could hardly believe that her wife's thoughts had immediately turned to getting as far away as humanly possible. Now that Fran was in the second trimester and had stopped feeling so sick and exhausted, she had far more energy for sex. In fact, she couldn't get enough of it; since her womb had grown with the pregnancy, she had started having explosive orgasms. So why was she talking about going to the other side of the world?

'I don't get it,' Rachel said, the pain of imagined rejection audible in her voice.

'Darling, don't take it personally. I'm not talking for the rest of our lives, my sweet. I just think it's time I saw where my ancestor Frances – Ahurewa or whatever her name actually was – came from. In fact, I probably have family out there, you know. I am part-Māori. Just imagine! That kind of explains my dark complexion, doesn't it?'

At that, Fran reached for Rachel's hand, provocatively moving it to touch the skin on her inner thighs, dangerously near places she knew darned well would arouse.

'You minx!' Rachel declared, removing her hands and holding them aloft as she declared unnecessarily: 'I hold my hands up!'

Fran pulled Rachel's hand back to where she wanted it.

After a very satisfying interval the couple resumed their discussion.

A Kind of Family

'So, OK, I get it. You go, my love. I get that you need to do this. Though I *am* going to miss your randy arse.' Rachel gave Fran a playful slap on her buttocks, causing giggles to erupt before Fran looked Rachel squarely in the face, holding one cheek and looking lovingly into her eyes.

'I'm going to miss you like fuck.' There was no doubting the sincerity in Fran's voice.

As the plane came into land, Fran sat bolt upright in her seat. This was a terrain she could never have dreamed of. The mountain range crinkled below her like giant purple brains. After a while she could make out a patch of green and a lonely, winding road leading to an isolated homestead.

Why would anyone choose to live this remotely? Fran wondered; her eyes fixed on the changing terrain below. Momentarily she wished she didn't have a bump in the way so she could shift even further forward, such was the pull of this landscape.

More roads appeared, some leading straight down the mountains while others snaked up in a series of hairpin bends. She could now make out what she thought might be some walking paths among the rough tracks.

And now, water. Tributaries joining hands to dance forwards into fast flowing rivers, which came in turn to the stillness of massive lakes. The river below her was a kind of turquoise blue, the like of which she had never before seen in any country of the world. This land seemed magical. She could see why Peter Jackson had chosen this country in which to film his *Lord of the Rings* movies. It was like entering a different world, not just a new land but a complete new set of shapes and colours.

The plane began descending between the mountains so that now they loomed up to the side of her and it felt as if she could reach out and touch the grass. She checked her seat belt and settled back into her seat, ready for landing.

The wheels touched down with expert ease, and pretty soon the plane came to a standstill, after which the engines graciously expired. As she queued to disembark, she saw helicopters flying between the mountains, taking pleasure seekers to see the sights. She had never seen so many helicopters in the sky at one time. Small private planes, owned she supposed by people from North Island or overseas, sat on the tarmac waiting for their rich owners to decide to fly them. Fran wondered if the owners had pilot licences, or whether they employed someone always on standby, to fly them whither they wished. She could not begin to imagine what such wealth felt like, but then neither did she wish to know. Wealth was as alien to her as the sights she was feasting on.

Collecting her bag from the carousel was amazingly quick, though the checks took rather longer. She had to complete a form containing a lot of questions including whether or not she had been walking in the countryside recently, and did she carry any seeds. Yes, and no. The customs official inspected her walking boots and gave the all clear, then she placed her bags in the x-ray machine. Finally, Fran was out in the open air and was immediately struck by an elegant and proud sculpture, of three Māori chiefs. Reading the legend, she learned the work was called *Haere mai e te manuhiri tuarangi*, which meant, 'Welcome, o visitor from afar'. Always interested in public arts, she noted the artist's name: Mark Hill. She would happily have stood there looking at the sculpture in a state of reverie brought on by a combination of pregnancy and jet lag, but her pre-ordered taxi arrived. The very relaxed, smiling driver got out to greet her, guessing by the look of her that this was the pregnant English woman he expected. He swiftly lifted her one small case into the boot and opened the back door of his cab.

As the driver pulled away from the airport Fran was in awe to see Lake Wakatipu so near. They drove beside the lake all the way into Queenstown, and then met it again on their way out of town and up the hill towards Fernhill, the district where she was to find her hotel. When she arrived at the hotel the first thing she did was to walk right through the bar to the back and marvel at the vastness of the view over the lake, towards the Remarkable Mountains. She was struck by an unexpected sense of coming home. To her own surprise, she began to cry.

Fran took a few days to get over her jet lag, sleeping in and missing breakfast more than once. On her third day she took the bus into town and walked around the streets near the lake, eventually settling on a Victorian Bath House now converted to serve coffee and light meals. It being early autumn but still quite warm in New Zealand, she was able to sit outside and watch the lake life. Shark-shaped boats dipped up and down in the water while other boats took people soaring above the lake in parachutes fixed to the back of the boat. Still more boats sped around the bay, off to other parts of the extensive connecting weave of lake and rivers. As she sat sipping her coffee, she heard a ship's funnel sound. It sounded like the foghorn on the Woolwich free ferry she remembered from her childhood on a visit to London. As she lifted her left hand to shield her eyes, in the distance she saw an old steamboat approaching. It moored some distance from where she was sitting but she decided since she had finished her coffee to walk round to the quay to see it. As she approached, she was struck by the long, excited queue of tourists waiting to board, many of them Chinese. She looked for the boat's name: the *Earnslaw*. On impulse she bought a ticket and joined the queue. Soon afterwards they were taking off across the lake, the succulent greens of trees and grass from the embankment reflected in the lake's clear water.

By the time she returned from her trip, Fran was tired. She hadn't the energy to stand in line for the bus and so she guiltily ordered a taxi. Once back in her hotel she flung herself on her bed and fell into a deep, contented sleep. When she awoke, it was dark. Rachel would be just getting up now. Fran grabbed her phone, opened Messenger and clicked on the video symbol.

Rachel answered at once, her eyes visibly swollen with recent sleep. She was standing in the kitchen, in her pyjamas. It was obvious by the way she was moving that Annie was at her feet, getting in her way as she walked across the kitchen to fill the kettle.

'Hello, darling,' Fran said, tears in her eyes as she saw her wife on the other side of the world. Such a strange invention, this technology that allowed her to talk to Rachel without any real delay, see her even, but not to touch. How she wished she could just reach out and touch Rachel and smell her special scent.

'Hello, sweetie. Sorry. Just let me fill this kettle. You know me. I need a coffee in the morning before I can function. Oh, Annie! Get out of the way!' Rachel put the kettle on, then turned to face her phone. But just as she was ready to talk the image blurred and Rachel sounded like a Dalek.

'Oh, shit! This connection is rubbish!' Fran felt the pain of separation even more, now unable even to see or hear Rachel properly. But something distracted her – a sensation in her belly akin to a goldfish turning over.

'Rache! Rache! I can feel the baby moving!' Tears of jet lag and joy mixed together now into one salty, hot mess. 'Rachel!'

But the connection was lost. Fran slumped back onto the bed, wondering whether or not she could face the short walk to the hotel restaurant. Before she could decide, she fell asleep.

The next day, Fran picked up her phone again. This time, her fingers trembled as she keyed in the number. It rang only twice before she heard a strong New Zealand accent on the other end.

'Hello? This is Aroha. Can I help you, please?'

Fran's voice hid from her like a shy child. She forced the air out as she shaped her words, hoping they would sound normal.

'Um…' She cleared her throat. 'Hi. This is Frances. I emailed you. My grandmother was Ahurewa. I think she was your grandfather's half-sister? That makes us second cousins, I guess. We have the same great...'

Before she could finish, there was a squeal of delight on the other end.

'Ohmygodohmygodohmygod! Where are you?'

'Um – I'm at a hotel up the hill – in Fernhill? I think you're out by the airport, aren't you? In Frankton?'

'Yees, yees. You have to come over! Do you have a car?'

'Er – no. I guess I could walk into town and get a bus out?'

'Don't you dare! My husband will be finishing work at lunchtime today. He can come and pick you up, if you don't mind coming here in a truck? It's just that we do have a car, but it saves time if he picks you up in that, and then he can take you home in the car later on. Come for lunch!'

'Oh, gosh, you are kind.' Fran wasn't sure how she felt about travelling in a truck with a strange man, but she was keen to meet someone who connected with her Māori heritage. And so, she agreed.

When she arrived at the small house near the lake, she was struck by how basic it was. The roof was corrugated iron, the walls paper thin. Fran thought it must cost a lot to heat. She felt humbled by this, glad of the fact that she and Rachel had a nice brick-built house with a proper slate roof, and central heating. She was also glad of her internal 'central heating', as she jokingly referred to the baby growing inside her. She didn't need the extra warmth here in New Zealand, but she would be glad of it on her return to winter in the UK – at least until Spring hit properly.

Her second cousin squealed an excited hello and clapped her hands, then grabbed the back of Fran's head, bringing their foreheads to meet before releasing her to look into her eyes. Fran took a step back as she saw herself mirrored in Aroha's features, if exaggerated. The same flat bridge of the nose though slightly wider, slightly darker skin and even darker eyes with the same straight, strong hair. Aroha must have seen it too as she seemed to be looking back at Fran with a smile of recognition. Behind Aroha, a cheeky little boy with similarly dark skin was holding onto her leg, peering out at the stranger. He whispered to his mum.

'Is she Pākehā, Māmā? What's she doing here?'

'No, my love. She's my cousin, and your cousin too. She's Māori. She's whānau[2].'

'Whānau?' Fran pronounced the word as she heard it; Fah-noh, puzzled as to its meaning and uncertain whether she had repeated it correctly.

'Yees. It means you're one of us. You belong to us, and we to you. We come from the same ancestor.'

After they had eaten a delicious lunch of eggs benedict, Aroha pulled out the family photograph album. Fran found it overwhelming to see pictures of all of Aroha's family including her siblings, offspring, parents, and her grandfather – Fran's grandmother's brother.

'What were you told about my grandmother, Aroha?'

Aroha became silent, fiddling with the pages of her album.

'Well, you've got to remember my grandfather was born after she disappeared. But he told me there had been a sister. His mother had told him about her before she died. She must have felt the need to get it off her chest, I guess. She had carried the secret for so many years, God rest

---

[2] The word whānau (pronounced fah-no) is often taken to mean extended family but its meaning is more complex. It includes physical, emotional and spiritual dimensions and can include relationships with whāngai (foster children) as well as those who have died. It is defined by descent through common ancestors traced through links of both sexes. (https://teara.govt.nz/en/whanau-Māori-and-family/page-1)

her soul. She told him there had been a little girl, but her daddy had been unkind to her and refused to care for her little girl despite himself being a rich Pākehā. I don't think he married her. In fact, I suspect he was her employer and no doubt got her pregnant without her wanting any of it. But I can't prove it. She didn't go into details apparently, though I do know she was in service at the time and couldn't continue to do her job as well as care for her little girl. I think he turned nasty. My pōua – sorry, grandfather – he always looked like a lost soul when he spoke of the sister he had never met. His mother never had any more children after him. She lasted until he was twelve, but she died with a broken heart, I think. He found her on the kitchen floor, her head in the gas oven. Of course, in those days it wasn't any longer a crime here in Aotearoa, but it still carried that stigma, so they hushed it up, him and his dad.'

'So, did you know the little girl's name, or where she had gone before you heard from me?'

'None of it, no. It was a complete surprise when I heard she'd gone to England. Such a beautiful name, too, Ahurewa.' Aroha looked up from her album, a look of softness in her face.

'You look a lot like my mother,' she said. Then her eyes wandered down to Fran's belly.

'Yes. Yes, I'm pregnant.' There was no point in pretending.

'Who's the lucky fella, then?' Aroha asked, with a you-can-tell-me-I-promise-not-to-tell look in her eyes.

'My wife.' Another secret told.

'Oh, gosh! No worries, Fran! We're not exactly orthodox around here either!' Aroha said, a laugh of relief in her voice. 'I was wondering how I would tell you about my brother. He's a stereotypical gay bloke. Still lives with our Mum!'

The two of them laughed together in that way that people laugh when they have just found out they have something in common that separates them from others. Something both special and not understood by the rest of humanity. Still smiling, Fran grabbed her cousin's hand and held it on her belly. The hand settled there, warm and welcoming to her baby. And then Fran felt another flutter.

The next day Fran decided to climb Queenstown hill. On the initial steep ascent she could feel her womb tighten, but it was not an unpleasant feeling. She was glad of the walking poles she had invested in. One thing about Queenstown was the plethora of walking shops. That, and the stunning views all around.

She was grateful for a seat positioned immediately after the first and very steep section as she looked out over the town watching paragliders descend from the gondola. It was an effort to get even this far up Queenstown Hill, but right now she needed to be up high, to find a new perspective on the events of the day before at Aroha's house. She was determined to reach the Basket of Dreams, a sculpture she had heard you could sit in with a wide view down into the valley below and over towards the Remarkable mountains, known locally as just 'The Remarkables'.

She felt a kick just to the right above her navel. Instinctively, her hand reached down to meet it. Another kick, like a call and response, an unsung song between her and her unborn child. Her breathing eased and her shoulders dropped. She could see the sun playing hide and seek between the trees and felt her whole body reach out towards its warmth.

Since she had known her grandmother had been adopted from New Zealand, Fran had found herself wishing she could ask her mother so many questions. The pain of never now being able to ask brought hot stinging tears to her eyes. Was the pain of separation somehow passed down the generations? Was this why Fran could never be a good enough daughter to Ahurewa's daughter? How could it be that a Māori kid ended up in the UK in the 1910s, adopted by white Europeans? Frances, the name she had grown up with, had not even been her real name. It was Ahurewa, meaning 'sacred place'.

A Kind of Family

Until yesterday she had not known much about her Māori relatives, most of whom lived and worked right here in Queenstown. In such a small town, there was a good chance she had already bumped into one or more of them without knowing. The thought made her head spin, and even without the pregnancy it was enough to make her breathless. Did she want to meet them all? How would they feel to find this Pākehā with a British accent at their door?

The past began to rearrange itself into a different order of meaning, and with it came new thoughts about her own identity – and that of her unborn child. The knowledge of her ancestry explained why Fran was always so much darker than the other girls at school, a fact that had puzzled her all her life and during childhood had given her peers an excuse to call her despicable names. Names that must not be called. How had her mother felt, hearing about the name calling? Susan never seemed to know what to do about it, whereas in all other matters she seemed to Fran's young eyes to be profoundly wise. She could heal a grazed knee, discern Fran's deepest thoughts, and predict the weather. But she was not dark like Fran, and so had no coping strategies to pass on to her beloved little girl when it came to racist taunts.

Fran now knew, or at least suspected, that her grandmother had had a white father. Fran's mother Susan had, mercifully for her in 1940s Britain, inherited her grandfather's eyes and lighter skin. She wondered how Frances - Ahurewa - had fared in London when she arrived in 1914, and later growing up. Now that she knew her grandmother's true identity Fran understood that, had she not been estranged from her daughter, her grandmother Frances would have recognised herself in Fran's dark features. It would have been bittersweet to be reminded of her own childhood identity, of her longing for the land she was born in and for the mother she was born to.

Fran looked at her watch. It was now 1 pm. The middle of the night in the UK. Time to move on. Her centre of gravity tipped as she hauled herself up. Such an easy thing to do just a few weeks ago, but now it felt like she was an old woman despite the new life growing inside her. Once on her feet though, the going was easier. She came to a wrought iron gate which had a jumble of images on it including the New Zealand fern, spirals, sun, water, fishes and birds. By the gate was the legend:

> *This pathway leads to our future. With each step, we seek the guidance and wisdom of those who have gone before us; we walk with a sense of hope, that those who follow in our footsteps beyond the year 2000 can do so with the same sense of pride in, and protection for this beautiful place.*

Fran thought of Ahurewa and wondered if she had ever walked up this hill. She stroked her belly, willing her unborn child to walk in her footsteps in years to come. As she approached a sharp bend to the left, she began to see stones piled upon each other – lots of them. She had seen this before in Queenstown, on the track to Sunshine Bay, and wondered what the significance, if any, was. Then, she saw another inscription to the right of the path:

> *Queenstown Hill*
>
> *This hill was once known as Tapu-Nui*
>
> *A hill which signifies intense sacredness*
>
> *Erected by the Queenstown District Historical Society*

Sacredness. A sacred place. Her grandmother's name, Ahurewa, meant sacred place. Fran stood for a while staring at the inscription, then began walking again, slowly and deliberately. She was glad now to be alone with her thoughts, to have time to absorb things before talking with Rachel. But she also felt unsettled in her bones. Where did she belong? She tried to picture Ahurewa's face – to conjure her up. What song would her grandmother sing to her, now? Would it call her to home? Susan, despite her failings as a mother, had always sung to Fran at bedtime. She also told stories of far-away places with names that Fran did not as a small child understand. Fran wondered whether Susan had known, whether consciously or not, about her own mother's heritage. Her mother's stories she now realised, were passed down by her own mother and linked to her lost mother, to Fran's grandmother's land and to this sacred place. Fran felt a deep longing for the times when she could ask her mother about the threads that bound them together. But those days had passed long before Susan's death. As she continued climbing, Fran was overcome by a deep sadness and regret about lost opportunities.

Fran tried to picture her grandmother as a little girl, plucked from her home and deposited in London. Was she dark, like her? Did she suffer being called names? Her hand reached down instinctively to protect her own baby. She remembered when she herself was five years old, losing her mother in a shop that had one way in and one way out. Susan had told her to wait outside because the aisles were narrow, and she did not intend to be long. But to the five-year-old Fran a few minutes without her mother was more than she could bear and so she went inside in search of her mother. Unbeknown to her, as she entered the shop her mother was paying at a till near to the exit. By the time Susan emerged, her daughter had disappeared. Fran later heard that her mother had begun searching frantically, up and down the street. In the meantime, Fran was searching inside, the panic rising inside her as she bit her lip to quell the tears. She must have run out just as her mother went back in, and instead of now staying put she ran down the busy road, crying openly, lost and desperate. Mother and daughter were eventually reunited in the police station, where Susan walked into a room at the back to find Fran tucking into orange squash and chocolate donated by doting police officers.

Meekums

Now that she had remembered how terrified she had been to lose her mother for just an hour, Fran felt she could touch the edges of how her grandmother must have felt, separated forever and sent out of her land and her culture. How must it then have felt for her grandmother Frances, to lose her own daughter when Susan decided to ban her from her wedding? And how must Susan have felt having made that decision, not to have her mother around when she finally fell pregnant? Fran felt a hot tear of compassion for both her unknown grandmother and her often difficult mother, burning into her cheek like an open wound.

Still lost in thought, Fran emerged into a clearing. There before her was a metal spiral structure, shaped like a flattened basket. The Basket of Dreams. The views beyond of Lake Wakatipu made her want to breathe in, to fill her lungs with the sacredness and beauty of this place. She sat on the edge of the basket, untied her boots, then flung her coat onto the metal to make a soft mattress. She lay down and drank in the sky above her. A bird floated high above, like a winged messenger carrying her dreams for her unborn child. The sky was clear and as blue as the lake below. Her breath came easy now. The baby kicked. She reached down with both hands and touched her belly. If Ahurewa's adoptive mother could love her enough to raise her, Rachel and she would be able to do the same with this baby. After all, Rachel had already got past her initial misgivings about becoming a parent. Fran whispered softly:

'Hello baby. I'm here. I'm your mother. And together, Rachel and I will give you your name. We'll choose a name that will be carried like a song on the winds to your ancestors, Māori and Pākehā. We will never leave you. We will love you forever.'

She rested in the basket of dreams for several minutes, the peace reminding her of the Quaker Meeting she now attended regularly. Then she quietly descended the hill, smiling at the walkers she met on her way.

A Kind of Family

As she said goodbye to her new-found family in New Zealand, Fran felt a sense of peace to have finally found her roots. But this was mixed with a deep sense of sadness for her grandmother who was never to return to New Zealand – never reunited either with her mother or, later in life, with her daughter. Fran left her whānau amidst promises to Skype and offers of beds that she knew could never be taken up by these economically deprived relations. But the bond was made, never to be severed.

The journey back to England was long and uncomfortable. Fran's thoughts on boarding the plane were all New Zealand and her Kiwi family, but by the time she got to Sydney she was impatient to get home to Rachel. Just two more flights, and she would be in her love's arms. On the second leg she watched a couple of classic films, but they began to blur into each other as the jet lag took over and she shuffled and twisted in her seat in an effort to get comfortable. Even in the discomfort though, she smiled as she placed her hand on her baby and felt the movements. There was a special human being growing inside her – her baby. Rachel's baby. Both Māori and Pākehā, but undeniably her whānau.

As she emerged into the hall at Terminal 1 of Manchester airport, the first thing Fran saw was Rachel's face, beaming at her with tears in her eyes that matched her own. The two women embraced, Fran's belly pressing on Rachel's. Fran smiled, and reached down to touch their baby.

'He or she is determined to say hello to the other mother,' she said gently, with an indulgent smile. Rachel just nodded, too choked to speak, and guided Fran towards her waiting car.

Life cycle

Fran didn't seem to believe her body could do it. When she got to forty-one weeks gestation, she confided in Rachel that it seemed to her as if birth would never actually happen and she would be stuck like this forever, in a permanent state of advanced pregnancy in which every movement seemed to take forever and leave her breathless.

Rachel spotted Fran considering her alien reflection in the mirror. Her belly protruded as if it had been stuck on her front, her rounded navel visible through all of her thin summer clothes. Neither of them could have imagined a belly could get so big. Whilst they both knew this large belly contained not just a baby but placenta and fluids, Rachel knew that the size of the baby alarmed Fran. Fran never having put anything bigger than a tampon inside her, Rachel knew it was impossible for Fran to imagine a whole baby coming out.

Their midwife, Angie tried to exude an air of confidence, but she had recently qualified and both Fran and Rachel had a sense she was winging it, with just a hint of Aussie brashness. They secretly thanked God that Angie would be accompanied by Susie for the birth – a much more grounded, very experienced British midwife. Plus, once Fran went into labour they would have the backup of Rachel's old boss, Freda. Rachel had worked with Freda when they were both new to their professions – Freda as a medic, and Rachel as a social worker. They had hit it off straight away, sharing socialist feminist principles which had even led Freda in later years as a GP to share her salary out with all of the employees at the surgery. That lasted until she became a mother and needed the rewards of her labours. In fact, they had both become more realistic and less idealistic over time, but the light of fervour that had united them all those years ago still bound them together.

Rachel had explained several months previously to Fran why she thought Freda would be a good choice of doctor for their home delivery. Angie had readily agreed, delighted to hear there would be friendly medical back-up. Freda had operated an open records policy at her surgery from the start of her general practice career, allowing any patient access to their own notes. It was a practice that was way ahead of its time. Rachel volunteered at Freda's practice while doing her PhD, which gave her access both to women who had experienced domestic violence and might want to tell their story, and also to her own notes. One day when she wasn't busy Rachel looked for her notes and was surprised at how quickly she found them. Holding them in her hands, while not breaking any practice rules brought feelings of guilt, excitement and apprehension. She sat with them in front of her on her desk, unsure whether or not to open them.

What she was looking for related to a time in her past when, after a particularly toxic relationship with a man she had contracted pelvic inflammatory disease. She shuddered as she remembered the consultant under whose 'care' she had been placed. He had treated her with derision bordering on disgust as he examined her first vaginally and then rectally, causing her to cry out in pain. When she looked back on the examination, she realised it was so brutal as to probably constitute assault though she could never have proved it at the time since this was before women were routinely examined with someone else present and so there were no witnesses.

Now, looking at her notes she came across two letters.

The first was written by her GP to the consultant:

4.3.1991

Dear Dr Featherstonehaugh,

I am referring this young lady to you. She has symptoms of pelvic inflammatory disease which seem resistant to the usual antibiotic treatment, though the laboratory was unable to grow anything following the most recent swab.

She claims she was 'raped' by her boyfriend with whom she has been living for the past six months. Whilst she may well have had an infection, this has been treated and I am convinced that her present symptoms are psychosomatic, though I am duty bound to seek your opinion.

Yours sincerely,

Niall Thomas, MB, CHB

The second letter was a reply:

17.5.1991

Dear Dr Thomas,

Thank you for referring this 21-year-old woman to me. I have seen her in outpatients and following rigorous examination I can confirm that she is tender on the right side of her abdomen.

A Kind of Family

I was unable to find any evidence of disease and would recommend that you tell her to go home, take two paracetamol and go to bed with a hot water bottle.

You might want to find out what she intends to do with her life following graduation; perhaps some gainful employment will take her mind off the break-up with her boyfriend, which I am sure is at the root of this psychosomatic presentation.

Sincerely,

Andrew Featherstonehaugh, MRCP, MB, CHB

As she folded the letters back into their envelopes Rachel was aware of acid rising from her stomach. She looked around to see if there was a bin, grabbing the nearest one just in case she might vomit. Her head felt like her study often looked, yet in motion; nothing was in order, and everything kept moving around, eluding her grasp.

Pulling her body together she took the only action she felt was available to her; she removed the two letters, placing them carefully in her handbag before stowing her notes back in the filing cabinet.

If her boss Freda ever noticed the letters were missing, she said nothing. The two letters still sat in a secret file in Rachel's filing cabinet at home, a dark reminder of past men's misdemeanours.

Finally, about ten days past her due date Fran told Rachel tremulously that her waters were trickling. The two women had already been told the baby had its back to Fran's back, which meant a long and painful labour. They both knew that if she did not go into labour soon it could mean a transfer to hospital, which might well result in an emergency C-section because Fran would be wired up and unable to move around; having read the books and gone to the classes, Rachel knew the importance of movement during early labour, to encourage the head to move down.

Mercifully, the day after Fran's trickle her contractions started. Both women went into overdrive, too excited to sleep. They rang the midwife, the doctor, and the acupuncturist, who came and painlessly inserted some needles and commenced moxibustion, lighting what looked like a cigar and moving it about near to Fran's skin at the base of her spine. Rachel busied herself around Fran, anxious to do whatever she could to alleviate the pain. She rubbed her back, went with her to the toilet, applied a cold flannel to her forehead, and wished she could take away the pain. Exhausted herself, she fought back the impulse to shut her eyes. At one point after about fifteen hours, Fran declared:

'I've tried everything now. All that's left for me to do is scream.'

It was five more excruciating hours before she had the urge to push. But that was not plain sailing either. They tried every position in the active birth manual and known to womankind. Eventually, while on all fours and shortly after Fran announced she could feel the need for a massive poo, Rachel heard excited shouts from Angie that she could see the head. After having a quick peek and confirming that she too could see the head – and a shock of black hair – Rachel moved behind Fran as they had practised many times, hardly able to believe that this was it. Their child was about to be born. Fran adopted a banana shape as Rachel held onto her. Rachel felt relieved to be able at last to do something she knew would be of benefit, as Fran leaned cautiously backwards to give her weight. The position had been chosen so they could both see their baby being born; they had rigged up a mirror at the end of the bed for this purpose. Shortly after this, Fran announced she could feel a burning sensation at the opening of her vagina. She breathed through it just as she had been taught, though Rachel could see by the look on her face that she was still unconvinced the baby could ever get through such a tiny hole. Still, there was no getting out of this

A Kind of Family

now. Rachel could feel a smile creeping across her face as she murmured words of encouragement to Fran. She could see the midwife working her magic, guarding the perineum with a large dressing as she encouraged Fran to pant. And then, there it was. The head, born, but seeming lifeless and looking very blue under the white vermix. Rachel tried not to show her anxiety, but there was no time in any case as another contraction came and Fran pushed with all her might – and out popped their baby. The midwife carefully placed the baby on Fran's chest, covered up to keep warm.

'Time of birth, 4.20 in the afternoon, August 4th 2015.' The midwife, despite having done this a few times already looked genuinely moved.

Rachel's eyes pushed tears out as if they didn't belong to her. She was beholding a miracle. Fran was cooing and looking like a mother already, a look of utter contentment and pure love on her face as she pushed the blanket away from their baby's face – a face that was turning from blue to bright red before their eyes.

Rachel moved out from behind her wife to sit by her side, making sure first that Fran was well supported with pillows. And then her tears turned to laughter as she lifted the blanket and saw two floppy red balls.

'Looks like we have a son, Fran!' She declared, through misty eyes. Fran smiled with that same nirvana-like smile, and nodded as if she had known this all along.

There was a moment's silence as Fran examined her son's tiny fingers and toes.

'Look at his hands, Rachel. They're wide but with long fingers. And he has dark hair! Isn't that amazing?'

The room fell silent again.

After a while Rachel whispered, a note of awe in her voice:

'That span will be good for playing the piano'. And in that moment her heart felt as if it might burst wide open, love pushing through her chest, pouring into her son like water gushing through a flimsy door.

Then she looked at Fran and felt the same swelling of love and gratitude and pride in her woman.

Once Fran had delivered the placenta and been cleaned up, and the two women were resting together on the bed with their son, Fran cradled the baby and offered him her breast, prizing open his mouth as she squeezed her areola between thumb and forefinger and waved it at his mouth. He poked his tongue out, tentatively licking the sweet colostrum then clamped his limpet-like jaws around her nipple. She winced, then looked up at Rachel with a look of utter contentment that said 'I will suffer any pain for this little boy'. Rachel smiled back, stroking the baby's dark brown hair as he exerted feather-like contractions on Fran's breast, with increasing urgency. Then he waited, still clamped on, and finally drank lustily of the milk he had just teased out of his mother. And the cycle began again.

'So, Fran. Are you happy to name him as we agreed, my love?'

'Yes,' Fran replied readily, looking down at her son with a look of pure love and indulgence. 'His name is Mikaere. Miki.'

Again unable to push back tears, Rachel stroked little Miki's cheek as she nodded.

'What a clever little boy,' Fran cooed.

'And what a clever pair of mummies,' Angie commented, her hand gently resting on Rachel's shoulder.

Rachel looked back at her, but was distracted by the sight of Aggie beyond.

Aggie sniffed and dabbed a slightly grey men's hankie to her nose and to each eye.

'Must bloody stop smoking. It's getting in me eyes', she declared with characteristic bravado.

Rachel simply smiled at her with a feeling of love and bonhomie that extended out from her new little family to the midwife, Aggie and the whole world.

A Kind of Family

Then Rachel turned back to take Miki from Fran. His belly full for now, he slept peacefully in her arms as she sobbed tears of gratitude.

The next few days and weeks hit both Fran and Rachel like a truck whose brakes had failed. Despite having read books, spoken to friends who had children and been to the antenatal classes, the sleepless nights felt like a form of torture that could potentially be exploited by an unscrupulous regime.

Despite feeling sorry for Fran that she had to endure sore nipples and after pains, Rachel felt a twist of envy in her guts that Fran was at least partially compensated by her hormones, which seemed to keep her in a state of perpetual bliss – though when she got low around the time the milk came in the situation was reversed as tears of desperation flowed readily in response to even the mildest of difficulties.

One of the things Rachel had been least prepared for, was the fact that even though she had not been the one to give birth she had fallen for their son like a soppy teenager in love. It frightened her that this little life depended on the two of them for his continued existence. The thought that some parents might exploit the vulnerability of their children sent panic surging through her body. To her shock, Rachel realised she would willingly lay down her life for Miki. She had never loved like this, so selflessly and so unconditionally, and she suspected the same was true for Fran.

Rachel was able to take three blissful months off from her university work, thanks to the university's parental leave policy. But the same wasn't true of her private work. She continued to be concerned about Adam, who still had been unable to tell her the story of the crash that left his fiancée dead. While not wishing to press him, Rachel felt instinctively that he would be unable to move on until he did.

It was two weeks after Miki's birth that Rachel sat in her consulting room, facing Adam. Today, he carried with him a single red rose, and

Rachel's first thought was one of alarm. What if he was falling in love with her?

He laid the rose carefully on the coffee table that separated them, then looked up at Rachel.

'I want to tell you what happened that night,' he began.

The roads had been wet, and a frost was predicted. They had been to his best friend's engagement party – the man who was to be his own best man, in fact. It was late when they left the hotel to drive back to the one where they were staying, just five miles away. There weren't many cars on the road, and Adam was feeling upbeat. He put some sounds on the CD. Stadium rock. Queen blared out as he sang along, one hand on the steering wheel and the other in his fiancée's lap. He remembered moving his hand up her skirt, exciting them both. He felt powerful, masculine, in control. The winding lanes of Kent presented no problem to him and he swerved his car as if it was doing an ice dance. Then, in an instant his two hands were on the wheel and his feet slammed onto both clutch and brake as he tried to steady the car in the face of an oncoming car that had jumped out of nowhere. Time slowed as he did this, but his car kept on skidding forwards. The impact knocked him out, and when he came round it was to someone knocking on his window, trying the door. He was aware of an extreme pain in his ribs and difficulty breathing. He couldn't feel his legs. It was a superhuman effort to reach for his keys and unlock the doors, after which he eased himself back. It was then that he looked to his left. His fianceé's head was at a grotesque angle, her eyes staring into nothingness with blood congealed on her face. Her nose was crooked, her lipstick smeared.

All through the telling of his story, Adam trembled. But he continued as if he had rehearsed this and was determined to get through it. Once the telling was over, his cry sounded like that of a wounded dog, hoarse and deep and wild. Rachel's stomach twisted when she heard the description of the dead woman. For a moment, she wished she was somewhere else. She instinctively wanted to rush home to Fran and Miki to make sure they were alright. She gathered herself to finish Adam's story for him.

'She was dead,' she said softly.

Adam looked up, tears dripping freely on the carpet between his legs.

'Yes. My darling, lovely angel was dead.'

The day she had to return to university, Rachel was reluctant to leave. She ran back to the door twice to kiss both Fran and Miki before getting into her car and speeding off, late for a meeting.

A couple of weeks after her return to work, Rachel had to go to Edinburgh. As external examiner, she felt unable to give her apologies to the Exam Board but it felt almost impossible to leave Fran and Miki for two whole nights. The morning she had to leave, she held Miki as she made coffee with one hand, reluctant to put him down. Her left bicep was growing strong with the effort of carrying several pounds on one arm on a regular basis. When the time came to say goodbye, she lifted his little body to her face, feeling his softness against her cheek and chest and willing herself to remember his smell while away. At that point, Fran entered the room.

'It's fine, silly! We'll be fine, and you'll be fine. You know the job backwards. Go and knock 'em dead, Drake.' Fran's voice sounded like a reassuring old record, familiar and confident.

But Rachel's misgivings were not just about the fact that she wouldn't see her little family for a few days. The time away just happened to coincide with a meeting Fran had arranged at one of the care homes where she normally worked. She had arranged for Roxy to babysit while she was out, a fact that perturbed Rachel. She didn't want to sound as if she didn't trust Fran's friends, but she knew Roxy had never had children of her own.

Rachel lingered on the doorstep. 'Are you sure Roxy will be OK?'

'Yes, I've written an essay on how to look after him. Besides, I'll have my mobile. All will be well. I've got to start getting used to being without him, haven't I? I'm going back to work soon. We don't all have generous university maternity pay, you know.'

Rachel felt a pang of guilt. She had offered to keep them all so that Fran could take more time off, but then Fran was stubborn and independent. She simply would not countenance it.

As Rachel left the house, Fran waved Miki's little hand at her, her face beaming with contentment and reassurance that all would be well. Miki smiled his special toothless, open-mouthed smile.

Rachel was grateful for time on the train to read a couple of academic papers that were vital to her own research. She hadn't wanted to open them while at home, feeling that her time off should be spent supporting Fran and getting to know their son, but it had been a strain as the work had piled up during her parental leave. As her train pulled into Edinburgh Waverley station she gathered up her belongings and headed for the Market Street exit, to begin her climb up the hill. She was glad that this time she had packed everything she needed into a smallish rucksack meaning that for once she wouldn't be carrying a case up the News Steps. She detested taxis, preferring always to walk, but sometimes she wondered whether she was being just a tad too spartan.

It was a lovely late autumn day, and unseasonably warm in the sun. Rachel felt another twinge of guilt amidst her enjoyment of the city and decided she would ring Fran as soon as she arrived in her hotel room.

Roxy turned up in a smart dark grey jacket, white shirt, and roguish tie with a loose knot to one side. On the bottom half she wore black jeans without any holes in them, and black pumps. Her hair had been dyed a sedate brunette.

'Wow, Roxy!' Fran was unsure what to say as she opened to door to her friend and one-time lover. Despite her lack of sleep and general disinterest in sex, she had to admit this was a hot look.

A Kind of Family

'Well, I thought I'd better show you I can look serious, when I want to, babe.' Roxy leaned forward and gave Fran a kiss on the cheek, lingering a little longer than is usual for friends.

Fran grinned as she opened the door wide to let Roxy in. Once inside, there was no time to waste. Miki had just been fed and put down for his nap.

'Right. Miki's asleep. Coffee's there. Don't drink it anywhere near him. I should be about an hour. You have my mobile. Nappies and all that shit are upstairs where he sleeps. He probably won't need feeding but there is some expressed milk in the fridge in a bottle, just in case.'

Roxy grinned.

'No worries, my Kiwi friend. It's all good.' This had become a standard joke between them ever since Fran had visited New Zealand. Roxy, having travelled the world, knew a fair bit about New Zealand culture and was only too ready to enter into this sort of banter with Fran – besides, Fran thought on more than one occasion, if Roxy kept things jokey between them it made it easier. She knew Roxy still missed Fran's presence in the house when she came home from touring. She had let it slip one evening when she rang Fran after a few pints in the pub with the band. Fran had prudently never told Rachel about the conversation.

The meeting went well, and dates were put in diaries for Fran's work to recommence. As she left the home she thought back to her postnatal examination, which was the last time she had left Miki. On that occasion, Rachel had been with him. She chuckled as she remembered an awkward moment when the (male) doctor tried to tell her that she could now resume sexual intercourse. Fran enjoyed telling him she was married to a woman, and had been having regular orgasms to assist her womb in its efforts to contract to its former state. The poor doctor had gone a mottled strawberry colour, from the top of his trendy T shirt to his hairline.

As she was crossing the road, still chuckling, she decided she must text Rachel to let her know how the meeting had gone. She stopped on a pedestrian island, because the lights had changed. Taking out her phone, she began texting.

Hi Rachel. Meeting went well …

Her phone leaped out of her hands, flying through the air to her right just as she felt an off-the-scale pain down her left side and her own body followed the phone in hot pursuit. She was almost calmly aware of being completely out of control. The descent was quick. Her whole body was one white hot pain. And then nothing.

Rachel again felt guilty as she turned the lock on her door, relishing the peace and quiet of being in her own hotel room. She had put the 'do not disturb notice' on the outside. Once she had boiled the kettle and was sitting with a brew in her hand she tried Fran's number. It went to voicemail.

Oh, well, maybe the meeting ran over.

Rachel opened her laptop to check emails.

She had just read a particularly long-winded one from the head of school about the proposed cuts and was pacing up and down her hotel room wondering what to do when her own phone rang. She saw that it was from Joanne and paused, puzzled as to why her sister-in-law would be ringing her.

The voice on the other end was almost inaudible. Rachel was aware of sounding irritated as she asked Joanne to speak up. She wasn't prepared for the deafening shout that assaulted her ears:

'Your wife is dead! I said Fran is dead!'

Rachel's heart seemed to punch up into her throat. She clutched to disbelief. This was some kind of sick joke – but she knew Joanne not to be vicious, despite her other faults.

Her voice wouldn't work. She swallowed, then heard her brother-in-law's voice as Joanne burst into tears that receded into the background.

'Rachel, I'm sorry. She insisted on ringing you herself. But she's beside herself, as you can tell. Rachel, I am so sorry, but you'd better come back.'

His tone was gentle, understanding even, and Rachel could tell his voice was cracking, too.

'Um... what happened?' Rachel knew she sounded flat, dispassionate. She had no energy for trying to do the right thing and empathise with anyone else. But she needed to know – to make it more real so she could start taking it in.

'She got run over, love. She'd just come out of the home she visits. She must have been distracted. She crossed the road. I think she was standing on an island in the middle. A lorry turned the corner a bit too fast, and went over the island. It was instant, Rachel. She didn't suffer.'

Silence.

'Er... Miki's still with Roxy at present. Shall we go and pick him up for you and keep him at yours until you get back?'

Rachel's legs seemed to have forgotten how to hold up the rest of her body. She felt her way towards the one chair, throwing off the clothes she had deposited there and sat down, her brain and mouth suspended in slow motion animation. She could see nothing.

She did not want to hear the implication that she was now a lone parent, looking after a small baby to whom she had not given birth. She just wanted to undo the events of the day, go back to this morning, and not have gone to Edinburgh. Eventually, hearing whispers on the other end of the phone she was brought back to the present, and the need to respond.

'Um... yes. I'll ring you once I am on the train and give you an E.T.A...'

Her voice sounded calm, but her guts were turning somersaults. She rushed to the bathroom, and vomited bile.

PART FOUR

Begin again

A Kind of Family

Friends indeed

The train journey back to Yorkshire seemed interminable. Rachel pretended to read as she took up her seat by the window. She put her headphones in but listened only to the noise inside her own head, which was a jumble of voices – her own, Fran's, and Adam's. Her client's account of his own car accident burned into her stomach like an acid attack.

As she approached the Scottish-English border Rachel forced some water down her, aware that her usual bodily cues for hunger and thirst were fugitive. She looked at her reflection in the window, checking whether her tears were visible to others in the carriage, but then decided she didn't really care what anyone else thought. She shifted in her seat, willing the train to go faster yet dreading what she had to face at the other end.

The story Rachel had up until now been telling herself about how life was going to pan out had gone into reverse. The narrative she had prepared included her and Fran getting old together. It included them both being there when Miki took his first steps, when Miki went to school for the first time, when Miki graduated (as he probably would), and when Miki brought home the person with whom he wanted to spend the rest of his life. Now that story had to be rewritten. But Rachel felt unprepared, deskilled, no longer a writer. She could not imagine a world without waking up to Fran every day, to her delightful zest for life – life! – and her often slightly inappropriate if not downright rude honesty. How Rachel loved and admired that openness which she (despite being a therapist) found excruciating herself. That honesty and openness was what had drawn Rachel to her in the first place, like an insubstantial moth to light.

Now Fran breathed no more. Rachel tried hard to take this in, but the thought made her body tremble. She drew her coat and scarf more tightly around her. Her body longed to reach out and touch Fran – the living Fran, who still existed somewhere for Rachel – just one more time, to breathe in her natural perfume, to hold and be held. More tears clouded her vision as she turned the page of her book in a vain attempt to keep up the pretence of reading. Perhaps people would think the novel was particularly moving. And then she heard and sensed rather than saw Aggie.

'Rachel? I know it's 'ard right now, an' I'm really, really sorry.'

For once, Rachel didn't have the energy to tell Aggie to fuck off, and besides the whole carriage would then be totally convinced she was definitely mad. Instead, she just listened, mollified.

'I do know 'ow it feels to be left a widow.'

A widow! What a strange and unexpected identity. Rachel wasn't ready to call herself a widow. But she had nothing else to do right now, and so she listened.

'It's 'ard. Really bloody 'ard.'

Rachel was vaguely aware that this was the first time she had heard Aggie swear.

'But it'll get easier. Take care of Miki. It'll 'elp.'

At hearing her son's name, Rachel's head became a centrifuge. How could she possibly be the mother Fran was to Miki? No! She had to have *time*. Time to get used to a life without Fran. Time to rewrite the story.

But Aggie's voice, and the sense of her presence, had gone. Rachel had never felt so alone.

When Rachel arrived by taxi from the train station, Jo and her husband had gone, to be replaced by Jane and Suzy.

'What are you doing here?' Rachel knew her voice sounded accusatory, but she didn't have the energy to be nice.

'Rachel, love, you rang me while you were waiting for your train. Remember?' Jane's voice was soft, like a mother speaking to a hurt child.

'Um… no. Where's Jo?' Rachel dropped her overnight case in the hallway, along with her handbag. This simple and familiar act brought more tears, as she contemplated never again being tidied up after and so never again being able to feel rebellious as she created her own special brand of chaos.

'She's gone to get some rest in her hotel. Roxy has gone home to tell the others. Miki's asleep right now, so you can have a cup of tea and put your feet up.' Suzy was already in the kitchen, putting the kettle on as she said this. 'And when he wakes, I'll go to him.' Suzy poked her head round the door, a bottle and bottle brush in her hand. 'I've been out and bought some more bottles and formula.' Rachel vaguely registered Suzy's concerned look. She swallowed, and immediately felt nauseous and dizzy.

Jane put her arms round Rachel's shoulders and guided her towards one of the sofas.

'When was the last time you ate?'

'Um... Can't remember. I can't eat, Jane. I can't.' And at that, Rachel broke down, sobs erupting unbidden from somewhere deep within her strangely remote body. Jane's caring came like a strong gust of wind to someone who is standing too near to the edge of a cliff. She could no longer stop herself from falling forever.

Miki's cries pierced Rachel as if some inconsiderate neighbour had suddenly started playing loud music late on a school night. She felt her body tense, keeping her eyes down until Suzy had appeared with him and safely administered the bottle she had prepared.

'Is there anyone else you would like us to tell, Rachel?'

Jane's question might as well have been about nuclear physics for the sense it made to Rachel. She struggled to put the words into a meaningful order, stalling for time with a puzzled 'Um...' as she looked up at her friend, her eyes not really focussing. All she could think of was wanting to be left alone, yet she dreaded the moment when her two friends would leave her. Panic set in as she contemplated a night with Miki on her own. For a while, she considered whether his Kiwi relatives might wish to adopt him, but Rachel decided now was not the time to think about such things. She forced her brain to work. If she could just get the immediate things sorted, she could then take the time she needed to be alone.

'Um... yes. I need people at work to know. I'll need bereavement leave. I wonder if Richard might let them know for me?'

Rachel thought, through her haze of confusion, that she noticed Jane bristle at this suggestion. Suzy answered:

'I'll contact Richard. It's fine. I'll share the load with Jane for that sort of thing. Give me his number.'

'Anyone spoken to Joanne? I don't feel able to have her here, to be honest. She might want to come back once she knows I'm here...' Rachel's voice trailed off.

'It's OK. I'll give her a ring,' answered Jane, now sounding back in control. 'I've got her phone number. Tell you what, if you want you can tell me where to find all of these numbers and emails and stuff. Give me a bit of scrap paper and I'll make a list for Suzy and me to work from. Deal?'

'Deal. Thanks, you two.' And once more, Rachel cried, this time with love for these two women who cared so much for her they were more like family than her own birth family had ever been.

The list got made and included (reluctantly) her own brother as well as Fran's Māori family. Suzy stayed the night, sleeping on one of the sofas. She reassured Rachel she didn't need to get up to Miki that night. She had everything under control.

As Rachel eased her painful body into their bed, she was overwhelmed by the smell of her wife encased in the bedding. It hovered round her, refusing to go away – a cruel juxtaposition to the battering news that was pounding at her life. Rachel grabbed at the duvet and wrapped her arms around a big wedge of it, breathing in her wife's familiar smell – a smell made by her live body and of which Rachel had never tired. She held on tight, willing Fran to be the body she held in her imagination, still alive, still present, still vibrant and funny and the birth mother of their son. Several hours later, just as the birds were beginning to sing their territorial songs, her arms began to relax enough to allow fitful bursts of sleep, from which she would surface to wail some more, clutching at her belly.

Rachel did not want to wake from her sleep. Today, a Saturday, she had to go and identify her wife's body. Jane offered to take her to the morgue, while Suzy looked after Miki. When they arrived, Rachel felt as if she had been superglued to Jane's passenger seat. She began shaking, staring straight in front of her.

'Rachel? Let's get this over with, love.'

But Rachel's body still would not move.

Jane got out of the car, walked round to the passenger side and opened the door. Rachel continued to stare, holding her breath and clutching her bag to her as if she were a refugee and these were her only possessions. Jane reached over her and unclasped the seatbelt, leaving Rachel adrift. Then a hand appeared in Rachel's vision.

'Come on Rachel. Let's do this thing.'

Rachel looked up at her friend. She noticed Jane's earrings, two pearl drops, and wondered whether she had seen them before. The hand moved. Rachel lifted her own leaden limb, and Jane swiftly caught hold of it. Inexplicably, Rachel was out of the car and on her feet. How did that happen?

The walk to the building was both endless and yet never happened. Time seemed to hop from one moment to the next with no intervening links despite the fact that in those gaps between moments Rachel felt like Major Tom, floating forever in space. And so, out of nowhere, she stood in a cold room, with Jane by her side and a man who slowly pulled back a cloth from what looked like a wax doll lying on a slab. The hair was almost black, strong and still shiny in places where it wasn't caked in a dark substance. The swollen eyes were shut, the skull misshapen and there were numerous gashes. Rachel could see the white of bone protruding from one asymmetrical cheek. But the lips looked familiar. Plumper, but perhaps more beautiful for that. They were Fran's lips. Under the cloth, a hand protruded. Her left hand, bearing the rings Rachel had bought her. They were tightly held by grotesquely oversized flesh, making her look obese instead of the very slim build she was in life.

Rachel's eyes flitted over the scene. This was her wife's body, but it was no longer her. Her beautiful body was battered, damaged almost beyond recognition. At the thought of this, her eyes filled with tears as she declared what she knew was expected of her:

'Yes, this is Frances Baker. This is my wife.'

And Jane was there, with her arms round her. Rachel knew Jane was expecting tears, but she felt numb. All she wanted was to get out of there.

Over the next few days, Rachel stared into the garden or into nothingness. Time seemed suspended like a fly in a spider's web. She ate and drank very little and would have taken even less without her friends to ensure nourishment was there and to encourage her to open her mouth and swallow. Occasionally, she looked at the clock to orientate herself or checked her mobile to see what date it was.

On the third day, a Sunday, Jane announced that she must work Tuesday, but she would take Monday off so that she could accompany Rachel to collect the death certificate, after which she would go back home. She promised to pop round after work on Tuesday. Suzy said she would stay another day or two, but when Miki woke instead of going into him she spoke with a new firmness in her voice as she folded Miki's newly-laundered clothes:

'That's your baby in there, Rachel, and he needs you.'

Rachel felt a burning liquid rise in her throat. Her head became a jumble of instructions she had never bothered reading, about how to sterilise bottles and make up formula. She knew how to change nappies, but how was she to buy more? That would mean going out of the house. She felt like a toddler digging her heels in, but she knew caring for Miki was not Suzy's job. She looked at her friend, then at the door to Miki's room – and forced herself out of the chair.

Picking Miki up, feeling the warmth of his little body against hers and his mouth rooting on her, the just-having-slept softness of him and the smell of baby products, Rachel felt calmer. She carried him into the living room, where Suzy was waiting with a bottle of formula. Suzy was smiling, and behind her Aggie was smiling too, pointing at Suzy and applauding.

Rachel sat in her chair, threw the muslin she was given by Suzy over her left shoulder, and gratefully took the proffered bottle.

'This one's on the house. Once you've changed him and got him playing on his play mat, you can come into the kitchen and I'll talk you through preparing the bottles for the day.' Suzy sounded like a primary school teacher, encouraging a young child to learn new skills.

'Well done,' she added.

After a few more days, the cards began to pour onto the door mat. Sometimes, Rachel would make the superhuman effort of getting out of the chair she sat in – 'Fran's chair' had now become her sanctuary – and would walk with deliberate steps towards the mat, stopping first to prepare herself for the precarious task of bending down to pick up the mail, then straightening herself first before slowly turning round to walk back and slump down into the chair. She tended to place the mail on the table beside her, unwilling to open any of it.

A Kind of Family

'Here's a coffee, Rachel,' Jane coaxed one evening. 'Why not open your mail while you drink it?' She dropped the mail in Rachel's lap, at the same time handing her a letter opener from her desk.

Rachel was vaguely surprised at how many people seemed both to know, and care. There were the predictable cards from Jane, Suzy, and one between Debs, Roxy and Feather. Jane's was simple, white with a kind of embossed pattern on it, whereas Suzy's had a quasi-religious message inside with a poem. The one from Debs, Roxy and Feather had a rainbow on the front, and an outpouring of words inside signed separately by each of them, testifying to how much they had loved Fran. Then came one from Richard, with a simple white dove embossed on white card. The message inside read: 'Thinking of you. Know I am here if you need me'. It was more than a week before Joanne's arrived, when Rachel realised she had not sent one to her. She asked Jane if she could get one but Jane stood firm.

'I think you should choose one. You need to go to the supermarket, in any case. It's time you started doing your own shopping. Suzy and I will help you make a list.'

Then came cards from work colleagues, including one very large one signed by lots of people whose signatures Rachel could not make out.

Jane helped Rachel find a funeral director. She settled on a cremation with a short humanist service.

'Rachel? I'm wondering who you might want to consult on the order of service. Maybe Joanne? And Roxy, Debs and Feather? Those three were like her family, after all, weren't they? Apart from you, Miki and Jo, I mean.' Jane's voice sounded apologetic, trailing off at the end.

Roxy stepped in and helped with the arrangements.

'I might not be a tour manager, but I see what they do. I reckon I can organise a gig. Funerals can't be much different.' Roxy blew her nose, hard. 'But I promise I'll consult you every inch of the way, Rachel. I'm not taking over.'

Rachel felt a tiny space opening in the centre of her chest, which rapidly closed over again like newly pierced ears that don't have earrings in them. The space felt too unfamiliar, too raw, and there was nothing to make it worth keeping open.

When the day for the funeral arrived, Rachel was glad Joanne and her husband and children had said they would meet them all at the crematorium. She travelled in one of the cars with Jane and Suzy by her side, along with Feather who sniffed the whole way there despite the hanky produced from Jane's magic bag. Roxy and Debra had said they would see them all at the crem. As the hearse arrived bearing Fran's body, Rachel's legs began to give way under her. Jane and Suzy stood one either side of her, holding her up, and Jane whispered 'You can do this, Rachel. We're right with you.' Rachel looked around to see where Feather had got to, but she was nowhere to be seen.

And then she spotted her, opening the door of the hearse to reveal the figures of Debra and Roxy both dressed in grey coat tails. They stood respectfully at the opened rear door as two men slid the coffin part-way out, then joined the two women as they held the coffin aloft. Rachel's lips parted as she saw someone emerge from the crowds to stand at the end of the coffin, also dressed in the same grey coat tails. At first, she thought it was a latecomer from the funeral director's staff. But no. It was Aggie, looking solemn, her body held erect as she made her slow progress with the others into the chapel. The crowds parted and everyone fell silent as they waited for Rachel to follow.

The service was mercifully short and included a song from Roxy, a poem written by Joanne's eldest, and a short but surprising testimonial from Feather, who with the aid of a microphone could be heard at the back of the room. She had painstakingly researched Fran's life and taken memories from Joanne, Fran's work colleagues, and of course her best friends as well as Rachel. Debra had put together a slideshow of photographs from Fran's life, which was projected onto the wall behind.

After the service they all piled into a working person's club nearby. Roxy had carefully selected the playlist after consulting the people who had been important in Fran's life. As she endured the endless procession of people come to offer their condolences, Rachel could see Aggie still in her grey coat tails, raising a glass to her, a look of love on her face that said 'Don't worry, you're not alone with this one, Rachel.'

Rachel was relieved when the day came to an end and she and Miki could go back to their home – despite the fact that this meant the start of a whole new life, the details of which she still hadn't worked out.

Help

It was one of those days when the mist seems to envelop you like a warm, comforting cloak. Rachel looked out the window, across the lawn and towards the tree – her and Fran's beloved copper beech – which in summer stood like a tall, strong woman with flaming red mane, now baring its wounds for all to see. Christmas and New Year had come and gone, Rachel sitting them out and dutifully turning up as her well-meaning friends required her to, even managing a sort of smile at times. She had been able to excuse herself before the fireworks started because she had to get Miki to bed. She cried herself to sleep as the New Year was heralded in with whizzes and bangs and cries of delight from nearby neighbours anticipating a bright new year ahead.

As Rachel sat staring, both hands round an oversized cup of steaming black coffee, tears seeped like an overflowing dam after unbearably heavy rain. The pain in her chest that always accompanied these familiar tears brought Rachel to her senses, and to the present. Miki would be awake in a few minutes, would need feeding, and then she knew she must get out of the house or go stir crazy. He always loved seeing the trees above him. Above all, she needed him to be occupied, to need her as little as possible, because she had nothing left in reserve to give him.

She heard mail drop onto the mat. More bloody cards. When would they stop flowing like her tears? It was a herculean effort to raise herself, walk to the door, bend to pick up the mail, then place the envelopes down on the table beside her. She couldn't face reading it just now, but she noticed one with a New Zealand postmark.

Rachel shivered. She felt the cold more these days. As she opened the wardrobe to pull out a cardigan, she saw Fran's clothes still hanging right beside hers. She knew that when she finally could get rid of them Fran's absence would still be there, like a photographic negative. Merely taking away a visual reminder would not erase her whole body's memory of the woman she loved – and who was now dead. She pulled on her light green cardigan, removing it from beside Fran's vibrant rust coloured dress.

And then, the cry. Not hers, but an urgent, angry cry, that said 'You should have known I would wake now and had the bottle ready for me!' Rachel forced herself to put down her coffee despite her impulse to run as far away as possible from the screaming rage that felt like an attack on her ears. She moved mechanically towards the sound. Then she tentatively opened the nursery door and on seeing him, swept Miki up in her arms and held him close as his little body struggled against her. She had already lined up the bottles for the day, with boiled water in them. She walked into the living room, placed Miki as carefully as she could into his bouncy chair and turned on the vibration so that the toy which hung on the bar in front of him began to rattle. He quietened and looked interested for a moment, then began the familiar grunting that always turned to further, desperate crying. But for now, he was safe, and this meant she was free to walk into the kitchen, speaking instructions to herself as she went in an attempt to stay present. She reached for the tin of formula, opened its metal lid, and looked inside for the scoop. It had become buried in the formula. 'Oh, damn!' Even the slightest mishap like this was liable to send her into desperate sobs, but she held it together and, with hastily washed and dried hands reached in and fumbled about for the scoop. Three scoops in the bottle, shake, take bottle to baby. She imagined Fran instructing her, making sure that their son would get what he needed as minimum care.

She carried the bottle into the living room, where Miki was once again beside himself with hunger and rage. She reached down into the bouncy chair, picked Miki up, and turned off the vibration. Miki was desperately rooting on her, his head turning frantically, his tiny mouth searching into Rachel's clothes. Rachel looked down at her son.

'Oh, Miki! I know you want your mummy's milk, not this bloody formula. I want her back, too, but we can't have her!'

Rachel sobbed as she spoke. She settled gently into Fran's favourite armchair, placing the bottle on the small table beside her. Instinctively, she settled Miki near her left breast, his right arm tucked into her armpit. She reached over for the bottle and placed it into his mouth. He immediately began sucking and swallowing, his sobs turning to contented murmurs, and as she gazed down at him, finally able to relax her tense body in sympathy with his, his eyes met hers. He stared at her for a long time as he fed, and once again her tears flowed, this time with some semblance of gratitude for this moment, and for this vulnerable, special little boy.

After the feed and a spectacular burp on Rachel's shoulder, Miki was happy to lie on his play mat and kick. Rachel was glad of this moment, when he was not cranky due to tiredness (yet), nor desperately, angrily hungry, nor in pain with some unexplained and incommunicable distress – and neither was he asleep, her waiting on tenterhooks to be woken with one or all of these.

The white envelopes beside her bothered her. She reached for one, tore open the envelope with her fingertips like a toddler who is still learning to tear paper, and bypassing the picture of a light in some woods on the front of the card she read the message inside. It was penned using real ink and written in a scrawling old-fashioned hand.

Dear Rachel, we cannot begin to imagine what you are going through. Fran was a dearly loved attender of our Meeting and

A Kind of Family

will be sadly missed here, but your grief must be like a mountain looming before you. Please know we are here if you need us. From all the overseers at Meeting.

Rachel sighed. Richard must have told them. Next, the envelope from New Zealand. Rachel guessed who this was. She couldn't face speaking to Aroha, but Jane had been good enough to skype using Fran's password. Rachel hadn't asked how the conversation went.

Dear Rachel, we were devastated when we heard that our lovely British cousin Frances has been killed. Words cannot express how we feel, but we feel for you more. We were so looking forward to Fran coming back one day with you and Miki. Please rest assured that you and Miki will always be welcome here. You are whanau, through Fran, who lives on in our hearts.

Aroha.

Rachel wandered back into the kitchen to her now cold coffee and drank it anyway. This was what life was going to be like, now. Her manager Elspeth had been very understanding since Fran's death; after the usual period of bereavement leave she had been encouraged to see her doctor and be written off as sick because, as Elspeth said, 'You're no use to man nor beast right now, Rachel – leave it to me. I will arrange cover.' Rachel had asked her clinical supervisor to contact Adam, who was her only client at the moment. She felt guilty about leaving him in the lurch, especially after what he had gone through. A part of her worried that he might become suicidal, but she knew too that she had done the only thing she could do and ended the work. Her supervisor would advise him on where to seek help. But now that the new year was underway, Rachel knew it was time to begin picking up the threads of her life and get back to work. Which left a huge problem to solve.

Even when she could get Miki into a nursery, how would she negotiate his needs in the evenings? That was when she tended to read students' work, write research funding bids, review papers for journals, write articles, prepare classes, answer a million and one emails, and do all the jobs she had previously carried out whilst pretending to Fran that she was on Facebook, because there was never enough time in her noisy, shared office with her needy students, and endless boring meetings. Something had to be done. But what? A nanny? Fran would never have approved of that, nor trusted one. No, it had to be someone who had a real commitment to them, as a family. For a moment, Rachel considered Fran's sister Joanne, but immediately rejected it. She had been devastated at Fran's death, and offered to help, but Rachel knew Joanne would want to control Miki's care and boss Rachel about. Jane and Suzy, although they had been right there for her as soon as they heard the news of Fran's death were realistically far too busy with their own lives to offer any consistent help. Roxy, Debs and Feather had all been round too, trying to help but Rachel was too acutely aware of their own grief. The fact of the matter was that none of these women would be able to live in, and that was what Rachel needed. And it had to be someone who understood her work as an academic.

Miki was happily swiping at soft toys dangling in front of him and so Rachel allowed her poor, heavy eyes to close, but her head was reeling. And then, she heard someone clearing her throat.

'Ahem!'

Rachel started.

'Aggie, fuck off. I can't cope with you being around right now. I need to be left alone, to think.'

'But that's where I come in, dear. Innit? That's what I'm 'ere for, you might say.'

'Oh, Jesus give me strength,' muttered Rachel. Aggie ignored the blasphemy.

''Ave you fought of – Richard?'

'No, no, no, no! Don't you see, you half-wit?' Rachel was past caring about Aggie's feelings. 'That would be too cruel. Richard has always fancied me. How could I ask him to move in? Jesus, don't you see? I am not about to start a fucking relationship with him, in case you have any bright ideas!'

Aggie smiled serenely, for once silent as she waited for Rachel to continue.

'Look. If I ask him to move in and help with Miki, to become a surrogate father without the perks of a relationship, how is he gonna feel, eh? It's just not fair.'

But, thought Rachel as her anger subsided, who else is there? She looked at Aggie as if inspiration might come, but she had to admit Aggie had a point. He was the only person that might just do it. But how could she ask? He would have to retire early…

Rachel sighed.

'Oh, OK. I suppose he can say no.'

But inside, she knew he would never refuse her anything it was within his power to give her.

Miki had fallen asleep on his play mat. Oh well. She went into the nursery, found a cover and laid it over him, settled into her own armchair, and opened a student's essay. She read the first paragraph three times, before closing her eyes.

Rachel looked down at her soy cappuccino. Richard waited patiently for her to begin.

He looked around him. They were the only two people in the café, other than a couple in their twenties who were so busy making out in a dark corner they were completely unaware of Rachel and Richard sitting in an alcove by the window. Outside, the traffic stopped and started as always. People, mostly students, walked by. Some seemed to be in their own private headphone world. Others were chatting animatedly in small friendship bubbles. To all intents and purposes, they were alone. Rachel appeared to have chosen well.

'I have something to ask of you, Richard.'

Rachel looked straight at him. Richard mused that it was impossible to make out what Rachel was thinking or feeling. When he heard Rachel was planning her return to work Richard had lamely offered to help, knowing he wouldn't have a clue what to do with a puking, screaming bundle of needs. He was relieved when Rachel told him she had it covered.

He thought he detected a pleading look in her eyes. He knew it was not borne out of longing for him. He'd learned aeons ago, that there was only one love in Rachel's eyes, and it was Fran. Miki had been Fran's idea, and Richard knew Rachel was almost as much at sea as he would be faced with caring for her dead wife's birth-son. Rachel was legally and in fact biologically his mother, and of course she had been devoted to Fran, but that didn't make her a natural mother. He knew she had done her share of the night-time nappy changes, but Miki was breast fed up to Fran's death. Richard found himself wondering, vaguely, what one did in these circumstances, to ensure adequate nutrition. Such things were a complete mystery, and he had no desire to be educated. He concluded that the look in Rachel's eyes was a mixture of grief for her lost love, and despair arising out of her own inadequacy with babies.

'Richard, are you listening to me? You don't seem to be here!' Rachel's voice brought Richard back with a bump.

'Sorry, Rachel.' Richard felt embarrassed that he had been daydreaming. He felt he owed her an explanation.

'I was just thinking how awful it must be for you right now. How are you coping, with Miki and all?'

A Kind of Family

Richard reached out and lightly touched Rachel's left wrist. He felt it move, almost imperceptibly, towards her body.

Bad move. Keep your hands to yourself, you stupid arsehole! Yet another reason to chastise himself. But then again, he had begun of late to stop apologising inwardly for liking her. He had behaved impeccably, after all. The touch was mere friendliness.

Nevertheless, he fixed his eyes obediently on her face.

'Right. You aren't making this easy for me. God, you can be such a prick at times, Richard!'

'Thanks Rachel. Honoured.' God, he was being sarcastic! Where did that come from? Despite Richard's attempts to be assertive with Rachel, he felt he had gone too far. It was much more comfortable to apologise.

'I'm sorry. I'm just a clumsy oaf. I'm all ears, truly.'

Richard smiled, warmly he hoped, and kept his hands in his lap.

'OK. Well, you see the thing is, I've been thinking about Miki. He really is the cutest little thing, and I'm absolutely devoted to him for sure. I can cope. It's just that, I feel he needs male role models in his life.'

'You can count on me, Rachel,' Richard chimed in, a little too enthusiastically. 'I'm going nowhere,' he continued, then kicked his own shin silently under the table.

'Well, I hope not. You see, the thing is, Richard – and I don't want you to misinterpret this in any way shape or form – I was wondering if you might like to move into the spare room and help me to bring Miki up. You see…'

Rachel paused, looking first at the gaggling students outside their window, then down to the froth left in her cup. She looked up again, squaring her face to his, and sighed audibly.

'You see, Richard, I'm not actually sure I can do this all on my own. I might make some absolute howlers, especially with a boy – what do I know about boys? And… well… I know I can trust you.'

As she finished her speech, Richard noticed her shoulders drop by several inches. She smiled at him in such an unguarded way, tears forming in her eyes, Richard's heart was like wax in the Mediterranean sun. He wanted to take her into his arms and love away her tears and pain.

He thought about what she was asking him to do. How could he consider it, feeling the way he did despite his efforts to distance himself emotionally? What would it be like, seeing her wrapped in a towel or in her nightwear?

'Rachel…' It was his turn to look away, searching for the right thing to say. This time, his eyes rested on the young couple in the dark corner, who by now were gnawing at each other's tongues. He decided to come clean.

'Rachel. This is awkward. I think you must know how I feel about you.'

'I know, I know.'

Rachel's cheeks coloured slightly. Richard couldn't work out whether this was embarrassment at his honesty, or shame at what she was asking of him. He hoped she had just a bit of compassion for him. He had spent years pussy footing around, pretending not to want her because his love (or was it just lust? All he knew was that he melted in her presence) was never quite convenient. But this was a big request and his feelings could no longer be put to one side. This time he had to be heard.

'Rachel, I know I only ever see you at work, but – well, I look forward to those times when we meet up. I confess I would have liked to be the man in your life, if you had been that way inclined. If I move in, I might just find myself longing for you. The truth is, that if I spend more time with you day to day, it's true I might go off you entirely…'

He managed a smile at this point.

'…but I fear it's far more likely that I will fall in love with you.'

Richard swallowed. He tried to gauge what Rachel was thinking and feeling, but she was giving nothing away. He decided to continue. In for a penny…

'I find it difficult enough at times, working in the same university and knowing you will never be in the slightest bit interested in me. My fear is, that I might find it unbearable to see you every day and live in the same house as you, much as I find myself longing to do just that.' Richard forced back the swell of emotions unleashed by this sudden disclosure. There was a silence that felt like a brick wall between them. Then a small voice penetrated the silence.

'I know. I'm sorry.'

Rachel looked genuinely contrite. Richard knew Rachel hadn't meant to cause him anguish. She was just desperate. But the look on her face offered him a small crumb of satisfaction and allowed him to go on.

'Rachel, it's hardly your fault that you don't fancy me. You know I was always very supportive of your relationship with Fran, and I'm truly sorry that you have lost the love of your life.' He knew his voice sounded strained. 'But do you realise what you're asking of me?'

Richard looked Rachel straight in the eyes with a frankness and vulnerability he knew he had never shown her before. He cradled his empty cup to stop himself reaching out and touching her.

'I do know, Richard. I'm so sorry. I know this is utterly selfish of me. I just don't know who else I could ask.'

That look of pleading again. How could he refuse? But what she was asking was madness. But then, it could be the start of a whole new life. He had had fantasies of retiring early, but feared a sense of purposelessness, and loneliness without his colleagues to say hello to each day…

'OK. Look. How about we start – with no promises mind – with me coming round to meet Miki? Let's see if I can hold him without dropping him.'

Richard forced a smile, trying to lighten the moment.

Meekums

The corner of Rachel's mouth twitched. She gathered herself upright and took another deep breath before she answered.

'So. How about we go pick him up from the childminder, straight after we're finished here? You can watch while I strap him into his car seat, and when I get him out again at the other end. Once we're indoors and you are seated in one of the armchairs, I'll give him to you to hold. I won't leave you with him long. I'll have to give him a bottle, probably, pretty soon after we get in.'

Richard's head felt slightly swimmy. Rachel sounded as if this was the last thing she actually wanted to be doing. Who was doing who a favour here? But then, maybe that was her game plan – to get him to feel she was the one doing him a favour. He had seen her in action at work. Rachel had a way of persisting when she needed to, which was why, Richard mused wryly, she was so good at her job. He smiled wryly.

'You really have thought of everything, haven't you? OK. Drink up.'

'I already have.' Rachel managed a smile back as she placed her coffee cup decisively on the table that separated them. Richard could see the relief on her face. He'd seen that many times, after hard won battles in the Exam Board, and in School meetings.

They walked silently to their cars, Richard's Porsche neatly tucked behind Rachel's car – Fran's old Punto - as she led the way first to the childminder, then to her house. She unlocked the front door before removing Miki from the safety of his car seat. He had fallen asleep during the ten-minute journey and was grumpy as she lifted him out. Then, before Richard had time to object he found himself comfortably seated in one of the ample armchairs, with Miki being handed to him.

'I'll just go and make up his bottle,' Rachel said, and disappeared into the kitchen.

A Kind of Family

Richard felt awkward, surprised that his left arm was aching with the effort of holding this small bundle. He looked around for something to prop under his arm, but everything was too far away.

'Well, there's only one thing for it, little fella,' Richard said, hoping he couldn't be overheard. 'We will just have to snuggle up.'

Richard tucked a foot underneath his buttocks and leaned back, resting his elbow on the arm of the chair. 'Hey! I'm getting the hang of this!' he whispered confidentially to an unimpressed Miki. He realised he could cradle the baby in just one arm, as his other hand wandered towards Miki's feet.

'Gosh, they're so tiny!'

Richard looked in wonder at how delicate and – yes, beautiful – Miki's feet were. It crossed his mind to wonder whether his own genes were responsible for any bits of this foreign little human being. He looked into the baby's face and noticed for the first time just how dark Miki's eyes were.

'Wow,' he remarked, dreamily. 'Wow, little fella.'

And then, the most amazing thing happened. Miki's face cracked into a lopsided smile, just as Rachel was returning with his milk.

'Oh, my God! He's smiling at you!'

'You're kidding. Surely he does that with everyone' Richard could not believe he might be responsible for Miki's pleasure. He looked down at Miki, who was still smiling with open abandon at him and had begun to kick, excitedly.

'I think you've got the job,' said Rachel at last. 'Do you want it?'

'When can I start?' Richard beamed at Rachel, then again at Miki. To his utter amazement, he was quite enjoying the sensation of being kicked.

Richard stared at his home computer. He had been avoiding this task for at least three days, which had led him to become the darling of the postgraduate research tutor since he had, in fact, finally completed the third-year report on his failing PhD student. Now, however, he had to face up to the hardest bit of writing he would ever do. He listened to his own internal coach, instructing him as he did his students:

If you don't know where to start, start anywhere. But get writing!

He swallowed, then coughed. He had a sudden urge to run to the toilet and throw up, but he firmly rooted himself to his chair.

'Dear Sylvia,' he began.

Good start. Address the Head of School by her first name.

'This is the hardest letter I will ever write. It is with great sadness …'

No. I don't want her bloody pity.

'It is with regret that I must tender my resignation.'

Good. Well done, Richard. Good. Now, keep going.

At that moment, his mobile rang. Richard leaped up, his heart racing.

'Hello?'

His hope turned to irritation as he listened to yet another pre-recorded message from some ambulance-chasing outsourced money-grabbing outfit. He felt better, having muttered some expletives at the unhearing person on the other end, then pressed the red button. His body felt heavy as he returned to his desk, and he felt tears close to his eyes. But this must be done.

Come on, Richard, he reasoned with himself. Man up. You know you have to face this sooner or later. Better to give everyone as much notice as possible. You don't want to have to deal with previously trusted colleagues avoiding you in corridors because they feel you've shat on them from a great height.

'Okay, okay. I'm doing it!' he answered himself out loud, then resumed typing.

'My reasons are personal. I would be very grateful if you could waive the normally required period of notice, so that I can have my desk cleared by the end of the month. Yours sincerely, Richard.'

Done! Richard pressed print, then neatly folded the letter into a university envelope which he had brought home for the purpose.

As he stowed it in his bag he felt as if someone else's body was carrying out the action. Tomorrow, he would deliver it by hand to the Head of School's secretary. He didn't want any chance of it going astray or getting into the wrong hands. He stared at his screen. This was going to be a long month.

Ahurewa

Rachel sat with her head in her hands, listening to Miki crying. She knew she should get up and go to him, but her legs were made of lead. As she looked out into the garden with snow receding and new life creeping through the earth, time seemed suspended. Today, a Sunday, would have been Fran's birthday and Rachel had asked Richard to leave her alone for the day. She was relieved that he had decided to go to Meeting for Worship then arranged to see some friends. Rachel squeezed her eyes shut in an effort to make the pictures in her head go away. Fran's reassuring face as she left for Edinburgh; Fran's body in the bed, ready for love; Fran giving birth to Miki, pushing him out with all her might. The pictures were all out of order as she struggled to hold onto them. Fran, in the morgue, no longer looking like herself in death.

Rachel raised her head to look out of the window, searching for new pictures to replace the ones that dominated her waking hours and overtook her sleep. Miki whimpered. She felt her body tighten, her ears prickling. The rest of her body did not move. As silence fell once more, she returned to the cocoon of her garden view.

There was movement at the periphery of her vision. It wasn't like Aggie to be so reticent, but then Aggie was, Rachel had come to understand, one for old-fashioned respect. Rachel sighed, and continued looking straight ahead.

'What do you want, Aggie?'

Not put off by her tone, Aggie shuffled into sight. The same droopy stockings were visible, though the tops were somehow held up beyond her ankles. The slippers had been replaced by a pair of black court shoes with kitten heels. Rachel avoided looking up, though she could see that the old apron was gone. Aggie was wearing a black skirt.

'Rachel…' Aggie hesitated as she clutched at her skirt. 'I really am so sorry for your loss.' Each word was clearly articulated, as if she had been practising in order to show her respect.

Rachel raised her head a little, still looking straight ahead, but the tears would not behave and stay back. She berated herself. She'd been doing really well of late, able to say Fran's name without choking. She pinched her lips together and wrung her hands. Only since Fran's death did she understand the wringing of hands, it occurred to her, as she found comfort in the feeling of her one hand being held tight by the other.

'Aggie, fuck off, there's a darling.'

Miki's whimper turned into a familiar, urgent cry. Aggie shuffled from one leg to the other, the taffeta of her skirt swishing as she did so, as if she were at a high school dance rather than come to pay her respects. She never did quite get the tone right. But then, Rachel realised, that was why she had grown to love her. Fran never quite got it right, either. But she was gone.

'Aggie, I don't know what to do!' The tears wrenched through Rachel's body.

Aggie visibly straightened, her tan stockings now making a slow progress downwards to lightly settle around her ankles.

'The first fing you will do, is to go an' get that boy!'

Rachel jolted, looking up at Aggie's face. She saw determination, mixed with an emotion she could not fathom. Rachel raised herself, walked into the child's bedroom, and reached out her arms to him. Miki reached back and immediately stopped crying. His thumb found his mouth as she cuddled him to her and walked back into the living room.

'And now, matey, you 'ave to change him.'

Meekums

Aggie delivered her instruction with a matter-of-factness that implied there was no point in arguing. Rachel put Miki down on the floor where she knew he was safe, then forced her legs back into his bedroom to retrieve the change mat, nappy bag, wipes and a nappy – all neatly stowed as they would had once been by Fran, in a basket beside Miki's cot.

For the hundredth time today, tears rose unbidden into her eyes, making it impossible to see. She groped around, feeling for what she needed. A light shone over her shoulder, the beam pointing at each item in turn, and Rachel knew it was Aggie, practical as ever, come to help her.

Eventually, Rachel found herself trudging back into the living room, which by now was bathed in the afternoon light. She placed the mat down before her and sat cross-legged, marvelling once more at how easily Fran had adopted this position.

Note to self: Must get a change station. If I'm finding this difficult, thought Rachel, I know it is ten times harder for Richard.

It helped to make plans, though she held on like a frightened child to doing things Fran's way.

Aggie remained silent all the way through the nappy change, though Rachel could see her shaking her head in disbelief. She knew Aggie disapproved of disposable nappies, and could almost hear her:

'In my day, we bunged 'em all in a great big pot on the stove an' boiled them! Never did me any 'arm, or my babies!'

But this time, Aggie held her tongue. Rachel was grateful. At last, the nappy change being over and a bottle made up, Rachel settled into Fran's nursing chair and offered the bottle to a whimpering, squirming Miki. His mouth attacked the teat and he settled into contented sucking and swallowing. Rachel could still smell Fran's scent on the chair. Surprised at how long the dead continue to inhabit the house in which they lived, she picked one of Fran's hairs off the arm.

'Oh, Fran! Why did you have to leave me?' Rachel sighed.

A Kind of Family

'Now, you know that ain't no way to go on,' Aggie scolded, but with uncharacteristic softness.

She moved into view so that she was facing Rachel and began shifting position.

'What is it, Aggie?'

Rachel could barely disguise the irritation in her voice, despite realising she was grateful for the company.

'I got somefink to tell you. It might come as a bit of a shock, so it's just as well you are sittin' down.'

More shifting from one leg to the other, accompanied this time by Aggie wiping her hands down her skirt, forgetting she was not wearing her apron. Rachel was sure she could see traces of sweat where Aggie's hands had made their rough progress.

She looked up, and her eyes met Aggie's.

'Don't fink ill of me, please, Rachel. I didn't want to tell you before now. But now you need to know. You see, I came to you for a reason. I knew you would be looking after my – Miki, you see.'

Rachel could feel her palms turning cold and damp. 'My?'

Aggie did not answer but shifted her weight back and forth like a four-year-old who wants the toilet.

'You said "my".'

Rachel stared at Aggie now, throwing daggers of accusation. Miki guzzled on, aware only of his intent to drink his fill.

'Yes. Yes, I know.'

Aggie now had hold of her skirt, revealing more leg than Rachel wished to see. She twisted the cloth between her hands.

'You know you found out Fran's grandmother was Māori? An' that she was adopted in the UK? Well, there's no easy way to say this, but that was… me.'

The last word was uttered with such quietness, her head bent forward, that Rachel was unsure at first whether she had heard correctly.

'Did you say – do you mean to say, that you are Fran's grandmother? But how can that be? Her name was Ahurewa at birth, and I know her adoptive parents changed it. But to Frances. Not Agnes!' Rachel's neck poked forward and up, like a goose whose young have been threatened.

'I didn't ask to come to this country!' Aggie stamped her foot, her hands clenched by her hips.

'My name is Ahurewa!' Tears leaped from Aggie's eyes. She wailed like a small child.

'It means sacred place,' she added as a whisper, wiping the back of her left hand across her face. Her breath stumbled over itself. Rachel could see Aggie pulling herself in, and in that moment, she saw the little girl who had had to cope without her mummy – and who was robbed of the one thing she still had from her mummy when she landed in England, her name.

'I know. We found out, remember?'

Rachel looked around her, as if searching for a missing piece of a puzzle.

'But that still doesn't explain things, Aggie. We were told her grandmother's English name was Frances.'

'It was. I changed it to my second given name Agnes, when I started goin' out wiv Stan. 'E 'ad a sister called Frances. We didn't want to confuse 'im, see? An' it kind of stuck.'

'But why didn't we know about this? I don't get it.'

Rachel wasn't sure whether to believe this story or not. But then, Aggie never lied.

'I did somefink very bad.' Aggie's knuckles were white from wringing her skirt.

Rachel stared at her. She had no intention of making this easy for Aggie.

Aggie sighed, her hands still clasping the cloth.

A Kind of Family

'I 'ad four boys at the start of the war. My youngest died as a baby, shortly after Stan was called up. The love of my life died, fightin' at sea. Stan's ship was attacked by a German U boat. There were no survivors. He never met his daughter.'

Aggie's voice was flat as she related this part of the story. She looked away, as if remembering the horror of receiving the telegram. Then she looked back at Rachel, her voice more severe.

'I was left to bring up all those kids on my own, still grieving for my baby an' for Stan. We were bombed out, during the war. I was terrified but I 'ad to put a brave face on it for my kids. Just like my own mother did for me.'

At this point, her voice nearly gave way. But she gathered herself together and continued. 'When my daughter took up wiv a seaman at the age of fifteen, I was terrified. When she got to sixteen and asked if they could marry, I refused my permission.' She began twisting the cloth once more. 'How could I? I didn't want my girl to go through what I'd gone through!' She looked away again.

'So I begged 'er to wait until she was twenty-five, just to be sure. I said if 'e loved 'er, 'e would wait. They got married in 1965, when she was twenty-four. By then she was so angry with me, they never invited me to the wedding.' She spoke through loud sobs now. 'I lost my māmā when I was little, and then my only daughter as a grown woman. Through my own fault!'

Rachel's training seemed to abandon her. She found she didn't know what to say or do, and so she just watched as Aggie's sobs subsided and her breathing became more regular. After a while, Aggie continued.

'I found out once I was over 'ere that my Susan went on to have two daughters. She 'ad to wait ten years for the first, then she 'ad a second one almost immediately. That daughter was called Frances after me, so I guess she must have missed me just a little bit by then. But I never saw Frances. Not until I made contact wiv you. That's your Fran.' Aggie slumped, her hands now hanging by her sides like two wrung-out cloths.

Rachel had suspected for some time Aggie was more than just another one of her voices, but until now she had managed to package her own experiences into previously held beliefs: there are no such things as ghosts; there is no life after death. Seemingly contradicting these beliefs, she felt it was important to hold the alternative position that just because we cannot see things that people who are 'mad' see, it doesn't invalidate their reality. Now everything she had held onto was slipping like seaweed from her grasp. She placed Miki's bottle down carefully on the table beside her and shifted her position. Miki had fallen asleep.

'Your adoptive brother, David, was my grandfather.' Rachel said flatly. 'Miki is genetically related to him, because we used my eggs…' Rachel trailed off, her eyes searching her sleeping son as if he could somehow help her make sense of all she was hearing.

'I know.' Aggie also looked at Miki, a look of pure indulgence in her eyes.

'Thank you for giving him a Māori name, she whispered. Then she pulled herself upright, wiping the back of her hand across her face.

'The good news is that I was long ago reunited with my māmā. It still 'urts when I remember being torn away from 'er—' She paused, swallowing hard. '—but now we never 'ave to be separated again. An' I made it up with Susan, my daughter. An', of course, through you I got to know my granddaughter – your Fran. We're all watching out for you and Miki. In Māori culture, which I 'ave been accepted back into since comin' over here—' at this point she clutched both hands to her bosom, '—we understand the importance of what we call whānau. It isn't all about blood, you see.'

'Yes, yes I know. Fran and I did our homework. I think you know she found some of your – and her – whānau, when she visited New Zealand?'

A Kind of Family

'Yes.' Aggie's shoulders went up as she beamed delight, still clutching her chest. But Rachel had a question for Aggie.

'Aggie?'

'Yes, Rachel.'

'Is Fran – is she alright?' She hardly dared ask. Rachel bit her lip, waiting for the answer.

'Yes.' The answer came with uncharacteristic softness. 'Yes. She's with you all the time, Rachel. You just can't see 'er.'

Then Aggie's tone changed as her eyes narrowed and her smile dropped like a discarded child's toy. 'I need to explain why I came to you in the first place. I wanted to make amends, through you an' Miki. I lost my own mother, and through my stupidity my daughter. I wanted to make sure you an' Miki were OK. And that you would learn from my mistakes. You need to make your own family now, Rachel.'

Rachel took the now empty bottle from Miki's lips, sat him up, and rubbed his back. Out came a magnificent burp, at which both Rachel and Aggie laughed. But Rachel's laugh turned immediately to tears. She looked imploringly up at Aggie/Ahurewa, her friend.

Miki was her own blood, given birth by the love of her life who could herself have claimed to be Māori[3]. Rachel wanted to ensure that one day Miki could visit Aotearoa and meet his Māori family, but in the meantime, he needed a proper family, here in England.

'Fran was the centre of my world. She gave birth to Miki. How am I supposed to create a new family for him, Aggie?'

'You will, Rachel, you will. Just give it time.' Aggie soothed.

---

[3] The Māori Affairs Amendment Act 1974 re-defined a Māori as "a person of the Māori race of New Zealand; and includes any descendant of such a Māori". http://www.stuff.co.nz/dominion-post/comment/4003888/The-racial-purity-train-left-200-years-ago

A kind of family

Richard and Rachel settled into a kind of domesticity that enabled Rachel to continue working at the university.

Rachel felt guilty at first. She sensed that Richard missed academic life. But then she watched on with envy of her own as she saw him fall in love with Miki. She could tell by the glow in his eyes and the gentle strength with which he held Miki. He seemed to enjoy the simple, physical tasks of parenting, whether changing nappies or playing 'round and round the garden', watching from week to week as Miki slowly began to anticipate the tickle at the end. She also saw Richard examining Miki's tiny body and she knew he was looking for himself in Miki's features. It wasn't difficult to see that Miki's hands had the same wide palm as Richard's. Richard had once told Rachel that as a boy he had been selected to play the only bass recorder in the school because of his wide span. Richard took to walking around the house barefoot, and Rachel noticed Richard had the same slightly bigger gap between his big toe and the toe next to it than between the other toes, just like Miki.

One evening, after Rachel had tucked her son up in bed and Richard had poured her the usual glass of wine, he coughed in her direction. Rachel looked up, stifling a sigh.

'How was your day, Rachel?'

'Cut the crap, Richard. I know you have something you want to say. Spill the beans.'

A Kind of Family

Rachel's patience with Richard's sensitivities had not eased over six months of living together. She missed Fran's forthrightness; you always knew where you were with her, Rachel would hiss whenever he failed in her high expectations.

'Sorry.' The apology did nothing to soften Rachel. 'I guess you know me too well,' Richard admitted, his face colouring. But he persisted. 'It's just that – well, now that I'm living here and doing so much childcare – not that I want to be paid for it,' he added hastily.

Richard had a good pension, having managed to negotiate an early retirement deal.

'It's just that, well, I've been thinking. Fran was a wonderful mother, and Miki was very lucky to have two such wonderful parents.'

Rachel's lips pursed ever so slightly; her shoulders raised as her breathing shallowed. She felt lightheaded and her feet suddenly felt a long way away. But he persisted, his voice tighter.

'And... well... I wondered if you might feel OK if he had two parents once more. He might, after all, one day want to find me in any case, and as you know he will have a perfect right to do so. I wonder how he might feel if he finds I am his biological father but was basically the nanny?'

Her worst nightmares. As Rachel listened to Richard's rambling speech she felt as if Miki was being ripped from her own womb. She stalled for time, her head a maelstrom.

'What are you suggesting, Richard?' Rachel's voice was hard, defensive.

'I would like to adopt him. I don't want to replace Fran – she was always his birth mother, and you were always his biological mother. But now that I'm here and it seems to be working, I would like— no, I would *love* to be his father. Officially, not just biologically.' Richard coughed.

Rachel stood up and began pacing the floor.

'No, no, no, no, no! I knew this was a bad idea!' She clutched her arms to her stomach, as if the rolls of fat she felt underneath were the baby she had never carried. She could see out of the corner of her eye that Richard was looking down.

'You can't!' Rachel turned on Richard.

'Rachel…' Richard began, quietly.

'No!' Rachel countered. Then she ran upstairs to her room, slamming the door behind her.

In the safety of her room Rachel stood with her back against the door, holding onto its solidity with both hands. She knew she needed to talk to someone who made sense. Instinctively, Rachel knew Jane was not the best person to turn to right now. Something had gone on between her and Richard, though Rachel was never able to get out of Jane exactly what it was. Just that he had 'been a dickhead'. And so, she rang lovely, reliable Suzy.

Suzy listened while Rachel ranted until she paused, exhausted.

'Lovey, I can fully understand how painful this must be for you. And of course, it's entirely your call. You are Miki's mum, after all. Fran was Miki's birth mum. No one can take any of that away from you, and it sounds like Richard is fully aware of that.'

Rachel drew breath, about to defend herself, but Suzy had more to say.

'Rachel, he wasn't asking for a relationship – just co-parenting, which is essentially what he's already doing.' Suzy paused. 'I know you don't want to treat him like the hired help.' Damn her! She's appealing to my principles, the arsehole, thought Rachel. 'All he's asking is to be Miki's dad. Is that such a threat? He isn't the sort of man who would take over, or take Miki away from you. Is he?'

At which point, feeling seen right through by her friend, Rachel sobbed.

As she returned downstairs around midnight after hearing Richard go off to bed Aggie was there waiting for her, hands on hips. She had rubber gloves on. She meant business.

'Now, you listen 'ere young lady!'

Rachel never allowed anyone to call her young lady, but she was in no mood to fight.

'All ears, Aggie,' she muttered as she slumped into an armchair.

'Good! Now, I know you miss Fran, but she's all right. An' she wants 'er boy to 'ave the best possible life 'e can.'

Aggie paused, while Rachel registered the fact that Aggie was delivering a message from her lost loved one. She felt her whole body begin to tremble.

'Fran an' Richard got on rather well, didn't they? 'E introduced 'er to the Quakers, I believe?' Aggie paused for effect.

'An' she knew 'im to be a nice sort of bloke. 'E *is* a good bloke, isn't 'e?'

Rachel nodded.

''E loves that boy. 'E's Miki's whānau. If 'e were not the sperm donor, but just a good mate, I bet you'd consider lettin' 'im adopt! I know what it's like to bring up kids on me own. If I'd 'ad a fella willin' to 'elp as 'e is, wivout expecting you-know-what in return, I fink I'd 'ave jumped at it.'

She waited while this sank in, and then:

'I know this sounds 'arsh, Rachel, but don't you fink you're bein' a bit unfair? After all, the man gives 'is sperm when you ask, gives up 'is job when you ask, moves in and does unpaid childcare, an' 'e never asks you for anyfink. Until now.'

Rachel looked up at Aggie.

'Jesus, you don't pull any punches, do you Aggie?'

'Nah, love. Did you ever wonder where your Fran got it from?'

And at that, they both laughed, and then Rachel cried. Again. She buried her head in her hands, and sobbed for her lost love, for her own selfishness, for the way she had treated one of her best supporters, and for her beautiful little son.

She felt a hand lightly brush her hair, and looked up, but Aggie was gone.

The day the adoption papers came through coincided with Miki's second birthday. Rachel insisted on buying a magnum of champagne. Jane, Suzy, Roxy, Feather and Debra were all invited to share it with them, and Miki put on his best smiles as he was trotted round the adoring group of friends. They each took turns in toasting the toddler and his parents, not forgetting the dear departed Fran. Even Jane said she was happy for Richard. Aroha Skyped early in the day, just before bedtime in New Zealand, to welcome Richard into Miki's whānau, and Joanne sent a message of congratulations, apologising that she couldn't make it as one of her brood had a major part in a school play.

That evening as they sat in silence together, Richard reading his *Economist* and Rachel reading a book she was reviewing, Rachel looked up and there was Aggie.

She looked different – younger. She looked stunning, in fact. Her dark brown hair tumbled onto her shoulders in soft waves, her body no longer constrained with work clothes. But it was the same Aggie. Her eyes shone like two well-polished jet stones. Round her throat was a necklace made of abalone shells – she recalled Fran saying that in Aotearoa they were called paua, pronounced like 'power'.

'I fink you know why I'm 'ere,' Aggie said softly. Rachel looked over to Richard, who didn't move.

'It's OK. 'E can't 'ear or see me.'

Aggie waited.

Rachel nodded silently, aware of a deep sadness at what she knew was about to happen.

A Kind of Family

'You've done a good job, Rachel. I'm very proud of you. Miki's in good 'ands, wiv you an' Richard for parents. You don't need me anymore.'

Hot tears began to trickle down Rachel's cheeks. She sniffed and searched for a tissue in her pocket. Richard looked up at her, concern on his face, but she smiled at him.

'Must be hay fever,' she covered. He smiled back, then returned to his magazine.

'I'll be off then. You won't see me again – well, not for quite a few years, anyway. But I'll be watching. Take care.'

And that was it. She was gone. Rachel blew her nose, then looked over at Richard, the wonderful, flawed man who shared her son, her life, her space but not her bed.

'Thank you for being part of Miki's whānau,' she whispered. 'And mine.'

Acknowledgements

I am forever grateful to the West Yorkshire writer Ian Clayton, for re-igniting my passion for writing. Out of his courses for staff at the University of Leeds (made possible by the innovative Jo Westerman, MBE) *The Scribblers* emerged, and it was there that Aggie first made herself known to me. Thank you to my fellow scribblers Nicky Bray, Maddie Redd, Chris Sykes and Alice Temple for loving her as much as I do, and for encouraging me to write more. I also want to thank my fellow writers in three other groups for their valuable writerly support over the years: an unnamed online writing group that emerged from a Futurelearn / Open University course; *Mossley Writers*; and *Oldham Writing Group*. The members of all these groups have stoically endured hearing and reading my work on countless occasions, offering both insightful critique and encouragement to keep writing when I might otherwise have lost my nerve.

Darren Rewi could have felt justified in wondering what this mad Pākehā was doing bothering him, but instead he gave me both his time and valuable insight into aspects of Māori heritage. He also checked part of my writing to ensure that I had written sensitively and accurately on the important and shameful topic of past adoptions. I am indebted to him and hope one day to be of service to him or his whānau.

I wish to thank the following people for their generous and detailed feedback on earlier drafts: Sue Aspinall, Jo Core, Irene Double, Jennifer Ferrazano, Irene Fordyce, Liz Ottoson, and Laura Wilkinson. My heartfelt thanks to Sue Aspinall too, for being willing to be interviewed about the process of assisted conception.

Without Cherie Macenka, this novel would still be sitting unread, on my computer. She believed in my writing, for which I am grateful beyond words. She has also responded with breakneck speed to my naïve questions and facilitated a painless editing process. My thanks, too, to all the staff at Between the Lines Publishing, including Liz Hurst during the editing process, and Jim Tetlow for working so creatively, patiently and enthusiastically with me to get the cover artwork just right.

Last but by no means least, I am eternally grateful to my husband and family, for putting up with my long hours at the computer, for continued good humour, and for helping me to believe in myself as a writer.

About the author

Born and brought up in working-class London, Bonnie crossed classes when she went to university in the 1970s, eventually gaining a PhD in arts therapies in the 1990s. In the 1980s she crossed the invisible borders from South to North in England, settling eventually in Greater Manchester where she still lives, and travelling annually to New Zealand to be with part of her far-flung family. Bonnie is the author of two books on the arts therapies, having pioneered Dance Movement Psychotherapy in the UK. An escaped academic, she now concentrates on writing novels and short stories. Her blog about becoming an older woman in the UK can be found at https://mamabonnie.wordpress.com/. *A Kind of Family* is her debut novel.

Lightning Source UK Ltd.
Milton Keynes UK
UKHW020438031121
393296UK00011B/701